THE CLOCKWORK ORACLE

THE CLOCKWORK ORACLE

David L. Drake

Katherine L. Morse

AJ Sikes

BJ Sikes

Dover Whitecliff

An L. E. G. Publication

Published by L.E.G.

ISBN-978-0-9903457-2-5

Published 2018

Cover Design by David L. Drake
Interior Layout by BJ Sikes

The gods have placed me here I see your future clear
My tales cross the earth but none can see their worth
I've seen it all...

—From "Cassandra Knows"
by Alyssa Rosenbloom and Nathaniel Johnstone

Contents

David L. Drake

The Labors of Pacioli's Apprentice

The rhythmic rustling of the Franciscan's robe softly echoed throughout his chamber as he checked and rechecked his sums. Sitting on a high stool in front of a long table, he lightly dragged his left index fingernail just below a row of numbers in the bound book of parchment, careful not to mar the meticulously penned values. His right hand moved in a counter tempo, rapidly pointing his quill pen at sums on nearby scrolls. After a bit of mental analysis, he uttered a satisfied grunt, inked his pen, and scrawled a number at the end of the row. The midday sun shone brightly into the Milan room, highlighting the deep reds and bright blues of the woven carpets and the hung tapestries.

A quiet voice at the room's entrance interrupted the Franciscan's solitary activity. "Maestro Pacioli? May I have a word?" The youth at the door was dressed in a green and blue doublet, dark green hose, and a blue pillbox hat. He carefully held in his green-gloved hands a large piece of rolled parchment.

"A moment while I complete this row," the patriarch grumbled.

After a few more sweeping movements, a decisive dipping of the writing instrument, a scratching at the end of the line of numbers, and then placing his feather down far from the book, Luca Pacioli turned to face his apprentice with a smile.

"How may I help you?" Before the boy could answer, he added, "What is that you have there? That looks like archival parchment from the library of Duke Ludovico Sforza."

"Maestro, you are correct. I have a challenge with my studies that perhaps only you can help me with."

The master accountant pointed to a section of table less cluttered with papers, bound books, and writing implements. The lad carefully unrolled his treasure, weighted the corners with various items from the table, and took a step back to allow his mentor to get a look.

Luca eagerly leaned over the scroll. "This is, of course, Ancient Greek. See the word endings? And...oh my! This is written in boustrophedon, the 'plowing style' of back-and-forth lines. See how every other line is written right to left, but also the characters are flipped as if in a mirror. And down here...near the end...all these numbers..."

"Yes, Maestro. Just like the language students before me, I have been assigned a document—this document—to decipher. What you see on this parchment is a transcription made eight years ago by the Historical Society of Milan from a folded-papyrus codex. One of the scholars from the Historical Society estimated the codex was recorded four hundred years before the Birth of our Lord, given its state and careful preservation in a wax-sealed stone box."

Luca Pacioli raised his bushy eyebrows, and then tipped his head back in a gesture he habitually used to signal a request for more details.

"I have read through the historical notes on...well...a set of objects. The codex was copied from a tablet found at Delphi. The historical notes state that Greek scholars found the original clay was deteriorating, so they copied the text verbatim to a folded-papyrus codex. They preserved the twenty-two-panel codex as best they could in a waxed-sealed stone box. But...this is a text unlike any other I have translated. Shall I go on?"

Luca Pacioli replied, "Please, tell the story."

The student, pointing out the passages, recited the story as best he could.

One chilly morning on Mount Olympus, while the stars were still high in the sky, Apollo and Artemis came upon their father, Zeus, leaning over a tablet covered with lines, symbols, notations, and tables. Zeus was so lost in thought that they had to interrupt him.

Apollo spoke first. "Father, master of the heavens, please let me know when I must begin the sun's trip for the day. And when shall I complete the sun's journey?"

Artemis also pleaded, "Father dear, master of the heavens, please let me know when I must begin the moon's trip for the month. And when shall I complete the moon's journey?"

Without looking up, Zeus replied, "My sacred task is to determine the intricate movements of the entire universe. The sun and the moon are but two grains of sand in the ocean of heavenly stars. Have patience, my son and daughter, and your questions will be answered."

But Apollo and Artemis were anxious to start their tasks, and they waited impatiently. Finally, Zeus handed them each two scraps of bark with lines and positions of stars and planets. "When the heavens appear exactly as you see here on this piece of bark, you may start your ride. The other piece shows the position of the heavens when you should complete your journeys." They both nodded their understanding.

Zeus hastily left to continue his other morning tasks. Both Apollo and Artemis held their first bark piece to the sky. Artemis exclaimed, "I must leave immediately!" and strode to her brace of horses.

Apollo groaned. "The morning star is far from its rise." He looked around for what to do in the interim. He scanned over his father's tablet covered with lines, symbols, notations, and tables. Apollo smirked. "I could build a mechanism that calculates much of this so that I do not have to wait for instructions from Zeus."

Over the next month, Apollo secretly worked on his mechanism of wood and brass. But he was frustrated with the complexity. In exasperation, he bemoaned his struggle with the difficulty of the task. "Not even the gods are clever enough to devise this mechanism."

At the sound of Apollo's exasperation, Athena appeared. "What has you so vexed, Apollo?" He knew of her deep well of wisdom and reason, so he showed her the challenge he had taken up to determine the movement of the heavens, the sun, and the moon. He showed her his initial diagrams for his apparatus. Finally, he showed her the faulty instrument he had fashioned. She smiled and pointed out its flaws, suggested a few simplifications, and offered a few improvements. He was overjoyed and thanked her, and said that he would plant an olive tree in her name at Delphi as a token of his gratitude. She smiled, thanked him for the wonderful gesture of the tree, and departed.

Apollo completed his mechanism within a week.

Luca Pacioli scrunched his face up and grunted mild displeasure. "The word 'week' is a bit modern for this text. If I remember correctly, it is a Judeo-Christian unit of time."

The boy pointed at the three-word phrase, and nervously explained his translation. "Maestro, the text refers to the passing of a single moon phase, specifically the first quarter, and I substituted a contemporary word."

The master sniffed, "You forfeit your integrity with alternative wordings, young man. Your readers will lose their trust in the accuracy of your translations. Stay with 'first phase of the moon.' It has an air of ancient text."

The boy nodded and continued in his interpretation.

> *Apollo secretly confirmed his mechanism worked properly through a series of surreptitious questions he asked of Zeus. Satisfied, he showed it to his sister, Artemis. She was overjoyed that together they could determine, on their own, not only the position of the heavens for their tasks, but also tidal fluctuations, eclipses, the passing of comets, and extreme weather. She begged that he build one for her, and he agreed to give a duplicate to her when she completed her next monthly voyage of the moon.*
>
> *When Apollo completed the duplicate in a few days, he decided to travel to Delphi to plant the olive tree to thank Athena for her aid. He covered himself in the robes of mortals so they would not recognize him. On his way, he passed the Sanctuary of Apollo on the slope of Mount Parnassus, where the oracle Cassandra lay writhing from the fumes of the decaying Python. When Apollo approached, Cassandra pointed straight at him.*
>
> *"My eyes burn with your luminous visage, dear Apollo! Please come to me and tell me of the future!"*
>
> *Apollo smiled at his devoted acolyte. "I command that only you may see me as a god on my journey to Delphi today. But I have a treat to show you. Here is a mechanism that reveals the movement of the sun, the moon, tidal fluctuations, eclipses, the passing of comets, and extreme weather." Without the notice of others, he showed her the workings of the mechanism. As a demonstration, he determined the next eclipse. She became entranced. "I must have one of these mechanisms!"*
>
> *Apollo realized that he could give Cassandra the mechanism*

that he had made for Artemis, and construct a new duplicate for his sister when he returned to Mount Olympus.

"Cassandra, my dear, you may have the mechanism. I made it for you!" He also provided her the knowledge to use the mechanism in instructions on a clay tablet.

He left and went to the site of the Pythian Games and planted an olive tree. When he finished, he declared, "With this olive tree, I give great gratitude to Athena, without whose help, I could not have completed the mechanism." At those words, an angry Athena appeared.

"How can you privately praise me for my assistance, when you tell the mortal Cassandra that you alone created the mechanism?"

Apollo was shocked at the charge. "Cassandra sees the future through me. Your assistance in the forming of the mechanism is none of her concern."

"The knowledge I give, I can take away." With that, Athena held out her hand toward Apollo, and his understanding of the mechanism melted away.

Apollo rushed back to his work, but he could no longer understand his scribblings. He tried for three more weeks to recreate his work, but when Artemis returned from her journey, Apollo was bound by his word to provide a mechanism to her, so he gave her the original, losing the example he needed to make duplicates.

Cassandra, unshackled from her dream-like glimpses of upcoming events, could now predict accurately the movement of the sun, the moon, tidal fluctuations, eclipses, the passing of comets, and extreme weather. This helped her in her predictions of the outcomes of wars, the health of babies, and the rise of new heroes.

Apollo grew more frustrated with his loss. He fumed and cursed his bad luck. In frustration, he ran to Artemis. "I must have the mechanism back, so I can duplicate it for myself! When I complete the task, I will return it to you."

Artemis stamped her foot in anger at her ill-mannered brother. "A gift given is gone." Apollo was shocked at his sister's dismissal, but agreed that, as a brother, he was bound by his word.

Apollo ran to Delphi, to the slope of Mount Parnassus, where the oracle Cassandra lay operating her copy of the mechanism. "I must have the mechanism back, so I can duplicate it for myself! When I complete the task, I will return it to you."

Cassandra stamped her foot in anger at the ill-mannered god. "A gift given is gone." Apollo was shocked at the mortal's dismissal, but agreed that as a god, he was bound by his word.

Apollo called to Athena, "I must have my knowledge back, so I can duplicate the mechanism for myself!"

Athena appeared and smiled at the ill-mannered god. "You wronged me, dear Apollo. The gift of knowledge I gave you is now gone. The scales of justice are again even."

"But a mortal cannot have a deeper knowledge of the universe's future than I! I will destroy the mechanism!" Apollo ran to the slope of Mount Parnassus where the oracle Cassandra lay sleeping. He stole the mechanism, and threw it into the middle of the Mediterranean Sea.

Athena saw his cruel act. She saw Cassandra awake and become distraught over the loss of the mechanism given to her by the god.

Athena appeared on the slope of Mount Parnassus and spoke to the oracle Cassandra. "I see that your mechanism is gone. I am here to replace it with a better one. Tell me the events you would like it to foresee."

Cassandra was wise with her wishes. Athena smiled at her clarity of mind and heart. Athena nodded and returned to the charts of Zeus; she swirled her spear into the ground, gathering the stone, gems, crystals, wood, and metals of Mount Olympus. With the help of Hephaestus, the god of fire and metalworking, she formed a new mechanism that matched the wishes of the oracle.

She returned to Cassandra, saying...

"That is as much of the story as I can translate. Most of the remainder of the story on the codex was so deteriorated, it could not be transcribed, as you can see."

"But what is all of this?" Luca Pacioli asked, pointing towards the writing near the bottom of the scroll.

"It appears to be fragments of descriptions, numeric tables, and directives, but so disjointed that I can't make sense of them. But if I were to guess, they appear to describe how to operate the two mechanisms. I had hoped that, with your knowledge of numerical tables, we could put the puzzle together."

Luca Pacioli made a disheartened face. "I think this is nothing but another fantasy myth of ancient deities. A physical mechanism built by the gods of the ancient past! Of course, no such thing exists. And certainly not two items formed by deities." He looked back at the sums that he had been calculating for Duke Sforza. "I have more important tasks at hand."

"Perhaps your friend, the inventor, could assist me. Leonardo da Vinci?"

"Oh, he is also buried in work. I recommend you record the tale, and move on to another parchment for translation. One with a more mathematical nature. Did you see any more texts by Archimedes on the nature of geometry?"

The lad nodded, bowed, and left the monk to his undertakings.

Katherine L. Morse and David L. Drake

Circles Within Circles

Madame Luminitsa, I wish to contact my dearly departed father, Edwin," implored the man in the brown bowler with the finely-manicured, curled mustache while surreptitiously evaluating his surroundings. Despite it being midday, the only light came from a cheap, baroque replica candelabra in the middle of the round table. The rest of the small sitting room was dark, owing to the deep green and purple drapes completely covering the walls and windows.

Tiny dots of light peaked through, testifying to the hungry attention of moths, probably the same ones that had snacked on the carpet underneath his feet, at least the bits not worn thin by human feet.

"Dearly departed?" interjected the man's companion, a blonde woman squirming uncomfortably as she was unaccustomed to the bustled day dress confining her. She sniffed at the spicy, stale odor of day-old incense.

"Please, dear Czarina, let me conduct my business with the medium. We can discuss your skepticism at home. Madame Luminitsa, will you contact Edwin Llewellyn for me?"

"Mr. Um...?"

"Er, the name is Llewellyn. Percival Llewelyn. I have consulted many reliable sources and I have ascertained that you are the most reputable gypsy medium in all of London."

"Sir, I am *Romani*, not *gypsy*. Mr. Llewellyn, I do not perform individual séances. You must return two nights hence at 11:30 PM," replied the medium. "I will consult the spirits. We will speak with your father only if he is willing."

***

"Dearly departed?" Dr. McTrowell prodded again as they departed the medium's studio.

"Well, yes, Sparky. Edwin Llewellyn is very dear to me and he has departed to Hawaii. I miss him," Chief Inspector Erasmus Drake said to his fiancée in a lightly joking tone. "I am sure those gypsies are involved in the recent series of break-ins, but I cannot deduce how they always know exactly the correct time to commit their crimes. It took Scotland Yard a month to find this connection between all the victims, because the perpetrators do not take advantage of the most obvious opportunity when the victims are at the séance. I commend the perpetrators for avoiding that glaring error, but I still must apprehend these gypsies."

"They're not *gypsies*."

"I beg your pardon?"

"They're not gypsies...or more precisely, they're not Romani." Sparky felt like she was repeating herself a lot today. "Madame Luminitsa mispronounced the name of her supposed people. She pronounced it with the emphasis on 'Ro.' A true Romani would have pronounced it with the emphasis on the second syllable."

"Perhaps she has adopted the English pronunciation," the Chief Inspector offered.

"You know how you tease me for pronouncing the name of my home town of San Francisco like I'm Spanish? One pronounces important words from one's native environs properly for the rest of one's life, regardless of the language one is speaking."

"Your linguistic gift is a never-ending source of amazement to me. Madame Luminitsa and her friends certainly have all the trappings: colorful drapes, incense, and a crystal ball."

"Erasmus, most of those things can be purchased at a street bazaar or a cheap antiques shop. But that crystal ball is something else. Have you ever seen one suspended in a cage like that?"

"No, I have not. Nor can I divine the purpose of the crank and gears. Perhaps you will have the opportunity to examine it more closely once we solve this case."

***

"Pretender! Liar! Out!"

"Madame Luminitsa, there is no need for such agitation," the Chief Inspector insisted in a tone he hoped was calming.

"Out! Out!"

Two large men in decidedly non-Romani attire stormed into the room on a direct course toward Drake. McTrowell sprang out of her chair and, with the element of surprise on her side, knocked the closest one flat with a single, squarely delivered blow to the jaw. The sight of his partner in crime being punched by the slight, blonde woman startled the remaining miscreant into inaction. The Chief Inspector took advantage of the hesitation and gave him a sharp rap on the skull with the heavy silver head of his walking stick. With barely a glance at the two men rumpled on the floor, Drake turned to McTrowell, "I do not know how, but they have found us out. The rest of the gang will be clearing out. Fetch the Constables!"

The airship pilot scurried out of the building as fast as possible in yet another ridiculously bustled skirt. As much as she was enjoying solving this crime with her fiancé, she was really looking forward to getting back to more functional clothing. "Constable Higgins, we're found out and Drake thinks they'll be clearing out! Around the back!"

The Constable blew two sharp, shrill blasts on his police whistle, bringing the rest of the Constables running from their nearby hiding spots. As they swarmed over the row house where the alleged medium kept her studio, Drake emerged from the front door dragging along one of the would-be assailants. "Higgins, take this one. The other one is inside manacled to the stove."

"Yes, sir." The Constable hustled the assailant away.

The Chief Inspector turned to his fiancée. "Sparky, my love, how are you?"

"I've had quite enough of these silly dresses and my hand's a little sore."

"I must admit, I never get tired of their surprised looks when your ferocious little fist connects with their face." He chuckled. "Before Madame Luminitsa began caterwauling, did you notice something interesting?"

"You mean besides the splitting headache the incense was giving me?"

Drake smirked at her quip, but got back to his point, "All the other crystal balls I have ever seen were clear. A 'medium' gazes into them and purports to see something that the rest of us cannot. Although the room was darkened and the sphere itself was obscured by a scrollwork cage, it seemed as though something was moving about inside the sphere."

Sparky nodded in agreement. "I thought I saw something black swirling about, but concluded it was the beginnings of a migraine brought on by the incense. I was on the verge of inducing Hippocrates' cure," the flight surgeon replied sardonically.

Confusion registered on her fiancé's face. "Vomiting, my dear; Hippocrates observed that vomiting produces relief from migraines. But more to the point, that 'crystal ball' was clear when we saw it two days ago."

"I agree. If it had been simply a crystal ball, I might have surmised that it was a different one. But my surreptitious observations of the enclosing cage did not reveal any obvious way to open it. As I cannot deduce a motive for expending the effort to switch the globes, I conclude that it is the same one we saw two days ago."

"I don't suppose you'd let me fiddle with it a bit before you return it to its rightful owner," Sparky pleaded flirtatiously.

"We shall see, my dear."

***

Chief Inspector Drake headed straight for his most reliable Constable as soon as he returned to Scotland Yard.

"Constable Higgins, hello! How is your progress...oh, you look quite agitated. Having any difficulty in your inquiries with the sketches?"

"I'm not sure, Chief Inspector."

Drake waited a beat for the Constable to supply additional detail. When the Constable didn't respond to the pause, Drake continued, "Please try to be clearer, Constable. Did any of the victims recognize the sketches of the thieves?"

"No, sir."

"Well, that is sorely disappointing." Drake ran his fingers through his hair, trying to think of a way to press the investigation forward.

Constable Higgins offered, "But, in most cases, the victims' servants or neighbors reported seeing men around on the evenings of the séances who look like our perpetrators."

"That much is to be expected. The thieves went to the victims' homes during the séances. My guess it that the perpetrators breached the defenses of the victims' homes, but did not enter at that time. Were the thieves seen again on the days of the thefts?"

"Not so far as I can tell, sir. None of the servants or neighbors can recall seeing the men again."

"Hmmm, a theft pipeline. Ingenious in its efficiency."

"Sir?"

"I apologize, Higgins. I admit grudging respect for the efficiency and effectiveness of these crimes. Before Sparky and I captured them, the two thieves were sent to the victims' homes while the medium engaged the homeowners in a séance. The thieves left holes in the homes' defenses, but did not risk the thefts at that time. There must be other members of the ring whom we have not yet captured. Since we have not captured them, we do not know what they look like, so the neighbors and servants cannot identify them. This 'second shift' of thieves must visit the homes when it is safe to perpetrate the theft. Since they have not previously visited the targeted homes, they do not risk being recognized. But how do they know when it is safe? Blast!"

***

Scotland Yard Captures Gypsy Thieves!!!!

Chief Inspector Erasmus Drake and his girl sidekick, Dr. 'Sparky' McTrowell, infiltrated a ring of despicable, notorious gypsy thieves. The Chief Inspector once again proved himself a man of action, protecting his scruffy frontier lady from the filthy vagabonds. Scotland Yard has cleaned up the whole mess, arresting the lot of thieves. Londoners can sleep soundly again.

—Bryan Briggs

***

Sparky threw the newspaper across the room, which exploded into a dozen wafting sheets of newsprint. "Protecting!? Scruffy?! If that slope-browed, drooling, Neanderthal reporter Briggs, had been present at the Annual Symposium of the Occidental Inventors' Society, I'd have given him the same treatment as I gave the Duke of Milton!" She punched into the air so hard her coat made an audible snap as she reenacted the incident with the Duke.

Chief Inspector Erasmus Drake took a deep breath and stood up from the dinner table to collect the disassembled broadsheet. "Which he would have so richly deserved, my love. You must not stoop to reading narrow-minded press reports. It only angers and distracts you. May we focus on dessert and the mystery of the perfectly timed thefts?" He gave the newspaper a few quick folds and tucks, and resettled into his chair.

"Yes," replied McTrowell, "you are right, my dear. Let's get back to the real work. Have you returned all the stolen property to its rightful owners?"

"Yes, everything except the gypsy trappings." Drake thought back over the inventory Scotland Yard had seized. "As we originally surmised, those items were all cheap bric-a-brac, probably purchased at a street bazaar, except for the crystal ball."

"Did your thieves tell you where they got it? Or give up their co-conspirators who actually executed the break-ins?"

"Neither. I have the sense that they fear something more than jail. I think we will have to deduce the rest without their cooperation."

Sensing her opening, Sparky asked, "So, when are you going to let me at that crystal ball?"

Drake chuckled softly to himself. "More port, dear?"

***

Gunari strode an angry circle around the campfire as he read the paper. "They called us *Gypsies*?! Blood and ashes on their houses!" he swore, throwing the crumpled front page of the Times into the flames.

His wife stepped in to interrupt his pacing and rubbed his shoulder soothingly. "Blood and ashes, *bater*. Now at least we know where the orb is being held."

"What good does that do us, Tshilaba?"

She shifted from comforting wife to stalwart partner. "I no longer need to seek it throughout London. Gather the *familia*. I will seek knowledge of its location and guardians in Scotland Yard."

"Well yes then, *bater*, let it be so."

***

"Dr. Pogue, thank you for offering the hospitality of your home and labs yet again." Sparky looked around the basement lab in Edmond Pogue's sprawling warehouse home in Shadwell. Others might have found the lab dungeon-like, but the airship pilot found its expanse and plethora of equipment luxurious. She happily anticipated experimenting in this room again.

"Dr. McTrowell, it's always delightful to have you here. Yin and I so enjoy your mechanical challenges."

"Even...that one?" The flight surgeon winced as she pointed at her colleague's mechanical arm. Nothing would ever erase her guilt over the loss of Edmond's arm from experimenting with the Electric-Powered Automated Cutting Tool she and Drake had sent from Paris. "We should have realized how dangerous the EPACTs are...we should have sent the warning in the crate instead of relying on the optical telegraph." She choked back a tear. "I should have been able to save the arm." She wiped away the tear with her kerchief and dabbed at her nose.

The inventor scientist ran the repurposed EPACT components of his arm through a few mechanical calisthenics. "Well, I'd say I got the best of it," he joked. Seeing that his jocularity was not soothing his friend, he adopted a more serious tone. "Sparky, Yin will tell you that she's had to save my fool life several more times since that night. And Esmerelda would confirm that I haven't the sense to come in from the rain. If it weren't for you I would have lost my life and not just my arm." He hugged her awkwardly with his human arm. "Not to mention that I get to wear a 'Dr. McTrowell-designed arm' every day. Now who else can say that?"

She sniffled back a final tear and smiled at his enthusiasm. "When did you completely abandon referring to Yin as Dr. Young?"

"When she was just outside of Portsmouth with you and Sergeant Fox, rushing out to the high seas to save the Chief Inspector; I feared I would never see her again."

An uncomfortable silence stretched between them. When Sparky couldn't stand it any longer, she cleared her throat. "Well, I'm going to set up the lab. I'll unpack my clothes after dinner."

"Mrs. Bingham can manage that for you."

"I don't want to trouble her. Besides, I'd rather she spend her energies on preparing dinner. As much as I love adventuring, I do miss home-cooked meals and hers are particularly delicious."

"Yes, I completely agree. Delightful!" And with that cheery rejoinder, Edmond Pogue left her to her labors.

Sparky surveyed the room. As far as she could tell, it was in exactly the same state she'd left it before she and Drake had been dragged halfway across the world and back to rescue his foster father. Not that she'd expected Dr. Pogue or his staff to bother with tidying up the basement room. The giant abandoned warehouse he called home had plenty of empty space and his own, cavernous basement lab was fully outfitted. She felt that tug in her chest again. As much as she loved the thrill of flying and her adventures with Drake, some part of her longed for a permanent home. She really must get on that, but today her attentions were fully on the crystal ball.

Unlike Edmond Pogue's claim of unabashed carelessness, Sparky's experience with the EPACT had introduced more than a spot of caution into her approach to mechanical explorations. She donned a leather apron, leather work gloves, and a pair of goggles for safe measure. *Observation first, then experimentation,* she reminded herself. She picked the object up and turned its metal cage over gently in her hands, taking care not to disturb the crank or gears. It was hard to get a clear view because the cage's scrollwork obscured the glass-like sphere inside. Even turning it over, she didn't see anything inside the orb. She had expected that it might contain some kind of fluid, but it appeared to be simply a crystal ball. What she needed was better light. That was the one disadvantage of Pogue's "dungeon" laboratories, no windows, so no sunlight. Sparky's mind wandered to the topic of light, specifically artificial light.

What a boon it would be to scientists if they had reliable, steady light sources to provide steady illumination to their experiments.

She stared into the dark, cavernous corners of the ceiling, pondering how one might meet such requirements. She'd read a story about such an invention by James Bowman Lindsay, who used electricity coursing through a white-hot filament, but nothing had ever come of it so far as she could tell. Ah well, a problem for another day. She glanced back down at the orb in her hands. Just as she started to consider taking it out into the sunlight, she caught a glimpse of something through one of the holes in the scrollwork. Without warning, a picture sprung into her mind, fully formed. A man in late middle age, judging by his white hair, stood proudly holding a glass bulb in his hand. His haircut was unfashionably short, he had no facial hair, and his suit was peculiarly plain and loose, as if someone had mixed up the tailoring of work clothes with a suit. And just as quickly as it came, it was gone, but still burned in her mind's eye. She felt like she'd just awakened from a nightmare and was in those first few waking seconds where one struggles to decide if the memory was real or not. She rubbed her eyes.

More light! Sparky thought. She scurried closer to the gaslight fixture mounted on the wall, clutching the device firmly. She held it up to the illumination. She could see the flames flicker, refracting through the crystal ball, but nothing else. *Bother!* She set it down carefully on the cabinet against the wall to consider her next step. *Wait, what was that?* Had she seen movement inside it of the sort that she and Erasmus had spied during the séance? She picked it back up. *Nothing.* She put it back down.

There it was again! Alright, time to stop flailing about like a schoolchild before this damnable device drives me to distraction.

Focusing as best she could through the holes in the scrollwork, she lifted up the device slowly, steadily, without changing its orientation in any way. She thought she observed a slight swirl of black flecks that settled and vanished as soon as she got the device close to her face. The swirl reappeared briefly as she returned the device to the cabinet top and then disappeared completely. Did it somehow react to the heat of her face? No, that didn't make sense or it would have reacted to the gaslight or the heat of her body. The wood of the cabinet? No, the workbench she'd had it on before had been wood. It must be something about the cabinet...or its contents. She opened the cabinet carefully so as not to jostle the device.

Well, wasn't that just like Edmond?

The cabinet contained a Daniell cell with an iron bar wrapped in a wire that ran between the two terminals. Pogue must have been experimenting with electromagnetism. The magnet was just sitting there as if he had no further need of it. Well, she would find a use for it. And she'd serendipitously ascertained that the device reacted to magnetism in some way.

Now, about that crank and gears. She fetched every candle she could find in the lab and assembled them into three quarters of a circle on the workbench, leaving an opening closest to the edge of the workbench through which she could work. She placed the device in the middle of the circle and lit all the candles. She had been tempted to carry the Daniell cell over and include it in her experiment, but too few equations and too many unknowns. She'd try that later. She began turning the crank slowly, observing the motion of the gears. She peered through the scrollwork, trying to discern any corresponding reaction inside.

Nothing. What could be the point of the crank and gears if they didn't do anything?

It was as if someone had just glued the gears on the cage. She cranked faster and focused her attention on the encased crystal sphere. She began to feel ridiculous. Here she was, madly cranking a useless handle staring at a blank piece of glass! Her ears began to ring. She stopped and rubbed her eyes.

Maybe, like Drake, it's left-handed.

She rotated the device 180° and cranked it with her left hand while squinting intently at the crystal ball with the same disappointing non-results. The ringing in her ears returned, accompanied by a headache like the one she'd experienced at the séance. Experimentally speaking, she was deadlocked. Her brain felt like stirring mud. For all her excitement about unveiling the mysteries of the device, at that moment her fondest wish was that dinner was ready.

***

Sparky breathed deeply as she strode into the dining room, inhaling the savory smells of Dr. Pogue's housekeeper's cooking. In truth, Mrs. Bingham was more like his mother or auntie than his housekeeper. It was clear that the combined energies of Dr. Yin Young, Mrs. Bingham, and Edmond's sister, Esmeralda, were all required to keep the scientist anchored in reality. Mrs. Bingham entered the room carrying the herbed pork roast from whence emanated the salivation-inducing aroma, followed closely by Drs. Pogue and Young. Sparky looked at the dining table; it was set for four. "Mrs. Bingham, are you going to join us for dinner?"

The housekeeper deposited the platter of roast in the middle of the table next to a dish of candied parsnips, wiped her hands on her apron, and brushed an errant strand of graying auburn hair out of her face. "Oh, heavens no, dear."

"Then why is the table set for four?"

The housekeeper smirked cryptically, popped open her pocket watch, and cocked her head to the side, waiting. The doorbell chimed several rooms away. She nodded at the time on her watch and snapped it shut. "Dr. Pogue, you might leave the 'left-handed' seat open," she suggested as she left the room in the direction of the front door. They had all just taken their seats when Drake entered.

Edmond Pogue perked up. "Chief Inspector, what a delightful surprise!"

Erasmus seated himself to Sparky's left. She gave him a quick peck on the cheek. "Apparently not much of a surprise to Mrs. Bingham, dear. You might want to brush up on your spy techniques if a housekeeper finds your behavior predictable."

Sparky's fiancée changed the subject to hide his discomfort. "Speaking of technique, how are you coming with the crystal ball device?"

"I've fiddled with it all afternoon and observed flashes of the behavior we thought we saw at the séance, but I fear it's too complex for my mechanical skills. Dr. Pogue, if you have a few minutes to spare tomorrow, I'd welcome your observations and analysis."

"Delightful." He rubbed his hands together in glee and motioned for everyone to begin their dinner.

***

Edmond Pogue turned over in bed for what felt like the hundredth time that night. He could never decide if this tendency of his was a blessing or a curse. If he could get the idea out of his head, he could get enough sleep to work on it clearly in the morning. But sometimes he had his best ideas just as he was waking up or falling asleep. Yin had tried to teach him meditation to clear his mind so he could choose whether to think clearly or sleep, but he could never sit still long enough to get the hang of it. Tonight, he was just tired and spinning in circles on the same idea without making progress.

Trains would run more smoothly, and therefore more efficiently, with less friction between the wheels and the rails. If only the train could float above the rails. Electromagnets could be used to push the train away from the rails, but unchecked, it would just push the train off the rails. Other electromagnets could be used to counter the repulsive magnets, but if they were too strong, the train would just clamp down onto the tracks.

It was no use trying to work it out in his head; experimentation was necessary. He stepped out of bed into his slippers, fastened his mechanical arm to the anchors in his stump of his left arm, shrugged into the robe hanging from his bed post, grabbed the hurricane lamp on his nightstand, and headed for his lab. He hoped the noise didn't wake Mrs. Bingham who always gave him a stern scolding when she caught him experimenting in his night clothes. Now if he could only remember where he had left that Daniell cell.

He paused at the bottom of the staircase into the basement. He remembered that he'd wanted the electromagnet away from his other tools during his last experiment with it. It was in the lab that Sparky was using. When he walked into that lab, he was delighted to see that his electromagnet was just sitting on the workbench. Well, that would save him a lot of time searching. And perched right next to it was the peculiarly encased crystal ball that was puzzling both Drake and Sparky. He really shouldn't interfere with Sparky's experiments, but his overriding curiosity got the best of him. He plopped himself down on the high stool next to the workbench and examined the scrollwork cage. He inspected the enclosure for any way of opening it without causing damage. After searching for a hinge or a removable fastener until he was bleary-eyed, he thought he could just make out a seam running between the intersections of some of the scrolls. Somewhere he had an awl that just might fit into the filigree without harming it. Now where had he put that?

He jerked upright, nearly toppling his stool and himself onto the floor. He must have nodded off because he'd had a burst of a dream that was perfectly clear. His vision was of himself opening the second drawer of the tool box on top of the worktable in the back, left corner of his lab. The awl was in the drawer.

Well, I often think most clearly when I'm falling asleep.

He grabbed his lamp and headed for his own lab. Sure enough, the awl was in the second drawer of the tool box on top of the worktable in the back, left corner of his lab. As he stood in front of the worktable with the drawer open and the tool in his hand, he remembered something that made him shudder. In his dream, he'd been wearing the same pajamas and robe he was wearing tonight. Despite his fatigue, he was nearly certain that he had never been in his lab in these same night clothes.

Maybe I should leave the crystal ball for McTrowell's attentions.

He put the awl back in the drawer. In his determination to find the awl, he'd left the Daniell cell in Sparky's lab. He shuffled back to the other lab to retrieve it.

He slouched back down on the stool, put his right elbow on the workbench, rested his head in his left hand, and closed his eyes. He tried breathing slowly for a couple of minutes to see if he would be able to sleep. No, there was no chance of that. He stared at the Daniell cell, trying to visualize how he could arrange multiple electromagnets to both attract and repulse a train from its rails. Maybe if they turned on and off rapidly. Maybe if the ones in the front were attractors and the ones in the back were repulsors. He stared at the ceiling and back at the Daniell cell. He stared at the workbench and back at the Daniell cell. He could tell he was too tired to work out this problem tonight.

I really need to give Yin's meditation concept another try.

He heaved a sigh, looking at the Daniell cell and then at the orb. This time he was sure he hadn't nodded off. He remembered clearly envisioning a very streamlined train, the likes of which had never been built. It had neither smoke stack nor coal car. In fact, it didn't even have wheels although it was following a set of metal tracks. It was racing across the countryside at impossible speed. The backdrop for this amazing conveyance was a single, conical, snow-capped mountain in the distance topped with a caldera. *That is enough for one night,* he thought. He snatched up his lamp and headed back to bed.

***

The salty, sweet smell of fried bacon drew Sparky into the dining room. "Good morning," she chirped brightly before she caught a look at Pogue's face. "Edmond! Are you feeling well? You're very pale!" Instinctively, she leaned forward to check his pulse and temperature. Standing over his breakfast, she realized what he was drinking. "Why are you drinking coffee? That's very unlike you."

"I just couldn't sleep a wink last night." He tried to smile, but it was a poor substitute for his usually infectious grin. "I had nightmares."

"Oh, I'm sorry to hear that. I have several recommendations to help you sleep this evening, although I suspect you will succumb to a nap this afternoon. I advise skipping the coffee and letting the exhaustion take its natural course." She didn't bother telling him that she plainly saw there was something far more important than nightmares affecting him.

***

"Please, everyone!" Gunari shouted to be heard above the din of the whole clan gathered within the circle of the familia's wagons. He climbed up on the steps at the back of his wagon so he could see everyone's faces. "We're all angry about the *fakers* stealing the *yak*." He waited for the collection of angry conversations near the fire to die down. "Revenge will come later. We must find what is ours and take it. The police have it. How do we get the orb back?"

"A cloud of fire will arise in the east! Many will die!" An old woman shrieked from her position well out of the firelight.

"Shhh, mama," soothed the younger woman standing next to her. She pulled her mother into her embrace and stroked the older woman's head through her scarf.

Tshilaba slipped away from her position near Gunari to join the other two women. She led them outside the circle of wagons and addressed the younger woman in hushed tones, "Florica, we must trust the men to return the *yak* to us. But I fear it will not be in time to withdraw Talaitha from its powers," she cast a sorrowful glance at the crazed visage of the older woman. "We must prepare for the worst and protect the circle. The time has come for you to begin leading Luludja on the path to the seeing mind."

"How can you say that? You see what it is doing to my mother! The seeing eye always destroys the seeing mind. We should call the *yak* the destroying eye!" The anxiety in Florica's voice rose with each sentence. "How can you ask me to sacrifice my little girl to this?" She buried her face in her mother's head scarf and began sobbing.

"Florica, I fear this more than you. Remember that I am next in the circle. We know that insanity awaits all in the circle if the *yak* never returns to us. We just don't know when. The circle has protected the world from the evil power of the *yak* since the time of King Bahrām V Gōr. Talaitha knew this when she joined the circle and she accepted the danger when she led you down the path to the seeing mind. I will protect the circle if it is the last thing I do with my sane mind. Prepare Luludja. I promise you that we will begin your mother's withdrawal as soon as the *yak* returns." Tshilaba circled back around the wagon and rejoined the *familia* gathered around the campfire.

"It's settled," Gunari ordered, "Milosh and Nicu will acquire the disguises. The *čhave* will find this *Drake and McTrowell* to get information." He glanced around, searching for his wife. When he caught her eye, Tshilaba made a concerned face and shook her head slightly. "Get to it!" he barked. "We don't have much time!"

***

"Drake! Drake! A minute 'o your time?"

The Chief Inspector stepped into the alley from which the young ruffian had called out. Understanding the value of keeping their relationship secret, the two walked shoulder to shoulder deeper into the shadows. "What is it Spike?"

"Sumpin' peculiar's afoot. A few days ago, a lad shows up actin' all helpful like, askin' can he join our..." Spike hesitated to use the word 'gang'. He and the Chief Inspector maintained the little fiction that Spike and his cohorts got by on strictly legal enterprises. He continued, "...troop. He talked funny, usin' some words I couldn't understand. I think he mighta been gypsy."

"Ah, Romani?"

"Huh? Anyways, I get to thinkin' that them gypsies usually travel together, like in clans."

"True," Drake interjected, abandoning his efforts to correct the lad.

"So, I'm thinkin' where's the rest o' his family? So, I asks around to some blokes I know in other...troops. They's all seeing the same thing."

"Hmmm, this sounds like they are planning to infiltrate as many gangs...er, troops as possible. This could be the beginning of a move to take over certain street enterprises in London. Thank you for bringing this to my attention. If it would not endanger your troop, would you be so kind as to grant entry to this young gypsy lad and report back to me on his activities? I am especially interested in any contacts he makes with other gypsies." The Chief Inspector turned to leave.

"But Drake, you ain't 'eard the strangest bit." The Chief Inspector stopped and turned back around. "All of 'ems askin' what we know about you."

"I beg your pardon?!"

"Every one o' the gypsy lads is askin' around about you an' how you catches thieves."

The Chief Inspector twisted one side of his mustache while contemplating the story. "Well, Spike, that is very interesting indeed. Thank you for bringing this to my attention." Drake reached into his pocket and extracted a couple of pence which he dropped into Spike's hand which was, unsurprisingly, outstretched in anticipation. "It is most imperative that you invite this lad into your ranks and provide me with regular reports. Use the usual methods." He nodded towards Spike's pocket into which the coins had disappeared. "There will be more of those."

***

"I guess it's good that I didn't return in my pajamas," Edmond blurted out as he entered Sparky's lab.

"Excuse me, Dr. Pogue! Whatever are you talking about?" Sparky asked, jerking her gaze up from her examination of the orb with a magnifying glass.

"I came down last night when I couldn't sleep. I was looking for the electromagnet, but I got interested in your crystal ball. I'm sorry for interfering with your experiment." Pogue affected a sheepish smile that only made him more endearing.

"Ah, I thought it looked like it had been moved. Frankly, I'm frustrated and would welcome your 'interference.' So far I've only ascertained that it responds to magnetic fields."

"Oh," Edmond responded, "well that explains why the electromagnet was moved. I couldn't figure out how to open the cage."

"Nor I."

"I'm afraid I didn't make any real progress. I nodded off...and had really strange dreams. I gave up and went back to bed."

Pogue's comment about bad dreams piqued Sparky's curiosity for two reasons. She wondered if that wasn't why he seemed so fatigued at breakfast. Of more interest was her memory of her own waking dream the day before. Was it possible the orb could affect one's thoughts. How would such an effect be achieved? Perhaps through mesmerism?

"Dr. McTrowell?" Dr. Pogue reached out to touch her hand. "Are you unwell?"

Sparky snapped out of her reverie. "I apologize. I had a similar experience, Edmond. Are you sure you were asleep?"

"No, not quite. I was sleepy, but I still thought I was awake."

"I was distracted, but I was sure I was awake as well. I was just wondering if the device was designed to mesmerize people. Could that be how it's used in séances?"

Pogue scratched his head. "I don't know much about mesmerism. Isn't it meant to draw out memories?"

"Yes."

"One of the 'dreams' I had might have been something I remembered, but the other seemed like it was an idea for new technology, a train that did not require wheels."

"I too was thinking about an invention!" Sparky continued hopefully, "Perhaps the crystal ball helps focus one's mind! Wouldn't that be marvelous?"

"Delightful! But how does it work?"

"Ah yes. We seem to be back to the original question. How does it work?" It was Sparky's turn to scratch her head.

"I have an idea. Yin has tried to teach me to clear my mind, a kind of meditation. She says it helps her focus."

This idea perplexed Sparky. "Dr. Young unfocuses her mind to focus it?"

Pogue nodded. "It does sound counterintuitive, but it seems to work for her."

"This reminds me somewhat of Indian vision quests."

"Indians like Jonathan Lord Ashleigh?"

"No, I meant the native people of my home. But Indians like Jonathan Lord Ashleigh also have yogis. I feel like we have arrived at a hypothesis and an experimental plan. Perhaps, if we can discern what it does, we will have a clue as to how it works. What do you think, Edmond?"

"Delightful! I will ask for Yin's assistance identifying a Buddhist monk."

"And I shall inquire with Lord Ashleigh whether he knows any yogis in London." Sparky paused to think about the happily tasty benefit of a visit to Lord Ashleigh: chai. She unconsciously smacked her lips. "I'm off. I hope to have information by dinnertime."

***

"Constable Higgins," Drake began as he exited his office. He scanned the outer office where all the Constables had their shared desks. Higgins was nowhere in sight. Ever since the incident at the hospital with Professor Farnsworth, Higgins had been the soul of conscientiousness and Drake had come to rely on him. Much as he dreaded the inevitable outcome, he turned to Sergeant Parseval. "Sergeant, have you seen Constable Higgins this morning? Is he out on patrol?"

The Sergeant nearly sniffed in disdain as he answered, "Constable Higgins is seeing to his uniform."

The Chief Inspector waited for a more informative answer. He counted patiently in his head to three before pursuing his line on inquiry, "What does that mean, Sergeant Parseval? Is he sewing on a loose button? Is he cleaning his boots?"

"Sir..." Drake would have sworn that the Sergeant was on the verge of snickering. "...his uniform has gone missing. The sot ought to lay off the drink."

Drake considered continuing his questioning, but had tired of the Sergeant's thinly veiled arrogance. He nodded to conclude the conversation and retreated to his office. He knew Higgins well enough to know that the man didn't drink to excess. And even if he had, for Sergeant Parseval to jest at the expense of another officer of Her Majesty's Metropolitan Police was unforgivably unprofessional.

***

Sparky let herself sink into the upholstered arm chair and drew in the enchanting aroma of the chai that Virat, Johnathon Lord Ashleigh's servant, had delivered to her hands just minutes before. She loved the sweet, spicy, creamy, Indian tea prepared at just the right temperature for sipping. Sparky was so entranced by the divine liquid refreshment, she nearly forgot the reason for her visit.

Lord Ashleigh, the young, half-Indian viscount, sat across from her with his own cup of chai, waiting patiently for her attention.

He noticed her distraction and smiled to himself. "Ahem," he began, "Dr. McTrowell, I believe you mentioned urgent business when you arrived on my doorstep. Surely it was not just an unquenchable craving for chai."

The airship pilot glanced guiltily across the rim of the bone china teacup as she gave its contents another substantial slurp. "And what if it was?"

Lord Ashleigh's characteristic mirthful, booming laugh erupted from his chest. "If you are in such desperate need, I can arrange for regular deliveries."

Sparky paused a moment while considering the possibility. It wasn't her primary business, but she had opportunistic tendencies that were hard to suppress. Momentarily she considered the bliss of drinking Virat's spicy, sweet concoction every day. She could get so much more work done! She shook her head to snap herself out of her tea-fueled reverie. "Splendid though that would be, that is not the purpose of my visit. Although, perhaps, we could come back to that topic later. Drake, Dr. Edmond Pogue, Dr. Yin Young, and I are engaged in a highly unusual investigation."

"This wouldn't have anything to do with the arrest of those alleged gypsies, would it?" He winked ever so slightly.

"Do you know absolutely everything that happens in London?" Sparky quipped.

"And in all of Her Majesty's empire if necessary. Remember, she has ten thousand eyes and ten thousand ears." His tone was less mirthful.

Sparky nodded. As one pair of those eyes and ears, along with her fiancé, Chief Inspector Drake, she knew all too well how much information flowed to Lord Ashleigh. Most people who encountered him were taken in by the external trappings of his life: half-British, half- Indian viscount; first Indian graduate of Oxford College of Law; flamboyant dresser; bon vivant, and for all that he had accomplished, young. He was the absolute opposite of everything one would expect of a spymaster, which is what made his cover so perfect.

"Indeed, it would," Sparky continued. "One of the items confiscated in the raid is an object with...unusual, and as yet, undetermined properties. Dr. Pogue and I think it might benefit from examination by a yogi. Do you know one in London?"

The viscount burst into laughter again. "Dr. McTrowell, I have never imagined you a spiritual woman."

She pulled a face that waxed between non-committal and circumspect. "It has more to do with the ability to control and focus one's mind than with spirituality, per se."

"Of course, dear Sparky, whatever you say," Lord Ashleigh replied archly. "As it happens, I know just the man. Shall I arrange a meeting?"

"Yes, please." She thought for a moment. "It might be better if he traveled out to Dr. Pogue's residence in Shadwell, if it's not too much trouble. I realize it might be a bit of a trip, but I think it would safer if we didn't transport the device more than necessary."

"I completely understand."

Sparky tipped her head far back to capture the last delicious drops of chai. "I don't suppose Virat made more?" She asked hopefully.

***

"Pssst! Drake!" Spike hissed from the cover of the alley.

Drake glanced around to ascertain whether he was being watched, bending over to make a show of tying his shoelace. Detecting no observer, he sidestepped nonchalantly into the alley and moved quickly into the deeper shadows, keeping an eye on the entrance to the alley. "Spike, what have you learned about the gypsy boys?"

"The gypsies? Most peculiar. They's offering to tell 'ow them thefts was committed. But they won' tell me. They'll only tell you."

"Have you heard the same information from the other troops?"

"Yes, Inspector."

Drake was getting suspicious. He was beginning to smell a conspiracy, and it smelled foul. "And what do they want in return?"

"Did I mention this 'ole business was peculiar? They ain't askin' for nuffin'," Spike answered with a look of intense seriousness.

"Yes, 'peculiar' might be one word for it, Spike," the Chief Inspector continued. 'Machiavellian' might be another."

"'Scuse me?"

"They want something and I am almost entirely certain I know what it is. Were you able to follow the young Romani lad who has joined your...troop?"

"No, 'e gave me the slip every time I tried."

"Well, they have certainly had centuries of persecution to perfect those skills." The Chief Inspector glanced over his informant's shoulder toward the alley entrance. "However, you have not done as well 'giving him the slip.'"

"Beg pardon?"

"I believe you have a shadow."

"Wot?" Spike flinched and started to turn.

Drake grabbed his sleeve to stop him. "Do not turn around!" Drake hissed. He continued *sotto voce,* "I am going to raise my voice so I can be heard. I need you to play along. Nod if you understand." Spike bobbed his head once. Drake continued, using his stage voice, "Spike, I am indebted to you for this valuable information. Scotland Yard has no leads on the methods used to commit these terrible thefts. Any other information you can supply would be rewarded commensurately."

Spike's face turned quizzical at the last word, but he played along. "AYE, CHIEF INSPECTOR DRAKE!"

Drake interjected in a whisper, "You don't need to shout. He wants to meet me. We just need to draw him out."

"Er, right. Thank you, Ghief Inspector Drake. I'll come to Scotlan' Yard wif you an' give a full statement."

Drake steered Spike by the elbow and the two commenced a non-threateningly casual pace out of the alley. When they reached the street, the young Romani boy was leaning against the building pretending he was just watching the carriages roll past. Drake looked down at him beneficently, "Good day, lad. What is your name?"

"Zindelo, Mr. Chief Inspector Drake."

Drake reached out as if to shake the boy's hand, but deftly grabbed him by the collar. The Chief Inspector blew two quick blasts on his police whistle, bringing a Constable running. He passed the boy to the Constable. "Take this boy to Scotland Yard," he ordered. "And keep a firm grip on him. I expect that he has exemplary skills of evasion. I apologize for leaving him with you, but I must run on ahead!" With that, Drake took off at a sprint in the direction of Scotland Yard.

When he arrived at Scotland Yard, the scene was complete chaos, just as he had expected. The desk sergeant was completely befuddled and overwhelmed by a swirling, wailing crowd of women, all Romani judging by their clothing and accents. It didn't matter what their complaints were; they were achieving their diversionary goal. Before he'd gone to the orphanage and then into the care of Edwin Llewellyn, young Drake had been a master of the misdirection game. Rather than wade in, he observed for a moment. The women had brought a swarm of unruly children with them. The children ran amok, tipping over inkwells, scattering papers, and jumping on furniture. They were playing the game too. Drake was looking for the one who wasn't. There! Sly as a vole, focused as a raptor, a girl in completely nondescript clothing was slipping into his own office, unnoticed in the mayhem. He dashed after her, closing and locking the door behind himself. She had just started a methodical search of his desk.

"Good day, miss. What are you doing in my office? In my desk?"

"I'm so sorry, sir," she actually curtsied. "I got lost."

"Well," he replied calmly, "that certainly explains you ransacking my desk."

"I, um,..." she made a break for the door. Recalling his own time playing this game, Drake stepped aside, knowing the door was locked, and dodging the inevitable kick to his shins. As she flew past, he grabbed her by the waist and held her at arm's length to avoid her flailing feet. When he joined Scotland Yard, he never imagined himself detaining so many children. The effort required all his upper body and arm strength to hold her up until she squirmed herself into a state of defeat.

He tucked the would-be thief under one arm and unlocked the door. No sooner had he stepped out of the door than the din subsided. As he suspected, Zindelo was supposed to detain him while the rest of the gypsies acted as a diversion so the girl could search his office for the device. When he exited with the girl in tow, they knew the game was up; they all hustled out of the station. He set the girl down. Without the diversion, she was no longer a danger. She too ran out the door.

Drake mused, *The Romani had taken a great risk exposing themselves in this way. That crystal ball must have immense value.*

It gave him cause to worry for the safety of Sparky and everyone else in Pogue's household.

***

"Good evening, Dr. Pogue. This is Yogi Suneel."

"Good evening, Lord Ashleigh, Yogi Suneel. Delightful of you both to come! Has Dr. McTrowell explained our experiment?"

"Yes, she has," replied the viscount.

"And Deva Raya has explained to me," continued the yogi, calling the viscount by his Indian name. "But perhaps you do not understand the nature of meditation. It is not like the fortune telling of the Romani. It does not see the future. It looks inward, not outward."

"Oh, yes, we understand," Pogue replied enthusiastically. "We believe the device helps you think more clearly, but only when your mind's unfocused. Since you're an expert, we thought you might give it a try and tell us if it helps you think more clearly than just meditating. We're hoping that might give us a clue as to how it works. Please, come this way," Pogue gestured in the direction of the dining room. He and McTrowell had decided it would be a less foreboding venue than the dungeon-like lab.

Drs. McTrowell and Young were already seated in the dining room, each with a pencil and notebook in front of her, ready to take notes on their observations. Pogue indicated the place at the head of the table to the yogi where the device rested. He nodded politely to the women and took the proffered seat. Pogue and Ashleigh stood behind the yogi in hopes of making closer observations.

"Before you begin, please think of a question or conundrum that you have been unable to resolve," McTrowell directed. "You needn't tell us what it is, but it should be in your mind as you begin meditating. Will that work?"

"Yes," replied the yogi.

"Then please, begin when you are ready." She and Yin sat poised anxiously with their pencils above their notebooks.

***

Between swigs of his beer, Sergeant Parseval teased Constable Higgins as he approached the pub's communal table, "I see you found your trousers."

"Sergeant Parseval, I must insist that you desist from ridiculing the Constable. It is unseemly," Drake protested as Constable Higgins found a seat and set down his beer. Drake continued,

"Although I am curious what happened." He settled back into his seat in the basement of Ye Olde Cheshire, enjoying a quiet evening with his companions after the unusually hectic day. He sipped his beer thoughtfully.

"I don't rightly know. I sent my uniform in for laundering, as usual," the Constable reported. "When I went to collect it, the laundress said it had gone missing. Just like that. She's always been so reliable, never lost anything before."

"So, what did you do?" the Sergeant asked, waving at the Constable's uniform.

The Constable gave the sleeve a perfunctory brush with his hand. "I bought a new one."

"That must have cost a pretty penny! Did she offer to pay for it?"

"She did, but it's not as if she could afford it. We agreed she could work the cost doing my laundry. I just hope she doesn't lose anything else or I'll never get even." The Constable took a long pull on his pint glass.

The Chief Inspector cast a sympathetic glance at the Constable. He knew full well that the Constable couldn't afford to pay for a new uniform. He remembered being a poor young bobbie. Sensing Higgins' discomfort with the discussion, he decided to change the subject. "That was quite a kerfuffle we had today at the Yard."

Grateful to have the attention off his own mishap, Constable Higgins responded, "Yes, what was that all about?"

"Most of the action was pure nonsense," explained the Chief Inspector, taking the opportunity to impart some of his experience to his younger colleagues. "It was meant as a diversion to draw our attention from the quiet, plainly-dressed little girl who snuck into my office." He digressed for a moment, "That was a clever tactic, using a girl whom we would be less likely to notice or suspect of criminal intent." He tucked that thought into his mental notebook and continued, "Her mission was to search my office. Almost certainly she was looking for the device that we confiscated from the ring of 'gypsy' thieves."

"All this trouble over a crystal ball. How absurd!" the Sergeant offered.

"She would not have found it in any case. It is safely in the custody of Drs. McTrowell, Pogue, and Young. They are performing a series of experiments to determine how it functions." As much as Ye Olde Cheshire Cheese was effectively Drake's home, he felt uncomfortable discussing this sensitive matter in such a public place. "Gentlemen, it has been quite an eventful day. I believe I shall buy you the next round." The Sergeant and Constable weren't fools; they didn't object, but just smiled agreeably.

As the Chief Inspector approached the bar, a bobbie loitering at the dark end of it detached himself and slipped along the back wall, avoiding Drake's notice. He strolled by the booths, deftly nicking Sergeant Parseval's helmet as he passed their booth. He was out the door before Drake turned around from the bar.

***

Yogi Suneel sat with his eyes closed for a full ten minutes during which time Sparky began fidgeting like a bored schoolgirl. Once or twice she opened her mouth to speak, but Yin silenced the flight surgeon preemptively with a finger to her lips. The yogi's breathing was so slow and steady that Sparky thought he might have fallen asleep, but he was still sitting perfectly upright, and yet relaxed. She wondered how he was going to gaze into the orb with his eyes shut tight. Just as her patience was about to expire, Yogi Suneel slowly opened his eyes half way and looked into the orb. She had the sense that he was looking into the distance, as if he could see clearly through the blue sphere and beyond. She made a note while observing that Yin was writing as well. A small furrow appeared in his brow; he seemed to be doing battle with it, struggling to will his face back to serenity.

He closed his eyes and slumped in his chair, breathing rapidly and shallowly in sharp contrast to his earlier composure. Concerned that the yogi had taken a bad turn, Sparky quietly put down her pen and grasped his wrist, checking his pulse. He placed his other hand on top of hers and opened his eyes slowly. "Thank you for your concern, Dr. McTrowell, but I am recovering."

"Recovering from what, might I ask?" She withdrew her hand and retrieved her writing instrument.

"I had a vision that could not have come from within."

Sparky raised an eyebrow. "How can you be certain?" She and the other three assembled around the table leaned in toward the yogi.

"Recall that you engaged me for my lifetime of experience with meditation. This vision was unlike any other I have ever had. I anticipated clarity..." the yogi began.

"That's exactly what Yin says," Pogue confirmed.

"Quite so," continued the yogi, "but instead I was met with confusion, a vision I cannot explain."

The prevaricating got the best of Sparky. "What did you see?"

"I saw people of all colors, living together, among the stars, clustered around the device as we are tonight."

The yogi placed his hands, palms down, on the tops of his thighs and returned to his earlier pattern of measured breathing. Sparky, Edmond, Yin, and Lord Ashleigh sat in stunned silence at this revelation. Breaking the silence, Yin asked, "Yogi Suneel, what was the question you imagined?"

"I was considering when humanity will find peace."

***

"Master An has asked to examine the device outdoors. We will go to the garden," Dr. Young announced perfunctorily.

Pogue interjected jokingly, "Apparently Buddhist monks prefer the fresh air of outdoors, although that's something of a dodgy proposition out here in Shadwell."

Sparky looked back and forth between Yin and Edmond. "You have a garden?"

Edmond smiled his broad, sparkling smile. "It's really more the Binghams' and now Yin grows interesting things too. Mrs. Bingham says it's beastly hard to get good veg and herbs out here, so she and the mister grow a few things. And Yin grows things I've never seen before. No idea where she gets the seeds. Sometimes I think she's doing botany experiments with me." He chuckled.

"A garden," Sparky sighed. "I wish I had a garden."

"I think you need a permanent home first," Pogue replied.

"Oh, I'm so sorry. I can make other arrangements for lodging. I didn't realize I was imposing!"

Edmond reached out to take her gently by the shoulder. "I didn't mean it like that. You're always welcome here. We find your company, and your experiments, delightful. Don't we, Yin?" Dr. Young nodded her head in agreement. "I just meant that you might want someplace to call your own. Someplace to share with someone special, like a certain handsome chief inspector." He winked at Sparky as he leaned over to give Yin a peck on the cheek.

Sparky sniffled involuntarily at the thought of a real home. She hadn't thought about her mother's little vegetable garden in years. It seemed unlikely that chilies would grow in the damp cold of England, but squash might have a chance in the summer. Pogue's words swam through her misty gardening memories, "...bring it up to the roof while Yin and I prepare the setting."

"Huh?" she replied somewhat incoherently. Then she mentally filled in the bits that she'd missed. "Oh, yes, I'll go fetch the device and bring it to the garden." She turned to head to the lab, and then turned back sheepishly. "Um, how do I get to the garden?"

"The spiral staircase at the back of the kitchen. Easy access for Mrs. Bingham." He trotted after Yin in the direction of the aforementioned kitchen.

***

Although Sparky had seen no indication that the device was at all fragile, she still took great care with it. At least that's how she rationalized keeping it wrapped in a heavy, soft cloth. Certainly, it wasn't that she'd developed a sense of dread about it. The iron spiral staircase proved especially tricky to navigate with her parcel and she was relieved to arrive on the roof without incident. The roof garden was a surprising oasis of serenity in the middle of Shadwell. It consisted of a half dozen raised planter boxes, one especially deep one with neat rows of carrots and potato plants. Another was a maze of scaffolding for pole beans and tomatoes. Yet another was a darling, compact herb garden. One farther on was full of leafy vegetables, probably cabbage and lettuce. She couldn't identify the seedlings in the other two boxes. A small shed, probably for potting, stood at the far end of all the boxes.

Pogue and Young had spread old blankets in the walkway intersection between the four nearest planter boxes and were in the process of arranging a dazzlingly colorful assortment of pillows on top. The pillows looked as though they had been borrowed from Lord Ashleigh's sitting room. Right on cue, the viscount popped up from the kitchen carrying another armload of pillows. Virat followed close behind him carrying a hinged wooden box with corners clad in brass filigree, and a glass flask filled with a milky tan fluid. Without a word, he handed the flask to Sparky. Virat passed the box to Lord Ashleigh who opened it in the middle of the circle of cushions to reveal a brass incense burner and sticks of incense. The barrister selected one stick, lit it, and inserted it in the burner. He gestured to Sparky to hand him the device which he settled on one of the cushions near the incense burner. Sparky was only too happy to relinquish her burden because she didn't need to open the flask to know that Virat had been thoughtful enough to deliver chai to her. It was all she could do not to drink it straight out of the flask. Yin announced, "We are ready," and headed back toward the staircase. Sparky followed close behind. Going through the kitchen meant getting a teacup to enjoy the warm present from Virat.

In addition to the teacup, Sparky also found Drake in the kitchen happily tucking into a piece of Mrs. Bingham's rhubarb pie. She remembered seeing the red stalks of the rhubarb in the planter box with the cabbage and lettuce. "Good afternoon, dear." She dropped a kiss on his forehead. He smiled up at her with red-stained lips. "Would you care to join us on the roof for our next experiment?" He nodded enthusiastically, devouring the last two bites of pie and wiping his mouth with a napkin.

"Thank you, Mrs. Bingham. It was, as Dr. Pogue would say, delightful." He handed the plate and napkin back to the housekeeper, and followed his fiancée up the iron staircase, struggling to maneuver his walking cane in the tight spiral. He nearly bumped into Sparky who had stopped right at the top of the staircase, standing with her arms akimbo.

"How did he get up here?" she asked, gesturing at the man wrapped in flowing robes seated on the cushion immediately in front of the device. "I was in the kitchen the whole time."

Edmond pointed to the edge of the roof on the far side of the planter boxes. "There's an outside staircase just over there."

Sparky could just make out a handrail coming up over the edge of the roof. "Then why did we come up through the kitchen?"

"It's easier from inside the house. You have to go around the building to get to that one. And it's normally locked," Pogue explained.

"Oh," Sparky admitted, "that makes more sense. It looks like we're ready to start." She extracted her notebook and pencil from her pocket, and moved to take a seat on the cushions with Drake and Pogue following closely behind. Yin was already explaining the experiment to Master An, at least that's what Sparky assumed since they were conversing quietly in Chinese. Master An nodded thoughtfully a couple of times. Yin sat back on her cushion and prepared to take notes which Sparky took as her cue to do likewise. Master An's actions were remarkably similar to Yogi Suneel's, although he sat cross-legged with his hands on his knees. He breathed quietly and deeply for a few minutes with his eyes closed.

Although Master An's eyes were still closed, Sparky thought she saw the black particles in the orb begin to coalesce. She tried to focus through the filigree, but what she could see from her position looked like swirling water.

It's probably just the light refracting through the filigree and crystal...and my exhausted imagination.

Her attention was diverted when, out of the corner of her eye, she spotted Drake moving. She hoped he wouldn't disturb the experiment with his action. She hazarded a glance at him to signal him to settle quietly when she realized that he was drawing the sword from his cane. As stealthily as possible, he crept toward the roof edge, using the planter boxes as cover.

Before Master An could open his eyes, Erasmus shouted, "Boarders!" Sparky thought this a peculiar thing to say under the circumstances, but knowing Drake's childhood at sea had probably taught him to use that term when intruders came over the edge of any structure. She jumped up to assist him as half a dozen Romani men with their faces obscured by brightly patterned scarves scrambled over the roof edge from the external staircase. She dashed into the melee, quickly realizing that the intruders were armed with knives. Her fists wouldn't be enough. She cast about for another weapon. Nothing! Maybe in the potting shed? She sprinted down the length of the planter boxes.

Drake shouted over his shoulder, "Pogue, get the master and the device to safety!" Pogue didn't need to be told twice; he scooped up the device and hustled Master An toward the kitchen stairs. Virat's ever-ready throwing knives materialized in his hands. He ran backwards after Dr. Pogue and Master An, securing their escape.

In a single, smooth movement, Yin leapt to her feet, grasped the piping at the collar of her dress with her right hand, and deftly pulling it up and away from her body. The cord of the piping disengaged the tiny swing clasps adorning the front of the bodice and the inside of both sleeves, instantaneously releasing the dress to reveal Dr. Young's gi. She flipped the latches at the ankles of her boots to release her feet. In three leaping steps, she was across the nearest planter box and flanking Drake. Lord Ashleigh balanced himself on the corner of the box nearest the outside stairs, giving himself a higher vantage point from which to deploy his throwing knives without endangering the other members of Her Majesty's Eyes and Ears.

Drake executed a circular parry with his sword against the nearest intruder, sending his attacker's knife flying off the roof while simultaneously doing just enough damage to his opponent's knife hand to dissuade further attacks.

Sparky yanked open the door of the potting shed. Shovel? No. Hoe? Not quite. Trowel? How much damage could she do with that? Garden fork? That would have to do. When she finally joined the fight, she realized that she had the most formidable weapon, but was the least useful. She stepped back from the fray, positioning herself to poke the intruders back into range of her compatriots.

Another attacker lunged at Yin. Perhaps she just looked like a tiny woman in her pajamas. The paralyzing, disarming block of her hand against his wrist and the crisp blow of the heel of her hand against his nose proved otherwise. Not that he was conscious to register the error of his ways. His unconscious body slumped into the path of his compatriots, forcing them to dodge around. One hopped up into the planter box growing greens.

"Not the rhubarb!" screamed Drake.

"Of course not, dear," Sparky called back, forking the assailant out of the planter box and onto the roof on his back. That was going to leave a mark.

"Gypsies!" spat Drake.

"Romani," Sparky corrected him.

"Really, dear, now is not the time for semantic hair-splitting!"

The exchange distracted Drake for a moment, allowing two attackers to come up from behind him. One attacker raised his knife, aiming it at the back of Drake's neck.

"Duck!" Lord Ashleigh shouted. Lord Ashleigh's twirling knife skimmed past the top of Drake's bowed head before implanting itself in the assailant's throat. With blood gurgling out of his throat, the attacker toppled over the edge of the building.

The other attacker dodged around the confrontation to pursue the orb and its protectors down the kitchen stairs. His quarry sat perched on the kitchen table, defended only by the slight Dr. Pogue. Knife in hand, the attacker advanced on the scientist. Pogue attempted to protect the orb with his body. The attacker lunged. Pogue whistled a sharp note, activating his mechanical arm. The arm flailed wildly, confusing the attacker, but failing to disarm him. The attacker lunged again, forcing Pogue to dodge away from the table. Sensing his opening, the attacker grabbed for the orb. Mrs. Bingham slipped from her hiding place in the pantry and brained the attacker with a cast iron frying pan.

"Well done, Mrs. Bingham!" Pogue exclaimed. "You would make a fine batsman."

Drake glanced down the outside staircase. There were no more members of the boarding party. He assessed the carnage: three down, one dead. "Sparky, is there any rope in that shed?"

Pogue popped up at the door to the kitchen stairs. "There's another one down here in the kitchen."

Sparky returned the garden fork to the shed and returned with a spool of heavy, hemp twine. "This is all there is."

"It will have to do for now. Please tie up these three. I will manage the one in the kitchen." Wearily he pulled his whistle out of his pocket and blew two short blasts to summon assistance.

***

Once the bobbies had incarcerated the living assailants and sent the dead to the morgue, the members of Her Majesty's Eyes and Ears convened back in Pogue's kitchen for tea and port.

"Given this second attempt to steal the crystal ball, I think it best that I relocate here for the time being, if that's not an imposition, Dr. Pogue," Drake suggested.

"That would be delightful! There's plenty of room."

The Chief Inspector was uncharacteristically agitated. "Lord Ashleigh, what do you think about calling in Sergeant Fox? Is he available? Dr. Young, you are the Sergeant's sparring partner. Do you know where he is?"

As the director of the secret organization *Her Majesty's Eyes & Ears,* the viscount was not used to taking orders; he was more accustomed to leading. He paused a moment before answering, recognizing that Drake's state of enervation was most probably induced by his concern for McTrowell's safety. Lord Ashleigh had observed more than once that, although the Chief Inspector truly believed her capable of taking care of herself, he never stopped worrying about her. She was quite the risk taker. "Yes, the Sergeant's presence would be an excellent precaution under the circumstances. I believe I can have him relieved from his current duties with Her Royal Majesty's Aerial Marines." He took a sip of his port. "May I make an observation from my experience at my father's court?" The assemblage nodded. "As interesting as that crystal ball is, it is not gold or encrusted with jewels. As the Chief Inspector has pointed out, this is the second attempt the Romani have made to recover it. This time they sent four armed men, all of whom were prepared to die; one of whom did. There are things in this world that are worth more than money. They are worth life itself. This device is one of them. Henceforth, we must treat it as such. Until we know what its value is, it must not leave this building and it must never be unattended. I will fetch Sergeant Fox. In the meantime, I suggest the rest of you redouble your efforts to determine its functionality." He graciously kissed Mrs. Bingham's hand before departing with Virat.

"Well," Drake interjected, "I am too enervated to sleep. I shall take the first watch."

"I will join you," McTrowell offered. "Perhaps we can discuss wedding plans," she quipped. Judging by the blank looks around the table, her joke had fallen flat. "Actually, I would just welcome the time to talk with you. Mrs. Bingham, would you please make us a strong pot of tea?" She pushed back from the table and kissed him on the forehead. "I'll meet you in the lab. Um, where is Master An?"

"I believe he has retreated upstairs to regain his equanimity through meditation. Would that we could all do the same."

***

"So," Drake started nonchalantly, "what do we know? Or what do we think we know?"

"It seems to interact with the observer's brain. I have absolutely no scientific or medical explanation for that," Sparky responded dejectedly. "It gives you visions, but sometimes they're like memories and sometimes they're fantastical and sometimes they're nightmares."

"What if it is not scientific or medical in nature?"

Sparky rolled her eyes. "Please let's not have that conversation about whether time travel is possible again!"

Erasmus looked at her lovingly. "I was not suggesting time travel..." He chose his next words carefully. "I am only suggesting that we suspend some of our rationality briefly to consider the implausible. Perhaps expanding our sphere of considerations will suggest a novel path forward." He smiled hopefully.

She snorted slightly in response. "That was a lot of words to say that we're just going to make up fantastical nonsense. But we're out of ideas and we have nothing but time. Let's try it. We're pretty sure the observer has some question in mind when they have the visions and the visions are related to the question. I was thinking about an artificial light source when I saw a man; Pogue was thinking about trains when he saw something like a train that might be an invention of the type he was considering."

Drake rubbed his chin. "Yogi Suneel was considering a question about the future of humanity when he saw people among the stars. Perhaps it is an *invention* invention."

Sparky stared at him incredulously. "It reads your mind and invents what you want?"

"That does sound outrageous when you say it like that. But I had a similar experience with Green Fantasy and the Colt Pocket 1849. Do you suppose Pogue has any of that Green Fantasy?"

She popped open her pocket watch. "I think he said he procured some for some additional experiments. We still have half the night. We might as well search the place." She surveyed the cluttered, cavernous lab. "That should keep us busy until Drs. Pogue and Young relieve us in the morning."

Forty-five minutes, and what seemed like a hundred sneezes, later, Drake found a single bottle in the back of a cabinet. It was only a quarter full. He held it up triumphantly for Sparky to see and sneezed three more times. Sparky patted the seat of one of the stools next to the workbench and carefully uncovered the device. "Have a seat, my dear. I'll fetch a notebook while you consider the invention you're curious about."

The Chief Inspector perched on the stool and considered the device and Green Fantasy with some trepidation. Not all of his experiences with the green elixir had been positive. The addition of the cryptic orb made this experiment somewhat questionable. His fiancée returned with her note-taking equipment.

"Have you thought of your question?" she asked.

"I have. Do you suppose I should tell you or not?"

Sparky pondered the question for a moment. "Every other time, the observer was either alone, so there was no one to tell, not that either of us thought we were 'using' the device, or, in the case of Yogi Suneel, he didn't say anything." She gave the matter further consideration before tearing the back page out of her notebook. "Here, write it on this and fold it up. We'll look at it together at the end of the experiment." She handed the page and her pencil to Drake who scribbled something quickly and folded the sheet of paper.

He took a deep breath and exhaled. He uncorked the bottle of Green Fantasy and swigged a large mouthful. He focused his mind intently on the question for a couple of minutes while he waited for the elixir to take effect. He opened his eyes and gazed into the depths of the orb.

"AAAAEEEEEE!!!"

"Erasmus, Erasmus! What's wrong?!"

The Chief Inspector flailed wildly like he was swatting away a ravening flock of raptors. Sparky grabbed at his arms, trying to get him under control and protect the device. He was strong, stronger than she remembered. And he weighed half again as much as she did. She pinioned his right arm behind his back. He smacked her in the face with his free hand. Stupid! She should have grabbed his dominant left arm first. Sensing she was running out of options, she pulled him backwards off the stool. Her efforts to control his fall failed. He landed on top of her, elbowing her in the stomach in the process. It took all her strength to roll him off her. She sat on his back, pinning his arms with her knees. It was like riding a bucking bronco. She tried rubbing his head to soothe him. His behavior was too erratic for her to check his pulse. It took him several minutes to completely stop thrashing. His breathing settled into a steady, slow rhythm. She checked his pulse. He was either unconscious or asleep, but the worst had passed. She rolled him onto his back as gently as possible and slouched against the leg of the workbench. She hurt all over.

***

"Urrrgh. Bleah." Drake tried to open his eyes. Even opening them slightly brought searing pain. He could feel every heartbeat in his temples as if his head were about to burst. His whole body felt battered, like the first time he'd repelled boarders. No, not quite. He didn't feel cut anywhere. Despite the throbbing headache, he tried to inventory the damage. He also didn't seem to have any broken bones. Perhaps he had been mugged. Whoever had done it was quite skilled to have inflicted so much damage without cuts or broken bones.

"Cack, urg."

"Darling, how are you feeling?"

"Blurgle."

"Don't try to talk," Sparky instructed him calmly. "I'm going to dribble a little bit of water in your mouth slowly." She opened his mouth gently and trickled in just a few drops to make sure he could swallow. When she was confident that he had swallowed safely, she repeated the process. After the fourth time, she asked, "Would you like to try to sit up?"

"Yus pull."

"I'll take that as a yes." She crouched by his head and hefted his torso from under the shoulders. Even the top half of his body was more weight than she could handle easily. She sat on the floor behind to hold him up. "Can you tell me what happened?"

"I do no' know. Waaas I mugged?"

"You don't remember? You drank some Green Fantasy and looked into the crystal ball. And then you started screaming and flailing. I got you onto the floor and held you down until you stopped. You've been passed out for more than an hour. What did you see?"

The Chief Inspector tried to remember through the fog of pain.

"Ahhhhh!"

Sparky clamped his arms against his torso to prevent a repeat of the previous assault. "Shhhh. You're fine. I'm here," she whispered in his ear. He relaxed and slumped forward.

"Can I let go?" she offered.

He nodded wearily. "Would you like some more water?" He nodded again. She handed him the cup. He managed to drink from it without her assistance. She continued to prop him up until she felt his own muscles take control. "Can you talk now?"

"I think so." He gingerly scooted around on the floor until he was facing her. As inappropriate as he felt it was to sit on the floor, he didn't have the strength to stand up. Gradually he opened his eyes. The first thing he saw was her blackened left eye. "What happened to you? Whom do I need to arrest?"

"Um, yourself."

"I did that to you?"

"Not intentionally, my love. As I said, you started thrashing about as soon as you looked into the crystal ball. Can you recall anything you saw?"

Drake shuddered. "Fire, everywhere. I was standing among low stone and mud brick houses. People were running around screaming in terror." He paused. "They were dressed in loose robes, like togas." He paused again, struggling to recall more detail. "There were hills with colonnaded buildings on them. Like temples." A more complete picture formed in his mind. "It was as if I were in ancient Greece...or Rome?"

"You said 'hills,' plural?"

"Yes."

"And everything was on fire?"

"Yes."

"That sounds like the great fire of Rome."

"It does."

"What question did you ask?" She pulled the piece of paper down from the workbench and read it. *How can we report social disturbances more rapidly?* "Why would you ask such a question and what does that have to do with the great fire of Rome?"

"I asked the question because civil authorities often learn of emergencies after it is too late to contain them," he replied matter-of-factly. "Rapid reporting would reduce damage and casualties. As an officer of the law, such a capability would have great value to me. If the crystal ball is an 'invention invention' as we surmised, I would like to know how to create such a capability."

"Hmm, I guess that makes sense." She paused to connect her thoughts. "And the great fire of Rome?"

"For this I have no answer." They stared at each other in confusion.

***

When Pogue arrived with Young in the early hours of the morning to relieve Drake and McTrowell, he gasped at what he saw. "Good lord! What happened to you two?"

Drake moaned. Sparky responded, "We did another experiment. It went horribly wrong, but provided valuable insight."

"Did it involve a bender and a street fight?"

"That's not too far from the truth," Sparky allowed, causing Pogue to wince. "Drake tried to use the device after drinking some Green Fantasy. We found a little bit you had left over from the last time you two experimented with it."

Trying not to feel like a potted plant, Drake added, "I had a vision of the great fire of Rome."

Pogue scratched his head. "How is that informative?"

Sparky continued, "For the sake of argument, let's assume that the device somehow interacts with the observer's brain. I'm completely at a loss to explain how, but no hypotheses work without this assumption."

"I'm willing to go along with that...for the sake of argument," Pogue replied.

"All the 'visions' we've seen before had two things in common: the observers were in a meditative, mentally unfocused state and all the visions could have been about the future," Sparky summarized.

Pogue thought about her hypothesis for a moment before nodding.

She continued, "But Drake took the Green Fantasy, so his mind was overly focused." She paused for that fact to sink in. "His vision seems to have been of the past."

"So, you conclude that an observer in a meditative state can see the future if they posit the right question," Pogue concluded.

"I know it sounds completely mad, but that's the conclusion supported by the facts at hand. It would certainly meet Jonathan Lord Ashleigh's definition of something 'worth life itself'."

As Pogue and McTrowell pondered the ridiculous danger of such a revelation, Young interjected, "Greek oracles used a brazier with incense or sat over a volcanic fissure ton achieve a hallucinogenic state."

Drake, McTrowell, and Pogue stared at her, stunned into silence by the enormity of the implication of her conclusion. Despite the lingering effects of the Green Fantasy and his fiery vision, Drake came to his senses first. "Whether you all are right or not, the device is clearly dangerous. I believe we should cease any further experiments until we have made a clear plan that accounts for all known dangers and contingencies." The effort of forming the entire thought and accompanying sentence drained the last of his reserves. "I am going to bed. Sparky?"

"Are you inviting me to join you?" his fiancée quipped.

"Er, no. Um, I just meant you might also want some sleep," the Chief Inspector stammered.

"I know, dear. I was just teasing. I knew what you meant." She winked at Pogue who was smirking slightly.

***

Erasmus stuck his head in the open door of Sparky's bedroom. "Are you all right, dear?"

Sparky put down the book she had just opened. "As I recall, you're the one who had the horrifying waking nightmare. I'm just tired."

"Hmm, how is your eye?"

"Ah, now we get to the heart of the matter. It aches a bit, but there's no damage to the eye itself. You've not endangered my chances of flying another airship regatta."

"I am very relieved." He approached the bed to kiss her goodnight. Only then did he notice her choice of reading material. "*Frankenstein; or The Modern Prometheus*? Is that a wise choice under the circumstances?"

"I read it when I was younger. I think, in some way, it influenced my decision to become a surgeon and a scientist. It made me wonder what was really possible. I thought rereading it as an adult might give me new perspective. To be honest, I was trying to take my mind off the Romani and that damnable crystal ball."

He kissed her on the forehead. "Good night, my love. I'll be just next door if you need anything."

"Likewise," she replied with a hint of teasing. As he turned toward the door, she flipped past the first few pages and gasped.

Drake spun back around. "What is it? Are you hurt?"

"It's the preface! Listen to this!"

> *As a child, I scribbled; and my favourite pastime, during the hours given me for recreation, was to 'write stories.' Still I had a dearer pleasure than this, which was the formation of castles in the air—the indulging in waking dreams—the following up trains of thought which had for their subject the formation of a succession of imaginary incidents. My dreams were at once more fantastic and agreeable than my writings. In the latter, I was a close imitator, rather doing as others had done than putting down the suggestions of my own mind. What I wrote was intended at least for one other eye—my childhood's companion and friend but my dreams were all my own. I accounted for them to nobody; they were my refuge when annoyed, my dearest pleasure when free.*

"Don't you see?" she continued. "Waking dreams! And she wrote about science that can reanimate dead tissue! Doesn't that sound like Mary Shelley knew something about our crystal ball device?"

"That is a fascinating conjecture, my dear, but how would we ever prove it. And what more would that tell us?"

"The question is, what more would *she* tell us?"

"My dear Dr. McTrowell, Mary Shelley is recently deceased."

"Yes, of course I'm aware. I'm also aware that she kept extensive diaries and I know who has them. I must get some sleep because tomorrow is going to be a busy day of research. Good night, Erasmus."

He kissed her again and departed.

***

"Dr. McTrowell, what a lovely surprise! Honestly, I never know when or where you're going to turn up. The Times only reports on your past adventures, but does a poor job at keeping me up to date on your current location," Isadora Blenheim blurted out enthusiastically. It was one of the things that Sparky loved about the painter; she spoke her mind. Many people found Izzy's forthrightness off putting. Sparky found it refreshing. Over the years they had known each other, they had spent many nights talking until dawn about art, history, food, adventures, and anything else that struck their fancies.

"Izzy, dear, I must apologize in advance. I haven't time for chatting and reminiscing. I'm on a mission of considerable urgency."

"Does it involve that dashing chief inspector and that ring of thieves you just broke up?"

"Miss Blenheim, you are entirely too smart for my own good. What I am about to tell you must be sealed in the sanctity and secrecy of the Ladies' Adventure Circle. Do you swear?"

"I swear by Athena and Diana."

"I need to see Mary Shelley's diaries."

The painter gasped so sharply she started to cough. "By the goddesses! What does Mary Shelley have to do with a ring of thieves?"

"If I'm right, it will be a story the likes of which the Ladies' Adventure Circle has never heard. But I haven't the time to tell it today. It needs the whole Circle...and wine. The diaries?"

"Yes, right away!" The painter dashed down the stairs into her basement. A minute later, Sparky heard Izzy's vault slam shut. That was another way in which Izzy was different. Even though she was an artist, she was abundantly pragmatic. She'd bought a row house that had previously been part of a bank, but she'd intentionally bought the section that contained the vault. If for no reason other than this, she was the secretary for life of the Ladies' Adventure Circle. She scurried back up the stairs hauling a bulging leather satchel. She nodded her head sideways toward her studio and

Sparky followed her. Isadora proceeded to lay the diaries out on her work table in chronological order.

"I'm looking for an early diary, probably around 1810. She might have been a teenager reflecting on her childhood. We're looking for any reference to an orb or a crystal ball or device with a scrollwork cage," the airship pilot explained.

"Czarina Llewelyn McTrowell," Izzy exclaimed, using Sparky's full given name which few knew, "I will haunt your ghost for eternity if you don't tell me the whole story when this is over!"

"I swear by Athena and Diana, but we really must find this. I'll work forward from 1807 if you'll work back from 1817."

The two adventurers flipped pages for half an hour, occasionally murmuring or chuckling at the youthful musings of young Miss Godwin before she became Mrs. Shelley. Sparky looked up from 1811. "I'm reminded why we acquired and preserved these. She really was one of us in spirit. Have you found anything?" She glanced down the table. "Izzy! You're supposed to be researching, not reading! Are you still in 1816?"

"I'm sorry. This is just so interesting. It's like I'm reading it for the first time. Like this...oh goddesses! I think I found it!" The painter pointed at the journal while backing away.

Sparky took Izzy's place in front of the open book and read the entry out loud—

> *Claire hired a gypsy fortune teller to amuse us. I have witnessed similar performances before, though none so convincing. Her full attention was instantly upon me. She seized my hand. "Look! See!" she admonished me and held her crystal ball to my face, encased as it was in ancient filigree. I thought her quite mad. It was as one of the waking dreams of my childhood, yet devoid of fog. In my mind, I saw a future where science rules morality. The dead are made living without care for the horror visited upon the living and dead alike. I slept not a wink for three nights straight.*

"By the goddesses, it's a gift!"

"Sparky, whatever do you mean?"

"Some people must be more capable than others to use the device."

"Czarina Llewellyn McTrowell, you can be so infuriating sometimes. What are you talking about?"

The flight surgeon gently closed the diary, kissed her friend on the cheek, and said, "Izzy, I promise the whole story soon. But now I must dash back to Shadwell."

***

Sparky shifted nervously from foot to foot as the members of Her Majesty's Eyes and Ears filed into Pogue's dining room and found seats. Drake shook the hand of the final arrival, a man with impossibly wide shoulders and precise military bearing.

"Sergeant Fox, a pleasure to be working with you again. Your martial skill will be very valuable in this case. I take it Lord Ashleigh has fully explained the situation?"

"He has."

"Very good. After we hear what Dr. McTrowell has to say, you and I will work on a plan to secure the perimeter."

"Yes, sir."

Sparky cleared her throat ceremoniously. "Thank you all for assembling on such short notice. I have interesting information. I have reviewed the diaries of Mary Shelley. As incredible as it may sound, her diaries confirm what we have inferred from all our experiences and experiments. An individual with the skill to unfocus their mind can use the device to see the future."

The members of Her Majesty's Eyes & Ears sat in stunned silence.

"Of course!" Drake nearly leapt out of his chair. "That's how the gypsies knew..." Sparky attempted to interrupt him, but Drake proceeded. "I know, dear, *Romani*. That's how they knew when to break into the houses without getting caught."

When he took a breath, Sparky did interrupt. "Actually, they weren't Romani. They were just thieves. But there appears to be something else to it. Apparently, some minds are more capable than others. Mary Shelley was one such individual. The thieves must have one among themselves as well."

Pogue interjected, "But all of us have been able to use it."

"All of us who have tried," Sparky corrected. "That may just be luck. We may all have...I hesitate to use the term...the 'gift.' But we've only been able to use it poorly, unclearly. Perhaps others, such as the Yogi Suneel, Mary Shelley, and the Romani are able to get very clear and lucid visions. I am beginning to consider the possibility," she felt queasy saying it, "that this gift may be passed down through families. Be that as it may, it seems to have some ability to foresee the future. It is even remotely possible that Mary Shelley is distantly related to the Romani." She stopped there because she felt completely ridiculous suggesting it.

Drake offered, "It would be invaluable to Scotland Yard. One could ask what the next crime a nefarious criminal is going to commit so as to catch the crook red-handed."

Sparky responded, "I also considered the possibility that it could predict the future of medicine or airship travel."

Jonathan Lord Ashleigh interrupted, "Our personal curiosity about the future is irrelevant. We must recognize the terrible potential of this device and protect it accordingly. I shall begin making plans for its permanent storage. The rest of you must redouble your efforts to secure it in the interim." Confident that his instructions would be followed, he stood and departed, Virat following closely behind him.

***

"Chief Inspector," Sergeant Fox reported, "I have removed the external stairs to the roof, glued broken glass to the roof edge, and attached a hinged bar with a quick release latch on the inside of the door down to the kitchen to block entrance from the roof. Mrs. Bingham objected. Something about cooking for a crowd without access to fresh vegetables."

"I advise making peace with Mrs. Bingham. It will go easier for you."

Her Majesty's Royal Aerial Marine nodded. "I'm prepared to stand guard on the roof tonight."

"Will you need food and drink for that mission?"

"Yes, I will, Chief Inspector."

"You will need to see Mrs. Bingham about that."

"I take your point, sir."

Drake continued, "I have installed a telescopic peephole in the front door and a bar as well. What do you think about a vat of boiling oil on the roof?"

"Sir?"

Drake gave the Sergeant a pat on the back and a grim smile. "It was a joke, Sergeant Fox. These all seem like extreme measures for a ragtag troupe of gypsies...er Romani."

"He who exercises no forethought but makes light of his opponents is sure to be captured by them."

"Ah, Sun Tzu. Quite apropos. Again, I take your point, Sergeant."

***

"Mrs. Bingham," Chief Inspector Drake began as he entered the kitchen, massaging his temples from the stress of two days of vigilance. He stopped dead in his tracks. The little Romani girl who had tried to search his office was standing in the kitchen handing a basket of vegetables to the housekeeper. He pointed directly at the girl and shouted, "What is she doing here?"

"She and her brother are delivering vegetables since you won't let me up to the garden on the roof," Mrs. Bingham replied.

Drake positioned himself between the girl and the door. "How did she get in?"

"Through the side door to the kitchen."

"There is a side door to the kitchen?! How did we not know about this? And where is her brother?" Drake sputtered in exasperation.

"It's at the back of the pantry."

"The boy?"

"Honestly, Chief Inspector, they're just children delivering vegetables. And, no, I meant the door is in the back of the pantry. I haven't used it in years, but you have made a fortress of the front door."

"That was entirely the point, Mrs. Bingham! Never mind. Where is the boy?"

"He's in the pantry putting vegetables in bins."

"Fetch him."

Mrs. Bingham returned from the panty in seconds, ashen. "He's not there."

"As I suspected. What is he wearing?"

"Blue pants, um, a flat cap, and a dirty white shirt."

"Fetch Dr. McTrowell!"

The housekeeper hustled out of the kitchen. Drake turned to the girl and reached for her. "You are coming with me." She ducked under his hands. He attempted to block her escape through the pantry, but his fencing reflexes failed him. She didn't move in the direction he expected. Instead she pivoted and ran up the spiral, iron staircase toward the roof. Her tiny size and youthful nimbleness hastened her ascent, leaving Drake struggling to negotiate the curve sideways. When she reached the landing at the top of the stairs, she opened the door a crack and slipped through. She stretched a skinny arm back through the opening to release the latch holding the heavy bar up. Slippery as an eel, she pulled her arm out and slammed the door just in time for the bar to fall in place on the opposite side. While the bar served its intended purpose of securing access to the kitchen from the roof, its location at the top of the spiral staircase obstructed anyone trying to reach the roof from the kitchen.

Sergeant Fox, expecting an assault from the street was caught off guard by the ruckus from the stairwell. By the time he regained his bearings, the girl was running toward the edge of the roof, unspooling what looked like a long shawl from around her waist. Hidden under the layers of cloth was a crude iron hook.

Drake reached the top of the stairs and began wrestling with the bar. He pounded on the door to get Fox's attention. Fox hesitated again. Drake shouted through the door, "Go after her!"

"Sir?"

"Catch the girl!"

Fox sprinted after the girl who latched the hook inside the edge of one of the planter boxes closest to the edge of the roof. She tossed the end of the rag rope over the edge. Putting one foot on the edge of the roof, avoiding the broken glass, she launched herself over the edge, grasping the rope in her hands. She spun around in mid-air, planted her feet against the wall, and shinnied down before Fox could even reach the planter box. He followed her, but his size required more caution navigating the glass and rope. By the time he reached the ground, she'd already disappeared down the street and into an alley. He took off running in pursuit.

***

Mrs. Bingham arrived in the lab breathless. "Dr. McTrowell,

Chief Inspector Drake needs you in the kitchen. It has something to do with a little girl. He was very agitated."

"Drake was agitated?"

"Yes, quite. He shouted at me."

"You're quite certain? He shouted? You're not exaggerating?"

"Dr. McTrowell, I know when someone is shouting at me. He was shouting."

Sparky turned to Pogue and Young. "If Drake is shouting, something is really wrong. Get the device to a more secure location." She sprinted up the stairs.

Realizing he was going to be too late to assist, Drake latched the door open again and awkwardly backed down the spiral staircase, determined to find the boy. He knew better than to think the boy had simply walked through the outside door of the pantry and disappeared. The Romani were engaged in a complex game of diversion and evasion the likes of which Drake hadn't seen since his days at sea.

No sooner was Fox away from the Pogue residence than a boy in blue pants and a flat cap detached himself from the shadow at the corner of the building across the street, crossed to the rope, and scaled the side of the building with the skill of an acrobat.

Sparky found Drake in the dining room. "What's wrong?"

"The Romani have infiltrated the house," he replied soberly. "That girl who tried to sneak into my office was in the kitchen with Mrs. Bingham and a boy, presumably her brother, was also here."

"Where are they now?"

"She escaped via the roof from whence Sergeant Fox is in pursuit. I have no idea whether the boy is in the house or gone. I have not seen him at all. Presumably he would be the only boy in the house, but how can we even say at this point?"

"I'll get started searching the house, but we need reinforcements," she opined as she headed for the stairs to the upper floors.

"You are right, my dear. I will summon some." He turned toward the front of the house.

***

Dr. Young pulled up the enormous keyring hanging at her waist, calmly flipping through the panoply of keys as she approached a large wooden door at the far side of the lab. Dr. Pogue followed her, clutching the orb firmly to his chest. When Yin found the right key, she unlocked the door, hauled it open, and waited for Edmond to go through. Before she could follow him, she was distracted by a noise behind her of something falling on the far side of the lab; she went to investigate. When she discovered it was nothing but a stack of Edmond's books that had toppled over, she re-crossed the room and proceeded through the wooden door, relocking it and verifying that it was secure. She turned to walk down the stone hallway that led to yet another portion of the warren of warehouses that Edmond Pogue had converted into his home and laboratories. She listened.

Was that dripping water or soft footfalls?

It was hard to tell the difference in this part of domicile given its proximity to the Thames and its proclivity for echoes. She found Pogue standing at the top of a ramp leading down into one of the larger labs off the stone hallway.

"What are you thinking?" she asked with trepidation.

"We could lock it in that cage we built for assembling the dragon's tooth automaton," he offered, gesturing at the makeshift enclosure that nearly filled the room. "It could be a good security perimeter."

"I am surprised at this suggestion given that you nearly died in that cage," she observed, the calm expression on her face belying the consternation the memory of that near-fatal incident induced.

"I was planning to put the device in the cage, not myself again.

That would be madness," he offered cheerily. He headed into the enclosure, Yin following cautiously. No sooner had he set the device down than they heard a high-pitched squeaking on the far side of the room. A boy neither of them had ever seen before was opening the water taps to flood the room. Young dodged out of the cage to stop him. Pogue followed close behind, slamming the cage closed and locking it. Before Young could reach the boy, he leapt to the side of the cage and scrambled, hand-over-hand, to the top. Internally, she cursed her decision to wear conventional clothes that day; the skirt, tight bodice, and sleeves made pursuit nearly impossible. Nevertheless, she tried climbing the cage, but her sodden skirt dragged her down and entangled her legs. Pogue clambered awkwardly up the cage from the opposite side, whistling what sounded like a discordant tune to control the opening and closing of his mechanical hand. As Pogue neared the top of the cage, the boy whistled a few notes, triggering the release of Pogue's mechanical hand and sending the scientist tumbling backward into the rising flood. Young broke off her pursuit and plunged in to rescue him. It took every ounce of her strength to drag both Edmond and her waterlogged dress up the ramp into the room. He coughed and spat out the foul liquid. "Thank you, my dear." He turned to face the boy perched on the top of the cage. "You can't escape. You might as well come down."

Without a word, the boy dove into the water flooding the room. Yin dragged herself around the edge of the room to close the taps while Pogue struggled to open the drains. When the water receded, the boy was gone. And so was the device.

***

Drake approached the front door and peered out the peephole. Contrary to his fears, there was no invading force of Romani outside. He unbolted the front door, swung it open, and blew two sharp blasts on his police whistle. Almost immediately, a Constable came running. Drake raised his eyebrows as the Constable entered the house.

Say what you like about Shadwell, but their constabulary is certainly prompt.

"Constable, search the house! You are looking for a young boy."

"Yes, sir." The Constable ran in the direction of the stairs to the lab.

Sergeant Fox returned by way of the front door, winded from his exertions. "I couldn't catch her," he admitted dejectedly. "She could have slipped into some bolt-hole I couldn't find."

Drake chose not to chastise the Aerial Marine. The man's own self-recrimination was clear on his face.

The Constable returned from the depths of the house with the soaking wet boy, shivering, wrapped into a ball in a blanket, and squirming in his arms. "What should I do with the boy, sir?"

"Take him to Scotland Yard. I shall deal with him there." He turned to Sergeant Fox. "Please find Sparky and let her know the boy is captured. I believe she is searching upstairs."

***

Completely sodden, Pogue and Young sloshed back out of the lab with the cage now devoid of standing water, boy, and aggravatingly, the device. Edmond looked at Yin and offered hopefully, "He has to be down here somewhere."

She pointed at the large wooden box she had carefully locked on the way in. It was wide open. They slogged upstairs where they found Drake in the dining room.

Drake looked up and asked, "What happened to you two?"

"The boy followed us into one of the basement rooms and flooded it," Pogue explained.

"That would explain why he was wet when the Constable found him." Drake observed.

Sparky and Sergeant Fox heard the last part of the conversation as they entered the room. "Which Constable?" she asked.

"I summoned a Constable as you suggested. He captured the boy and is taking him to Scotland Yard," Drake replied.

"That's peculiar. Wasn't that terribly fast? I had only just begun searching."

Drake considered her observation. He had a bad feeling. Turning to Pogue and Young, he asked, "Where is the device? Why is it unguarded?"

Pogue answered sheepishly, "We think he snatched it while we were dealing with the flood."

"He picked two locks to acquire the crystal ball and to escape," Young added.

"Dammit!" Chief Inspector Erasmus Drake swore, slamming his fist onto the dining room table. "He must have had help!"

"Erasmus," his fiancée replied in surprise, "I didn't think you even knew that word. Surely this isn't the first time you've been bested."

"That is true, but our plan was solid. The 'Constable' must have been one of them. He must have been sent to aid in the boy's escape. It was as if they knew exactly what we were going to do at each step."

"Both the girl and the boy were in the house at some point. Perhaps they used the device to project our course of action?" Sparky asked more than suggested.

"But the device was never unattended, not for a moment."

"So, either they have a way to foresee the future without direct access to the device or they outsmarted us and predicted everything we would do." McTrowell looked at Drake with a questioning look.

"Either possibility is too terrible to consider."

***

Gunari stood on the deck of the ship, dressed in an ill-fitting constable's uniform, watching the white cliffs of Dover shrink into the distance. He wrapped his arm around his wife's shoulder, pulled her close, and kissed her on the forehead.

"The circle is restored. We must never let the *yak* slip away again."

"Bater," Tshilaba replied.

The skinny little Romani girl appeared on the deck, hand in hand with Florica. Tshilaba took the girl's face in her hands. "Luludja, you are the future of the circle. You are the one foretold by the prophecy. Never before has a member of the circle been able to use the *yak*'s power from any distance. Do not let this be a source of pride. It is a responsibility and a burden. Do you understand?"

"Yes, *tanti.*"

"Good girl." She kissed the girl on the crown of her head. "Let us go release your *bunícă* from the *yak* so she may live the rest of her days in peace."

"Will grandmother be better?"

"She will be like any other old woman. She will no longer have the power of the seeing mind, and it will no longer torment her. She has served our people and earned this comfort."

BJ Sikes

Enjoy!

BJ Sikes

Prophecies of an Electric Man

Paris, 1880

Being the personal Doctor-Scientist for the aging Queen of France wasn't as glamorous as Adelaide had expected. She propped her elbows onto her scarred mahogany desk and let her head sink into her hands. The brilliant electric lights in the laboratory were crucial for her work but gave her a headache. She longed to go back to her suite at the Palace and sit in the glow of the gas lamps. But she was just too busy for that luxury. The Queen's constant demands as her aging mechanisms broke down kept Adelaide busier than she had anticipated. She had been required to attend formal dinners every night for the past week, trussed into a tight corset and bustled evening gown. Now the Augmented nobles residing in the Palace of Versailles had discovered her mechanical skills. How would she find the time to develop improvements in Her Majesty's mechanisms, as well as create a self-actuated automaton to replace her?

The air in the cluttered laboratory grew warm and heavy as she sat scribbling. Adelaide pushed herself to her feet but a twinge in her back slowed her. She winced. The new pains in her muscles made her feel much older than her thirty-two years. The machine parts piled on the floor and the cabinets overflowing with tools oppressed her. She scowled at the mess. A stroll in the gardens would clear her head.

She walked towards the door but a glimpse of the covered figure of her automaton on a workbench stopped her. She had been working on it for months in secret, but her progress was slow. It was vital that this project, the Automated Dauphin, be complete before the Queen stopped functioning altogether. Adelaide intended to present it to the Presidente le Scientiste and the Academy as a successor for the childless monarchs. She gnawed at her lip, unsure about leaving now rather than working on the project.

The door to her laboratory creaked open, breaking into her musing. She raised her head. An older man limped in. His embroidered silk outfit and powdered hair marked him as a courtier. His face was drawn, a mixture of discomfort and disdain. He spotted Adelaide and called out, his voice shrill.

"Madame le Scientiste! I must insist that you repair this accursed mechanical knee of mine. I simply cannot bear it anymore."

She restrained a sigh but couldn't force a polite smile onto her face. She was not a born courtier with perfect manners drilled into her from birth.

"Monsieur le Comte. *Bon jour.* What sort of difficulty are you having with your knee?"

The noble stomped closer, clicking with each step. He waved a pale hand at his knee.

"It clicks. Could you not hear it? Can you imagine how embarrassing it is to click as one walks? It is insupportable. You must repair it immediately."

Adelaide bit her lip. The mechanical knee was not her invention nor had she installed the device. Why did the comte think she could help him?

"Monsieur le Comte, would it not be more appropriate for you to seek the counsel of your own Doctor-Scientist?"

The man looked affronted and crossed his arms.

"Why would I do that? You're right here in the Palace. Isn't that why you're here? I'm sure it would be an easy thing for a brilliant young scientist like yourself to repair."

Adelaide tapped her foot. Who gave him that idea? She bent to make a cursory examination, then straightened and forced a smile.

"I am afraid I'm not familiar with this particular type of mechanical knee joint. I don't know if the clicking is part of the design or a malfunction. I'm sorry, Monsieur le Comte, but you will have to consult with the Doctor-Scientist who installed it."

The comte's nostrils flared and he tossed his head.

"I see that your reputation is greater than warranted. I should have known better, after the death of that poor de Laincel girl. *Bon jour,* madame."

He limped out, grumbling, his knee clicking with every other step. Adelaide stood shaking and pale.

Bastard. How dare he imply that it was my fault that Marie-Ange died?

Images of Marie-Ange de Laincel, the only recipient of Adelaide's artificial heart, raced through the scientist's mind. She had been so beautiful, a petite, pale girl with a bad heart. Her death at an unknown assailant's hand remained a mystery. Adelaide's vision blurred and she dragged a hand across her eyes. Her efforts to save the girl's life had been useless. Marie-Ange had died a few short weeks before on the work table beside the one where the automaton now lay. The table remained bare, a reminder of Adelaide's failure. She wondered why the Palace guards were still unable to discover the killer. It shouldn't be too difficult. Adelaide had turned over the paint box bomb to the Guards herself. How many painters had been at the Palace that day? The guards must be incompetent or possibly even negligent. She needed to question the Captain of the Guards to make sure he was continuing the investigation. Energy filled her and she strode into the hallway, determined to find out what was going on.

The Palace corridors thrummed with the business of the Court at Versailles. Ministers and their staff hurried along, dodging drifting petitioners lost in the vast Palace, and sauntering courtiers searching for amusement. Adelaide stood at the doorway of her laboratory, hands on hips. She hesitated, trying to decide where to search for the Captain. Adelaide knew only a few areas of the Palace. She shrugged and headed towards the front of the vast building. Guards were always stationed there to control entry into the Palace. She could get directions to the Captain's location from one of his men.

Adelaide slowed her march down the corridor as she drew next to a statue depicting Aquarius as a young woman. Adelaide closed her eyes for a moment. She had found Marie-Ange collapsed on the marble floor in front of this statue. How long would it take before she could walk past this spot without that stab of pain? A trio of giggling young noblewomen drew up behind her, spurring Adelaide to move. She glared at them over her shoulder. They ignored her, caught up in their own world. Had they known Marie-Ange? They were of similar age. Did they know anything about Marie-Ange's death? Adelaide smoothed back her hair and paused, turning to face them.

"Mademoiselles? Have you a moment to speak to me?" Adelaide was vividly conscious of her provincial accent and her face flushed. The girls exchanged looks. One giggled. The tallest of the three, a willowy brunette, shrugged.

"What does the Royal Doctor-Scientist need from us? We have no need of your notorious Archimedean Heart, madame. We three are fit and healthy."

Adelaide's flush deepened and her palms grew damp. When she replied, her tone was brittle and probably not as obsequious as the noblewomen would expect.

"Did you know Marie-Ange de Laincel?"

The girl dropped her gaze and sniffled, the picture of misery, but it struck Adelaide as forced.

"Please, madame, we are grief-stricken. Poor Marie-Ange. Her Majesty was so very fond of her."

Another of the young noblewomen spoke up. She did not wear the mask of mock-sadness her companion did. Perversely, Adelaide liked her better.

"At least she escaped marriage with Mercoeur. Do you know he's already casting about for a new bride? I shudder to think which of us will be caught."

Her compatriot hissed at her.

"Be still, Aurelie. Madame does not need to hear about our romances."

Adelaide tilted her head to one side. She had not heard that Marie-Ange had been averse to her betrothal to Mercoeur.

"Why would she not wish to marry Mercoeur? He is young, wealthy..."

The girl who had remained silent until now burst out.

"Because she didn't love him, madame! She loved another!"

Her friend pinched her arm and shushed her.

"Idiot, you swore you would never speak of that."

"Why does it matter now she's dead?"

The girls glared at each other for a moment, then seemed to remember where they were. They all curtsied, a quick bob, then spun on their heels and hurried away. Adelaide stared after them.

So Marie-Ange had a secret lover? Who was it? If Adelaide could find out, she might have a clue to the girl's killer or possibly an ally to help her investigation.

She continued her search for the captain through the Palace corridors. This new clue in the investigation might help his efforts in bringing the killer to justice.

When did I become so blood-thirsty?

***

The high ceiling of the *Palais d'Industrie's* main hall soared above Adelaide's head and hundreds of excited voices echoed around her. She approached a group of fellow scientists, but as Adelaide drew near, the huddled men fell silent. One scowled over his shoulder at her. She recognized them. They were the preeminent electrical scientists in the world but seemed to have no interest in admitting her to their exclusive clique. Adelaide wondered if they even knew her name. She veered away from them, unwilling to risk wrecking on the shoals of their disdain. She sighed and fanned herself with her program. The overheated hall filled with other scientists, inventors, investors, and gawkers. Most were men. Lady scientists were more drawn to botany and the like. She knew of one female volcanologist, but women in the physical sciences were few and far between, even in the supposedly enlightened society of France.

Adelaide cast a look around the hall, spying exhibits that she was interested in viewing. She consulted her program, then marched towards a table displaying a new motor design run on electricity. If it could be miniaturized, she might be able to use it in her automaton.

A flamboyantly dressed man stepped into her path. He looked like an eccentric inventor, someone who lurked in the upper reaches of some noble's chateau because he embarrassed his family too much to be seen in society. His dark eyes arrested her progress. She stopped short. His expression unnerved her. His gaze was too penetrating. She felt like an insect under a microscope. Falling back on old habits from when she felt inferior around the nobles at

Court, she raised her chin and stared at him down her prominent nose. It struck her that he was a little shorter than her, quite a novelty. Adelaide waited for him to speak. His smile seemed too broad and didn't meet his eyes. He bowed deeply but managed not to break his hold on her eyes.

"Madame Doctor-Scientist. It is an honor to encounter you at this place."

His accent was as odd as his diction. Adelaide couldn't place it, but from the look of his high cheekbones, dark hair, and olive skin, he was from the East, perhaps near Russia. She nodded, an abrupt gesture, finished almost as soon as it began. She didn't feel the need to be overly polite so her tone was as abrupt as her nod.

"Monsieur. I don't believe we've met."

His smile wavered a bit then strengthened.

"You are correct, madame. Your reputation precedes you into this venue. I have longed with all of my being to meet the inventor of the Archimedean Heart. And now I, most fortunate of men, have encountered you here."

Adelaide felt her blush rise across her cheeks. She clenched a fist and breathed deeply, willing her blood to cool. Who was this sycophantic stranger? His flattery reminded her of someone she'd rather not remember.

"I thank you, monsieur...?"

"I am Yalanchi Peygember." He announced his name as if she should know it. Adelaide waited for him to continue. He seemed a little flustered, uncertain at her lack of recognition. Sighting the new motor over his shoulder, she stepped around him.

"Good day, Monsieur Peygember."

She caught sight of him frowning as she passed him.

"Madame, please, I have need of speaking to you."

Adelaide kept moving but deigned to look at him as he jogged to keep pace with her stride. She huffed out a breath.

"I can't imagine why."

"Please, perhaps I can make an appointment?"

"Monsieur, I am a busy woman."

She glanced at the magnificent clock hung high above the hall, indifferent to its beauty. She hoped it was accurate. Adelaide needed to return to the Palace by four o'clock for the Queen's treatment. Time to view the wonders of the Exhibition was waning. She didn't want to spend it talking to this strange little man.

"I won't waste your time with frivolity, of this I promise you, madame. Please, just grant me a little time and you will be happy for this."

He wasn't going away. He seemed likely to buzz at her like a fly all afternoon if she didn't get rid of him somehow. She leveled a glare at him.

"You may come to my laboratory at the Palace tomorrow at eleven in the morning, sharp. I can give you half an hour, no more. Don't be late. This had better not be a waste of my time."

He grinned with what looked like all of his teeth showing.

"I thank you deeply, madame, for your generosity. I look forward to spending more time in your company when I show you the magnificent artifact I have acquired."

He bowed again. She didn't bother to respond but darted around him, heading to the beckoning exhibit. Perhaps the Palace guards wouldn't let him in tomorrow so she wouldn't be bothered.

***

Adelaide was enjoying the quiet of her laboratory when the door banged open. The Captain of the Palace Guards stood in the doorway, hands on his hips.

"Madame le Scientiste, I must protest. Your interference into my investigation is not welcome or needed." His face was pinched into a scowl. Adelaide moved towards him but a wave of exhaustion slowed her down. She had stayed up most of the night working.

"Captain Girard. Please, come inside." She gestured for him to shut the door. He complied, the ferocious look not budging. "What is the problem?"

"Madame, I was told by one of my men that you were harassing a member of Her Majesty's Court with inquiries into the murder of Mademoiselle de Laincel. The Comtesse de Volney was most distressed by your questions."

Adelaide sank into a chair and closed her eyes for a moment.

"I did not intend to disturb the Comtesse. I merely wished to know about the painter she had recently engaged."

The captain stalked closer and towered over her.

"Ah, I see, so you must have been attempting to commission a portrait? I did not realize that doctor-scientists were in the habit of having their portrait painted."

Adelaide pursed her lips. Was he commenting on her less than pleasing countenance?

"Captain, I was trying to help. I thought if I inquired about a possible—"

He held up a hand to silence her. She gritted her teeth but complied.

"I thank you but it is not needed. Please rest assured, we will discover the murderer of Mademoiselle de Laincel. Without your help."

Captain Girard gestured in the direction of her automaton. Adelaide glanced over at the workbench and winced. She hadn't covered the Automated Dauphin.

"What is this machine you are working on, madame?"

Her shoulders tensed as he sauntered over to the workbench. He leaned over and scrutinized the automaton's face, then the exposed machinery in the torso.

"Fascinating. What does it do?"

Adelaide got to her feet and joined him at the automaton's side.

“It receives input from multiple sources, analyzes the information, and synthesizes a response.”

Girard sniffed, his mouth downturned. He poked the automaton’s arm.

“That’s all? Can it do anything else? Can it move? It seems like it would be strong.”

Adelaide reached down and switched on the automaton. His eyes glowed with a gentle blue and a humming rose from his chest. The hum grew into a whir and the Automated Dauphin levered himself into a seated position. Adelaide saw Girard blanch and step back from the metal figure. Even sitting, he was taller than the captain by a head.

“He can’t hurt you, Captain Girard. He has limited physical abilities although his calculating speed is rapid. I expect him to be very useful.”

Girard’s snapped his head to face her, disgust twisting his mouth.

“He? You call this thing a ‘he’?”

She reached out and stroked the automaton’s arm. He seemed to be gazing at her, waiting for something.

“It seems impolite to call him an it, don’t you think, Captain?”

“I think that it is odd to call a machine a him. Do you also have a name for your pet mechanical man?”

Adelaide felt a blush flood across her face. She daren’t tell the Captain of the Palace Guards that she called her creation the Automated Dauphin. He might call the Police Secrete.

“Why no, of course not. Should I? Perhaps I should call him Jean or Henri?” She giggled once, but managed to suppress the second. Henri? Where on Earth did that come from? Naming her masterpiece after that debaucher, the artist Henri Desjardins would be preposterous.

“Jean? Madame, are you mocking me?” The captain drew himself up taller and stared down his bulbous nose at her. Adelaide blinked, confused.

“Mocking you? I don’t know what you mean, Captain.”

He waved a hand at her and frowned.

“Humph. Never mind.” He stared at the automaton sitting on the workbench. Besides a regular whirring from its torso, it made no sound. “I don’t understand why you’re creating such a thing. It has no use as a soldier. It cannot assist as a service unit in the Palace.” His face creased in frustration. Adelaide smiled at the automaton.

“When my work is complete, you will understand. It will do amazing things for France and her people. Won’t you, my dear?”

Captain Girard stared at Adelaide.

“I see. Well, I’ll leave you to your work, madame.” He scuttled out of the room without waiting for a response.

***

Adelaide looked up from her notes.

“What are you doing here?”

She glared at the intruder. It was that man who had intercepted her at the Exhibition. He opened his eyes wide.

“Madame, we had an appointment. Yesterday, you told me to come at eleven in the morning.”

It seemed the Palace guards had let him in, even though she had neglected to inform them of the man’s arrival. The Captain must have been displeased after their argument.

“Oh, yes. I did, didn’t I?” she sighed. ”What do you want from me?”

“I need to speak to you, to show you this magnificent invention I have discovered.” He clutched a wooden box to his chest. His dark eyes held hers captive. She shook free of his gaze and glanced at the box. He must be another inventor attempting to lift himself higher in the academy using her reputation. Adelaide raised an eyebrow.

"I have enough inventions of my own to work on. Why would I be interested in yours?"

"No, madame, you misunderstand my inexact wording. I apologize; French is not my native tongue. I did not create this wonder. I liberated it from a pack of savages who had no need of it. It's very old, ancient in fact, but as you can see, most intricate in design."

He swung the lid of the box open. Adelaide sniffed, not bothering to look into the box. She sneered at the man.

"I see. And why have you brought this stolen artifact to me? Did I strike you as a dealer in stolen goods?"

He closed the box with a sharp click. His obsequious smile faded from his face, revealing the haughty, proud set of his features. Adelaide hadn't noticed them before. His glare looked almost noble. Who was this man?

"Perhaps I was mistaken. I had heard the Royal Scientist Physician of the French Court was a genius, capable of wonders of automation. I believed that she would be intrigued by this ancient marvel I have in my possession." His gaze slid towards the automaton lying on a nearby workbench then back to Adelaide. "Especially if it could assist her in her current endeavours."

Adelaide flushed and stuttered. She looked away from his intense gaze. Her failure to make progress with the automaton mocked her, and made a lie of her reputation as a mechanical genius. The machine, while splendid in appearance, was still just a jumble of parts. The Dauphin was a toy, a novelty, rather than the replacement monarch Adelaide intended. Adelaide swallowed, her throat tight. She kept her gaze on the automaton.

"I am a modern scientist, monsieur. I am unsure how this ancient marvel could be of assistance in my work."

"This device is said to be capable of many things. I thought it would intrigue you."

She examined the foreigner, his bright eyes taking in everything. Perhaps this odd man was right. Perhaps his mysterious device could help her automaton function properly.

"I see. I may have been hasty in my assessment of your motives, monsieur."

"Peygember. My name is Yalanchi Peygember. I am a collector of antiquities, visiting Paris."

His tone had changed. He sounded almost genial but his smile didn't quite reach his eyes. What was he up to?

"You believe this artifact that you liberated would interest an inventor of automatons?"

He nodded and placed the box on her desk.

"Please, madame. I invite you to examine it." He opened the lid of the box. Nestled in a bed of velvet sat a glowing glass ball filled with strange mechanisms, surrounded by a filigreed metal cage.

Adelaide narrowed her eyes. It was unlike anything she'd ever seen.

"Very pretty. What is it?"

Peygember threw his arms out in an expansive gesture.

"It is an oracle, madame, an oracle created thousands of years ago. It foretells the future."

Adelaide snorted and an indelicate laugh burbled out of her.

"Really? An oracle. My good sir, I am a scientist, not a fortune teller. Perhaps you should sell it to the Romani at the fairgrounds."

He reared back and his eyebrows shot up.

"Romani? Who said anything about Romani? This has nothing to with them, nothing."

Adelaide regarded him. He seemed about to burst with indignation. She had touched a nerve.

"Regardless of who you sell it to, I am a scientist, and have no need of a fortune telling device. What I need is an artificial mind for my automaton. I don't suppose you happen to have one of those in your collection?"

She gestured towards the automaton on a nearby workbench, wires pouring out of it like a fountain. She hadn't replaced the faulty actuator yet. Peygember approached the prone mechanical man, curiosity writ across his features, his indignation faded.

"Magnificent. You truly are a mechanical genius. What does it do?"

Adelaide sighed.

"Not a great deal, I'm afraid. He will do as his program cards tell him to do, but I have repeatedly failed to make him self-actuated."

He circled the figure, peering into the opened chest cavity.

"Fascinating. Why do you wish it be self-actuated? I understand of course the obvious novelty of such an invention."

Adelaide ambled to the side of the automaton and smiled down at him.

"I call him the Automated Dauphin. He will be the voice of France's people. He will hear their every need and rule them justly. No emotion to corrupt his power. Pure reason. With the Automated Dauphin ruling us, France will no longer be subject to irrational monarchs and their greedy relatives."

Her voice rang out with the conviction of a true believer. Peygember stared at her.

"Madame, that is a lofty goal but I must ask, have you the blessing of the current monarchs for this project?"

Adelaide's face sagged. She bit her lip.

"They have no surviving children. This could be their son. I just need to convince the ministers to allow the Automated Dauphin to ascend to the throne. Once he is fully functional. Otherwise the duc d'Orleans will return to France with his *Naturalistes* and they will banish Science."

Peygember tilted his head towards her.

"Perhaps you could use the orb in your clockwork prince? The orb, it has fantastic powers, unheard of in this time."

She gazed into the distance, pondering the idea.

"He's electrically powered," she corrected. "An oracle as a brain? It is somewhat intriguing. It might work."

Peygember clapped her on the shoulder.

"This is excellent news. I will leave you to your experiments. I will return in a week to hear of your remarkable progress. I bid you good day, madame."

He slipped from the laboratory before Adelaide could even rouse from her reverie to respond. What was this Peygember going to get out of this? Was he expecting to be co-inventor of the Automated Dauphin? She glanced over at the orb awaiting her, tempting her with its mysterious inner workings. The brass encasement glimmered under the lights.

Perhaps it can make the Automated Dauphin work as I plan. I can worry about what Peygember wants later.

She examined the strange globe, trying to make sense of its structure. She brushed a finger across the filigreed metal surrounding the glass globe. It felt strangely warm. She drew her finger back and closed the lid of the box with a soft click.

***

With a weary hand, Adelaide pushed open the heavy door to her laboratory. She felt as if she hadn't rested at all. The orb sat on the workbench. Its inner mechanisms glinted under the electric lights. She thought she had closed the box before she left the night before. She must have been more tired than she thought.

Adelaide studied the orb. She had never seen anything like it and had no idea of its functions or how to activate them. She bit her lip, shrugged and turned away. The sight of the table where Marie-Ange had died brought tears to Adelaide's eyes, as it so often did. Such sentimentality was unlike her. She pinched the bridge of her nose and squinted against the threatening tears.

Tears were useless. They wouldn't bring the young girl back to life nor would they avenge her murder.

Adelaide growled. She was still no closer to discovering who had killed Marie-Ange. The Captain and his Guards were useless. The killer could still be visiting the Palace, blissfully unaware that he had killed Marie-Ange. No, he knew what he had done, Adelaide was sure. He must be confident that his crime would remain undiscovered. She wondered if he planned to kill again. Why had he chosen Marie-Ange as his victim? Or was she simply in the wrong place at the wrong time? Adelaide's guts churned. Her failure to solve the mystery was disrupting her work and making her ill. She was constantly nauseated and couldn't eat. Sleep was difficult at best.

Perhaps this supposed oracle will help me find out who murdered Marie-Ange?

Hope flickered in her. She approached the orb and picked up a magnifying glass to take a closer look. The workings baffled her. It resembled a spherical astrolabe but on closer inspection, it was filled with intricately carved intermeshing metal gears. Adelaide lifted the artifact and turned it, examining the encasement. She prodded the metal then at her touch, part of the orb's encasement shifted and opened without a sound. The orb lay inside, revealed.

Adelaide hesitated, her hand hovering over the encasement's opening. She took a quick breath and plucked the orb out of its cradle. She rotated the glass orb on its axis. A series of depressions on one side caught her attention. She pressed her forefinger into one and the material in the depression seemed to soften under her touch. Adelaide drew in a quick breath, surprised at the sensation. She probed another depression with a second finger. The same softening occurred. She fit another finger into a depression. Part of the mechanism shifted inside the orb. A series of indescribable images, like a strange dream, shot through her brain and intense lights seemed to blind her inner eye. She gasped and tried to put the orb down but it felt somehow fused to her fingers. Her body grew hot then cold. The images grew more coherent.

She saw the Automated Dauphin, striding down through the gardens of Versailles, surrounded by courtiers. She stood next to him as he sat on the throne. The images changed, coming faster. Explosions, men screaming, dirt clods flying around them. A comet streaking across the night sky. A man in a soldier's uniform, limping. A woman wearing a shockingly short dress embracing him. The sun eclipsed by the moon. People running down a metal-walled corridor, chasing someone. She saw herself again, in her laboratory, gnawing on a hunk of bread.

Adelaide trembled and rested the orb on the bench, still unable to remove her fingers from the depressions in its surface. The orb seemed to release her fingers and she jerked her hand back. She shook her head, trying to rid her mind of the disturbing images. The orb was not a sham, despite her earlier suspicions. Did Peygember even know what he had entrusted to her? Could the images be visions of the future? None of it seemed real. Who were those people? Were they born of her imagination or would they exist at a later time? Perhaps the images meant that her invention would succeed as planned. A wave of dizziness struck her. She leaned against the workbench and panted, trying to clear her head.

Once the vertigo had passed, Adelaide examined the orb again. She took care not to touch it. It had some inexplicable power, but would it give her the knowledge she needed? It seemed to activate with just the touch of her fingertips. Did she dare repeat the experiment?

I wish there were someone I could trust to help me with this project. Or even ask about it. Peygember didn't seem to know much about the orb, just that it could be useful.

She reached her hand towards the orb, tempted to try again. Adelaide halted. Her hand was shaking. She was dimly aware that it wasn't just her hand. Her whole body was trembling and weak. Food. She should probably eat before working anymore. She grabbed a bread roll from the ever-present tray of food the servants left her and tore off a bite. A sense of déjà vu struck her.

How odd. I just saw myself doing this. Could the orb really predict the future? Or was that a coincidence?

She shrugged and kept chewing.

***

The Automated Dauphin laid immobile on his table. His blue eyes glowed. Adelaide perched on a stool at his side and scribbled in her notebook. She shook her head and scowled at her prone automaton. The orb was certainly having some effect. The Automated Dauphin was speaking more clearly but the spontaneous words pouring out of him made no sense. She wondered what was creating the words. She had not installed a speaking program card in the automaton,

The peaceful messenger will be forgotten? The people of the world wonder and follow the Beast?

What is that supposed to mean?

Adelaide wished she knew more about this mysterious glass orb. Was it acting as a sensorimotor as she had first assumed? It nestled inside the automaton's chest like a strange parasite. Adelaide squinted at the orb's inner mechanisms. None of it made sense to her, despite her years of working with automatons and other machinery. She pushed back a strand of hair and took a deep breath, then poked her finger into one of the depressions on the orb's surface. Something shifted at her touch and a piece of the internal workings spun. She pushed harder and more parts of the internal mechanism moved. The automaton spoke again.

"The town of the south is seduced by the white horse. The queen of the stars will bring forth the prince of the night."

Adelaide threw her hands up. She glared at the automaton.

"What are you talking about? That's just a lot of nonsense! Oh, listen to me, I'm talking to an inert lump of metal. Yes, you, you are a useless collection of gears and wires. You may be handsome but you're still an idiot. Or am I the idiot?"

She stomped to her desk and sank into her squeaky chair. Her notes on the orb and the automaton lay like torn petticoats, scattered across the scarred wood surface of her once-fine writing table. Her scribbles and diagrams made sense an hour ago but now with new evidence before her, she needed to redo her calculations. The babbling nonsense the automaton spouted wasn't helping Adelaide's work.

She glanced up at the ormolu clock, its gaudiness incongruous in her messy laboratory. It was almost midnight. Adelaide was sure it had only just been seven o'clock. She couldn't remember if she'd eaten dinner.

She shook her head. It didn't matter.

She had work to do.

Peygember was waiting to hear of her progress and she was sure the Queen would summon her in the morning.

Another distraction from her work. Her head throbbed and her mouth was dry.

Adelaide looked around for something to drink. The Palace servants usually left something on a tray, knowing she rarely ventured out for meals. Yes, on the floor next to her desk sat a tray. It held a carafe of wine and a platter of dried-out cheese and sausages. The smell of the meat turned her stomach. Adelaide poured herself a glass of deep red wine, ignoring the food. The mice could have it, as long as they left her wires unchewed. The wine was rich and fruity. It went down smoothly. She poured herself a second glass and sipped it, then returned to her work table and the notes she'd left strewn about. She squinted at one of the pages then riffled through the pages to another. She nodded to herself. Adelaide finished the last of the wine and lurched to her feet. She swayed a little.

"I know the problem," she announced to the empty room. "The orb has to be connected to the central actuator. That will fix it. I'm quite sure." Even to herself, she heard the slur in her words. Perhaps this wasn't the best time to make alterations to the automaton. Adelaide ignored the niggling voice and stepped over to the worktable. She bit her lip and considered the orb, then reached in and undid three connections, her fingers fumbling. She let out an exasperated huff at her clumsiness, then grabbed a different wire. Her hands shook. She connected the wire to the orb then dug around in the torso of the automaton for more wires. Adelaide swore at herself and tried to steady her hands. The connections finally clicked into place. She flicked a switch to engage the program and stepped back. Clicking and whirring noises rose from the automaton. Adelaide waited, watching. The whirring grew louder and the automaton sat up. Its head turned towards Adelaide, eyes glowing.

She shivered. What would he do?

At this point she had no idea. She moved back and the automaton seemed to track her movement. She gasped. Her wooziness cleared. A clear voice, with just a hint of the mechanical, filled the laboratory.

"Madame le Scientiste. You must beware. Enemies surround you. The peaceful messenger will be forgotten. The town of the south has been seduced by the white horse. None remain to support you."

Adelaide gaped. Gone was the senseless chatter he had spouted before, but it had been replaced with...prophecy? Had her Automated Dauphin turned into some kind of oracle? Had the orb taken over his functioning?

"Automaton, your program is faulty. False predictions are not in your capacity. Your purpose is to speak as the voice of the people, and to rule them justly."

She shook her head at her stupidity in addressing the

automaton. He wasn't programmed to receive auditory input yet, just the input from the program cards.

"The voice of the people has spoken through me. You must beware. The man with dark curly hair will set up a trophy. Rain. Blood. Milk. Famine. Weapon. Pestilence."

What nonsense was this? Was he responding to her words or was he incorrectly processing the card data she'd installed earlier? The strange orb must be interfering with the command processes.

A wisp of her hair tickled her nose. Adelaide pushed the offending lock from her face. She wrapped her arms around her waist and stared at the automaton. His eyes seemed to stare back. The whirring sound grew loud again and the automaton lay back down on the table. The glow in his eyes faded and he was still.

Adelaide swayed on her feet, trying to decide whether she had been subject to an exhaustion-induced hallucination. Did it mean anything? Should she tell Peygember about this new development? She closed her eyes and rubbed them. Her body ached with fatigue. The clock chimed. One o'clock in the morning.

I need to sleep.

With one more searching look at the silent automaton, Adelaide turned and left her laboratory. She stepped onto the marble floor of the hallway, her boots clicking. The checkerboard floor glinted in the moonlight. The bright electric lights had turned off earlier that evening. The hallway was empty and her footsteps echoed as she moved away from her laboratory. She paused in front of the statue of Aquarius. She knew there would be no sign of Marie-Ange's death there but couldn't resist glancing down. It looked like the rest of the corridor. Only Adelaide knew differently.

"You still seek answers."

Adelaide started, heart racing. She wheeled around, looking for the voice's origin. The hallway was full of shadows but otherwise empty.

I'm exhausted. Hearing things.

She rubbed her hot face and crusty eyes.

"I saw who killed her."

Adelaide gasped. The voice was right there. She looked up at the statue. Had its face changed expression? Impossible. She looked around for the source of the voice but saw no-one.

I really am tired. I need to get some sleep.

With another glance at the statue, she turned.

"He killed her right here in front of me."

Adelaide suppressed a shriek. Her heart pounded and her legs quivered. That statue was talking to her. She raised her eyes. It seemed to be staring back at her.

"Who killed Marie-Ange?" Adelaide whispered, her voice rough.

The marble face of the statue was still, its expression tender. It didn't respond. Adelaide shook her head, annoyed with herself. How could she expect a hallucination to make sense? She strode away, toward her rooms. A faint voice came from behind her.

"The painter."

Adelaide growled and kept walking.

"The painter? I knew that. I just need to know which one."

She barreled around a corner, not watching where she was going until she ran straight into one of the Palace Guards. He rocked back on his heels and put a hand out to steady her.

"Madame le Scientiste, are you well?"

The young man looked alarmed. Adelaide snarled up at him.

"Watch where you put your big, clumsy boots. It's the talking statues you should be minding, not me."

She pushed aside his restraining arm and stepped around him. She muttered curses, then halted. Turning, she met his confused stare.

"That statue, it told me it knew who killed Marie-Ange. You should interrogate that statue. It said the painter killed her. I knew that, I was the one who found the paintbrush near her body."

The guard tried to hide his smile.

"The statue told you this, madame?"

A wave of hot fury filled her.

"Don't laugh at me, you incompetent boob. Talking statues are a lot better at finding her murderer than you are."

She wheeled around and stalked away.

***

The ticking clock hanging on the wall of Adelaide's laboratory seemed to grow louder. She put down her pen and scowled. A walk in the gardens would clear her mind. She pushed to her feet, and her muscles protested with a twinge of pain. She groaned and rubbed the small of her back. Yes, a walk was needed.

She strode to the door, resisting the urge to glance at her work as she passed tables and shelves of items needing repair. It would wait. Adelaide pulled the heavy door open and stopped short. Two men stood there, both looking surprised at her unexpected appearance.

"Adelaide—er, Madame le Scientist. *Bon jour.*"

It was Valmont, the man who had broken her heart when they attended the Academy together. He had taken an inspector position. She winced. Her laboratory was in no shape for an inspection. She looked at the other man but didn't recognize him. Valmont gestured to his companion.

"Madame le Scientiste Coumain, may I present Presidente le Scientiste?"

Adelaide sucked in a quick breath. The president? Here? Had he somehow heard about her Automated Dauphin? Was he coming to take over her project? She cast a look behind her. Her automaton was covered with a sheet. Good. Perhaps they wouldn't notice him. Remembering her manners, she dipped a quick curtsey.

"Presidente le Scientiste. It is an honor to meet you and welcome you to my laboratory. Please come inside."

Their faces were hard, unsmiling, as they entered. Adelaide frowned in response as they passed her. Valmont sauntered towards her desk and began leafing through her notebook. Adelaide's palms grew hot and moist. What would he make of her notes?

The president surveyed the room. She saw his gaze linger on the piles of broken machinery littering the floor.

"I—I have no assistant at present. Please forgive the disarray."

The president met her eyes.

"I know. She was executed for treason, as I recall."

Adelaide flushed. Was he implying that she too was traitorous? Perhaps her work with the Automated Dauphin could be seen that way, but Adelaide knew better. She knew its true intent.

"Yes, she was a saboteur. In league with those Naturalism terrorists. I caught her destroying my work..."

She trailed off. The president was edging closer to the automaton.

"And what work did she destroy? Enhancements for Her Majesty?"

His voice was edged with something. Sarcasm? Anger?

"No, nothing like that." Adelaide's heart raced.

The president whirled to face her, his face dark with anger.

"No, she didn't sabotage enhancements for Her Majesty because you haven't been working on any, have you, madame?"

Adelaide shook her head and struggled to explain.

"Time, there hasn't been time...so many demands..."

Valmont broke in. He held her notebook.

"You have not had time because you've been working on an unauthorized automaton, as you painstakingly detail in your notebook. Where is this automaton?"

His gaze roved the room until he spotted the prone figure of the automaton on a table. Stepping over to it, he whipped the sheet away. The metal face, its prominent nose distinctive, gleamed under the lights. The president gasped.

"What is this? It looks like His Majesty."

Adelaide looked from the automaton to the aghast faces of the men. How was she going to explain this without being accused of sedition? She couldn't demonstrate the automaton's function. It wasn't ready yet. Valmont sneered.

"I see you've been wasting your time creating a facsimile of His Majesty. While a worthy tribute, I think helping the real King would have been a better use of your time and the Crown's money."

The president gazed down at the automaton, his mouth turned down. He spoke in a low tone.

"I expected better of you, Madame."

"But, monsieur, it's not fully functional yet. It will do wonderful things once I've figured out how to initialize the feedback automatically. The people of France will have a voice, you see, and our weak flesh will no longer matter."

Valmont raised an eyebrow at her pronouncement and barked a laugh.

"What madness are you speaking?"

Adelaide faltered. She creased her brow. Madness? She wasn't mad. The concept of the Automated Dauphin was perfectly reasonable. The people of France needed this technology. It was the next step in evolution. Why couldn't they see that?

"It's not madness. I must explain—"

The president held his hand up to silence her. His stony glare chilled her and she shivered.

"I don't need to hear more from you, madame. It is plain to me that you are in dereliction of your duties to Their Majesties. I have no choice but to remove you from your position at the Palace. Furthermore, the Academy of Science no longer requires your service."

Adelaide's body went numb. Her breath stopped for a moment. She shook her head, denying what she was hearing. How could they be so close-minded?

"No, no. You can't...my work is essential, it must continue."

The president cast another glance across the untidy room, a sneer across his face.

"You have twenty-four hours to remove yourself and your rubbish from this room. Come, Valmont. We must find a competent Doctor-Scientist to assign to Their Majesties."

He turned and marched to the door trailed by Valmont. Neither looked back. Adelaide slumped against a workbench. Her corset stays dug into her waist but she was past caring.

***

Adelaide sat at her desk, staring at nothing. Tall, disordered stacks of papers and notebooks on the desktop almost hid the rest of the laboratory. All of her calculations and notes about the Automated Dauphin. She needed to get up and pack them all, but her body refused to move. How could this be happening to her? She knew her cause was true and yet here she was, just a few short hours before she would be ejected from the Palace. Where was she going to go? She had nowhere to stay, let alone carrying stacks of boxes and a very large automaton. Adelaide had never lived alone and wasn't even sure where to begin. She had no friends or even friendly acquaintances at the Palace to ask. Returning to her family's tiny cottage in Sanery was out of the question. It was an obscure fishing village with no amenities or resources to help her with her work.

And she hadn't spoken to her parents for years. They might not even be alive.

Adelaide bit her knuckle, willing herself not to cry, but the hot tears spilled down her cheeks. Silent sobs shook her. She bit down harder and the pain stilled her tears. Her knuckle throbbed. She brushed her hand across her damp cheeks, then cast a bleary look at the papers in front of her. Which pages among the stacks were essential? Perhaps she could leave behind the records of her failed experiments and just take the most recent documentation. Adelaide reached for her leather satchel and shoved her notebook into it.

She lurched to her feet. The automaton was too big to fit into any of the boxes the Palace servants had brought in. Adelaide searched the room until she found the long coffin-like box he had arrived in from her laboratory at the Academy. She dragged it over the automaton's workbench and winced. She could barely move the box. How was she going to get the automaton inside? And then move the box? She placed a gentle hand on the automaton's chest, careful to avoid touching the orb.

I wish you could walk out of here with me and show them all how wrong they are to dismiss my idea.

Memories of her vision from the orb filled her thoughts. The Automated Dauphin promenading in the Gardens of Versailles, surrounded by admiring courtiers. Herself at his side as he sat on a throne, dispensing wisdom. Adelaide had believed for a moment that they were true predictions, but the possibility faded with every minute closer to her ejection from the Palace.

A soft knock roused her from her reverie. Were they here already to remove her and her belongings? With a soft pat on the automaton, she faced the door.

"Come in."

The door creaked open and Yalanchi Peygember's dark head appeared, peeking around the door. Adelaide groaned. She had forgotten all about him.

"Monsieur Peygember. This is unexpected."

The small man entered the room, his eyebrows drawn together in confusion.

"*Bon jour,* Madame le Scientist. I did mention that I would return in a week and it has been that much time."

Adelaide heard her former title with a sinking heart.

"Please, monsieur. I am just Mademoiselle Coumain now." She blinked back the hated tears. Would she ever be her usual stoic self again?

"I beg pardon. I addressed you incorrectly before? I apologize, I do not understand."

Adelaide raised her chin. She grasped at self-control.

"You were correct when we first met, but I no longer have the position of Scientist-Doctor, monsieur."

Peygember's expression grew more confused. He glanced around the room as if looking for answers.

"I am afraid I do not understand the French system of scientists. Something has changed for you?"

Adelaide nodded. Change was an understatement. Her whole world was turned topsy-turvy.

"Yes, monsieur. I am leaving the Palace today. The Presidente le Scientiste has dismissed me."

Peygember gasped.

"Dismissed? This is preposterous, dismissing a scientist of your caliber. Why would he do this thing?"

Adelaide smiled, a bitter cast to her lips.

"I neglected my duties to Their Majesties by spending so much of my time on their replacement."

Peygember looked over at the automaton, his face solemn. He approached it and stood next to Adelaide.

"This is then partly my fault. You spent many of your hours working with the orb, did you not? Attempting to make it function within your automaton?"

Adelaide shrugged. She met Peygember's eyes, level with her own. They were full of sympathy.

"I still haven't made much progress, I'm afraid. He spouts nonsense most of the time. If only I had more time to work on him, but I have to leave the Palace today."

"What will you do? Have you someplace to go?"

Adelaide shook her head.

"No, I have nowhere to go. I don't know what to do. I don't even know how I will manage to lift the automaton into his carrying case."

Peygember patted her shoulder. Adelaide generally hated being touched but his patting felt comforting.

"If you will allow me to assist, I can provide you and your automaton with a refuge. My townhouse in Paris has room enough for all."

Adelaide jerked away. What was he proposing? What kind of woman did he think she was?

"Monsieur, that would be improper."

He stood next to her, his hand still in the air where he had been patting her shoulder. His face reddened.

"No, madame...mademoiselle, I was not proposing anything improper. Just a temporary refuge for you until you find a place of your own."

Adelaide grew warm with embarrassment. Why had she jumped to that conclusion? Had her previous experience with Henri clouded her judgement?

"It is my turn to apologize then, monsieur. I can not afford to recompense you for your kind offer. I have no income. I am in need of a patron to support my scientific work."

He smiled with a sad twist to his lips.

"I would be honored to offer you patronage, but my funds will only stretch to hospitality, I am afraid. I do have an idea that you might consider. If it is successful, I think we can find you a patron."

Adelaide's interest was piqued.

"Indeed? That would be optimal. What is your idea, monsieur?"

He rocked back on his heels and put his hands in his waistcoat. A brilliant purple paisley today, Adelaide noted.

"We attract a patron by exhibiting your finest creation."

She frowned.

"The Automated Dauphin is not ready. I have much to do before he is fully functional. I can't exhibit him."

Peygember's smile took on a mischievous slant.

"You underestimate what you have already accomplished. Your automaton moves and talks. No matter that he talks nonsense. We can advertise him as the Electric Prophet. Wealthy people denied the power and mysteries of the Court would be intrigued by the idea, I assure you."

Adelaide snorted. The Electric Prophet? What a ridiculous name.

"He is the Automated Dauphin. He has a higher purpose than titillating bored rich people."

"Yes, yes, of course. You have explained this. But you say at present that he is not functioning as the Automated Dauphin, correct?" She nodded. He continued, his voice soothing. "We will show him as he is and his potential will be obvious to all, especially those who would be a patron of a brilliant scientist such as yourself. We earn money exhibiting him and you find a patron. Do you not find this beneficial?"

She pushed an errant wisp of hair behind her ear and considered the proposal. Would it really gain her a patron? That would be the answer to her dilemma.

"Perhaps. You think people would pay to see an automaton walk about and spout nonsense?"

"Yes. It's all in how we tell them about it. People love mystery and occult. But we can not refer to him as the Automated Dauphin, mademoiselle. We do not wish to attract the notice of the Police Secrete, you understand? Even a whiff of sedition is dangerous in Paris, I have been told."

Adelaide nodded. Her assistant, were she still alive, would confirm Peygember's words.

"Very well. We had better get a move on. I don't have much longer before the guards escort me out. Can you help move the Automated Dau—automaton?"

They struggled with the weight and bulk of the mechanical man, but managed to get him into the case before the guards appeared. Captain Girard himself came to escort her out of the Palace. Adelaide disliked his smirk but said nothing. She cast one last look back at her laboratory, strewn with her discarded life, before pulling the door closed.

***

The automaton sat upright on a straight-backed chair, his arms resting against his torso, hands on his thighs. Adelaide had to keep reminding herself not to think of him as the Automated Dauphin. To help with this, Peygember had suggested she dress the automaton in a formal suit. His unmoving features reminded her of the Queen, her former patient and someone she'd probably never see again.

Adelaide felt a twinge of regret that she hadn't helped the Queen more. The monarch's ancient body was failing despite the modifications Adelaide made to her old-fashioned clockwork augmentations. And now who would help her? Would the Queen fade away without the proper care? Adelaide took a deep breath and placed her hand against the automaton's cold cheek.

The automaton's mouth gaped open in a permanent look of surprise. His glittering blue eyes used the same technology Adelaide had used for the monarchs. She had created his features and installed his eyes before ever seeing the Queen up close. Now she wondered if the likeness would be too much for the audience.

Peygember had promised that an illustrious group of wealthy merchants would be in attendance for her automaton's debut. Adelaide wasn't sure now if it was such a good idea, but they were paying well for the novelty of being the first to see this mechanical marvel. A fully operational electric man, and a prophet at that.

The tickets had sold out within hours.

Peygember was in front of the theater, turning away people who didn't already have tickets. He had deliberately booked a smaller venue, he'd told Adelaide. The appearance of exclusivity would tempt those with the means to afford his outrageous ticket cost.

Adelaide surveyed the stage, empty except for her creation seated in the middle of the stage. He looked forlorn, lonely. Adelaide shook herself. Sentimentality was a ridiculous emotion. It only led to trouble.

Heartbreak. Bad decisions.

Anger and shame arose in her at the memories of her brief, ill-conceived love affair with Henri Desjardins, that artist from Montmartre. She still wondered if there would be consequences from her moment of weakness, possibly even a child. In a way, she was glad that he had fled France. She wouldn't have been able to bear seeing him at a chance moment, perhaps in the crowd gathered outside for a peek at the Electric Prophet. She snorted at the sobriquet. Peygember had insisted they dub her Automated Dauphin with the name. He had argued that her name, with its whiff of sedition, would bring the Police Secrète to their door. Adelaide had acquiesced, but she knew her invention's true purpose and could not shake the desire to see it fulfilled.

And if there is any truth to the prophecies it spouts, then perchance...

She could hear the audience on the other side of the curtain, their voices high with excitement. It was almost time for the show. Adelaide looked around for Peygember. He would be the master of ceremonies at this event, leaving Adelaide to linger in the wings. She needed to check the automaton one last time. The orb was still not predictable in its functioning. Perhaps one more turn would format the mechanism into a more synchronized alignment. She shivered a little as she approached the seated figure. Working with the orb was not a pleasant task. The prospect of more nightmare visions did not tempt her to make adjustments, but she wanted the audience to understand the power of her machine. If it went well tonight, she could find another patron to fund her experiments. Showing the automaton as if he were a sideshow freak didn't appeal to her, but it did have the potential to be lucrative.

Adelaide placed her hand on the automaton's shoulder. Would tonight's performance upset him? As if he heard her thoughts, the automaton turned his head towards her. The sound of whirring and clicking from his neck grew and his monotone voice reached her ears.

"Do not be concerned, madame. All is well."

His head turned to face front and the whirring faded.

Adelaide took a step back. She hadn't initiated his startup sequence. He shouldn't be able to speak without it, let alone move. Had she really heard him speak? Was it the orb speaking and moving her automaton? She rubbed the back of her neck. She wished again that she had a clue how the orb actually functioned.

"Our audience awaits the spectacle. Are we ready to begin, Mademoiselle Coumain?"

Adelaide started at Peygember's voice. He stood in the wings, resplendent in his evening wear. She was still in her scientist's drab black dress. She had no other clothing.

"I just need ... I need to ... to check ... please wait?"

She fluttered her hands in Peygember's direction, then at the automaton. One more check. She had to adjust the orb. Something wasn't right. Peygember's forehead creased.

"Are you well, madame? You appear pale. May I fetch you a glass of water?"

Adelaide let out a high giggle. She needed to get him out of there so she could adjust the settings on the orb.

"Water? Yes, water. Water would be lovely."

She leaned over the automaton and unbuttoned his dress shirt. The orb in his chest pulsed under her fingers and she hesitated. Adelaide sank her teeth into her lip, exhaled and reached for the depressions in the orb. A wave of sound and light crashed over her, a flurry of images moving too fast to comprehend.

She keened.

It was too much. A chorus of voices wailed and screamed in her mind. She pressed harder until she felt a click inside the orb, then snatched her fingers away. The cacophony in her head cut off and she shuddered and gasped.

We'll see what that does.

With trembling hands, Adelaide re-dressed the immobile figure. She caressed his face and darted close to lay a furtive kiss on his forehead. She stared into his glowing eyes.

"Don't worry, *mon cher,* I'll be right here. Please do what you're told."

She straightened and smoothed the front of her black gown. Peygember appeared in the wings, bearing a glass of water. Adelaide grimaced. Why was he carrying water around? He was supposed to be preparing for the show to begin. She gestured towards the automaton.

"We're ready now, Monsieur Peygember."

***

The curtain was going up. No time to back out now or making any more adjustments to the orb. Adelaide could hear Peygember on the other side of the curtain, extolling the wonders of the automaton. She shrunk against the side of the stage, out of sight. A spotlight shone on the automaton and his metal skin reflected the light. His eyes glowed a beautiful blue. Adelaide crossed her fingers that he would follow the program she had set for him. Stand, walk to the front of the stage, bow. Then he would speak the mock prophecies she and Peygember had concocted.

She hoped.

Her stomach soured and her corset felt too tight. With a start, she realized that the automaton was moving, responding to Peygember's commands. His mechanical voice carried as he initiated his greeting sequence.

"Good evening, ladies and gentlemen of Paris. I thank you for attending my debut performance."

The audience clapped, a polite gesture. They weren't impressed yet. So far, he was obeying the script she had generated. Adelaide watched him stand and pace towards the front of the stage. His step was steady. Adelaide leaned out of her hiding place to watch him bow.

He's graceful for a mechanical man. I did well.

She smiled to herself. Now it was time for the pretend prophecies. As programmed, he spoke, his voice booming.

"I am the Electric Prophet. Hear my predictions. Take note of them. The queen of the stars will seduce the prince of the night. The god of justice foretells peace, but the peaceful messenger will be forgotten. The white traitor will burn."

The audience tittered and murmured at that. The so-called prophecy was vague but Adelaide and Peygember had hoped it would intrigue the jaded Parisians. Adelaide leaned further out to watch the automaton lift his arm, pointing at a man in the center of the room.

"You! You will deliver the enemies of all the lands and humble the mighty of the peoples to bring upon their heads the reward of the Wicked and justify the Judgement of Your Truth on all the sons of men. A cloud of fire will arise in the east. Many will die."

The man's neighbors turned to look at him. The laughter grew but with a shrill hint of fear. The man singled out by the automaton seemed annoyed, his face drawn into a scowl. Peygember thought it would be entertaining to point to a single audience member while the automaton was prophesying, but perhaps he had been wrong in his estimations of their audience.

The automaton swiveled on one foot and strolled along the edge of the stage. Adelaide was reminded again of her vision of him. He seemed so noble in his fine evening clothes under the glare of the stage lights. He stopped in front of Peygember, seeming to wait for further instructions. Peygember waved his arm towards the automaton's chair.

"Return to your seat, automaton."

The automaton at first seemed to obey Peygember. He paced towards the chair, but then stopped and turned to face the audience.

"I am not an automaton. I am the Electric Prophet. Heed my words. The clockwork sovereign, the aberration of nature, will stop short when the people of the world follow the Beast."

The audience gasped and grumbled. Loud protests and shouts erupted.

"How dare you?"

"Ridiculous!"

"This is treason!

"Who is causing this machine to speak such lies!"

The automaton had not been programmed to say that. Heart in her throat, Adelaide watched him, waiting to see if he would sit back in his chair and shut down as instructed. He lifted both arms in the air and his voice raised to a shout

"Peace will return to Europe when the white flower again takes possession of the throne of France."

A roar rose from the audience at this final pronouncement. They sounded like words taken from the Naturalistes' propaganda. This audience was most definitely composed of Royalists. Angry Royalists who were getting to their feet and approaching the stage, yelling. Adelaide looked to Peygember. He was staring with wide eyes between the oncoming audience and the automaton. She gestured for him to come to her. Peygember sprinted across the stage, dodging a tuxedoed man clambering towards the automaton. Was the furious guest going to attack her mechanical man? Adelaide froze. They could destroy him. She needed to get her automaton away from the enraged crowd.

"Automaton! Come to me."

He turned his head to face her and paused. She waved him over. The angry tuxedoed man loomed close to the automaton, raising a hand to strike the mechanical man. Others had climbed onto the stage now. Peygember reached her side, panting, his face pale and sweating.

"We need to leave, Adelaide. These people are going to tear us apart for threatening their queen."

Adelaide shook her head and pointed back at the stage.

"I can't leave him; we need to get him out."

She watched as the angry man hit the automaton and yelped in pain. The mechanical man turned to face his assailant and shoved the man off his feet into the oncoming crowd. Adelaide heard screams of pain and fear as people tumbled to the floor. She trembled.

He definitely wasn't supposed to do that.

The automaton turned and stomped towards her. His immobile face seemed to be fixed on hers as he approached. Was he going to attack her too?

He halted in front of her.

"Madame, we should leave."

Adelaide glanced over his shoulder. The crowd behind him was hovering together, muttering. Soon enough they would pluck up the courage to make another move. Peygember grabbed her arm as an audience member pulled a rapier out of his walking stick and glared at her.

"Adelaide, we have to go now."

She let herself be dragged along. The trio fled into the backstage area, heading for the back entrance of the theater. Adelaide's sides ached from the fast pace but she kept moving. She cast a sideways glance at the automaton, tromping at her side. He had not received instructions to hurry along with them. He had become self-actuated. What would the orb do to him next?

***

Adelaide slumped against the dusty carriage cushions. The dark interior of the hired hack reeked of old wine and cheap perfume. She wrinkled her nose against the smell. Opposite her, the automaton sat, muttering, his eyes glowing. Peygember sat next to her, silent. She tried to understand the automaton's words. It sounded like "sorrysorrysorry."

Her companion broke the silence.

"That did not transpire as I expected."

Adelaide cast a glance at Peygember and laughed without a trace of mirth.

"Monsieur Peygember, I would never have agreed to exhibit the automaton if I thought it would be such a disaster. This entire situation has been a complete disaster. I have lost my position, my automaton has gone rogue, and I'm running away from an angry crowd of would-be patrons with their accusations of treason ringing in my ears."

She leaned her face on her hands but couldn't bend far in her over-tight corset. Peygember reached over and patted her knee.

"Yes, it was, as you say, a disaster. I apologize, mademoiselle. I would never have suggested this plan if I had thought it would prove to be so deleterious to your career or your person."

She pulled her leg away, more from habit than distaste at his touch. She raised her head and smiled to soften the move away from him. He returned her smile with a wistful, almost sweet expression. It was an unfamiliar expression for him. She wondered what he was thinking. Adelaide glanced at the automaton.

"I think I must be as much to blame as you are. I agreed to experiment with the orb. I really thought I could get my automaton to work as I intended. But, do you know, I can't understand what came over me at the Palace. I heard and saw bizarre things when I worked with that orb. I said and did things not like myself." She shook her head, remembering the talking statue.

"It has a strange power. Do you think the automaton spoke true prophecies tonight?"

Adelaide shrugged.

"Who can say? They were seditious even if not true." She peeked out of the carriage window. "If someone reports this to the Police Secrete, we will be in deep trouble."

Peygember drew his heavy eyebrows together in a frown. He gestured at the automaton.

"Can you control it? What if it speaks words of sedition in front of the authorities?"

She bit her lip and shook her head. Her voice came out a whisper.

"I have no control over him. He could be the end of us. The Police Secrete execute traitors. My own assistant was taken and executed just on my word that she was a traitor."

He hissed a breath inward and drew away from her.

"Why would you do such a thing, mademoiselle? What wrong did your assistant do?"

A familiar ache lodged in Adelaide's chest as she remembered that evening. She had been reeling with guilt and spent passion from her forbidden tryst with Henri. As she had sat quietly trying to decide what to do, she had spied her assistant attempting to destroy the Automated Dauphin. Adelaide had lost her temper and summoned the guards to arrest her assistant. How to explain all of that to Peygember? She barely understood her own reasoning.

"You must think poorly of me. I had my reasons. She was a

saboteur."

She caught a little sigh escaping his lips, but he remained quiet otherwise. Adelaide stared out of the window, away from the searching eyes of Peygember. The wide avenues had given way to the old twisting lanes of Paris. She didn't know which arrondissement they were in now, but it was far from the bustling theater district.

"Where are we going?"

"I thought it best to go where there is not so much scrutiny. I instructed the driver to take us to Montmartre."

Adelaide gasped. Was he joking? Did he know about Henri?

"Montmartre? Why not to the train station? We should leave Paris as soon as we can."

Peygember screwed his mouth into a grimace.

"Ah, I did not think our situation so dire. You are right. I will instruct the driver to take us to the Gard du Nord. I believe it is close?"

Adelaide nodded.

"What about him? We can't let him stay active. He could say or do anything."

The mechanical voice of the automaton grew louder and startled her.

"Madame le Scientiste. You must remove the orb from my workings. I am a danger to you. Remove the orb and I will no longer function independently. I will no longer be a danger. My words distress you. You must remove the orb and remove these words."

Adelaide's eyes filled with sudden tears and she swallowed hard. Removing the orb would render him into a metal puppet once more.

"Automaton, do you realize what you are asking me to do? You would not be capable of anything without input."

She could have sworn a metallic sigh echoed within his chest.

"I understand. The orb controls me now. You would control me without it. The orb makes me do terrible things. Please, madame, please remove it from me. Remove it before it can no longer be removed. Already it takes over my functions."

Adelaide and Peygember exchanged looks. He nodded. She stood, balanced for a moment as the carriage rocked back and forth, then sat down next to the automaton. He turned his head towards her and the light from his eyes dazzled her for a moment.

"Are you sure?"

Her voice was soft and tender, the voice of a mother speaking to her child.

"Please."

She reached for the buttons of his dress shirt and unbuttoned them with trembling hands. The light was dim inside the carriage, except for the brightness of the automaton's eyes. Adelaide didn't remember his eyes ever being that bright. Her fingers fumbled with the connections. She brushed against the orb. It seemed to throb against her fingertips. She shuddered and pulled away.

"I need more light. I can't see a thing."

The automaton inclined his head and his opened chest cavity was illuminated with the glow from his eyes. Adelaide drew a deep, shuddering breath and grasped the connections between the automaton and the globe nestled inside his torso. She pulled them free, leaving pieces of wire attached to the orb. Adelaide cautiously grasped the orb and drew it out. The automaton's eyes faded and he stiffened against the carriage seat.

"Automaton? Can you hear me?"

There was no response from the stilled automaton but she felt an answering tingle from the orb. She shrieked but held tight to the artifact. A deep revulsion of the thing filled her.

"Adelaide? What's happening?"

Peygember leaned forward and grabbed her shoulder. She looked up at him, her face frozen in horror.

"What do I do with this thing? It's trying to talk to me."

He drew back, his mouth twisted in fear.

Her vision clouded and Peygember, the automaton, even the carriage faded from view. Adelaide was in a foreign-appearing room with gleaming metal walls and flashing lights on low surfaces. A woman, seeming to be unaware of Adelaide, moved stealthily towards a man sitting with his back towards her. She raised a dark cylinder and fire shot out of it. The man slumped onto the floor. Adelaide screamed and found herself in Peygember's arms. He was shaking her and calling her name.

"Adelaide, what's happening?"

She fought down the bile burning in her throat.

"We need to get rid of this thing. Now." She peeked out of the window of the carriage. The dark waters of the Seine glinted in the moonlight next to the carriage. She dropped the window and with all of her strength, tossed the orb into the river. She sank back down onto the carriage seat. "There. That's done."

Peygember looked as shaken as she felt.

"You did the right thing. The good thing. This was the good thing to do." His French was unraveling. She didn't understand all of his words but they certainly weren't French.

"Now what do we do? Orb or not, we still have this very distinctive, though no longer functioning, automaton who looks very much like the king of France. The Police Secrète will be looking for us. And I am still no closer to achieving my goal. If I ever will."

Peygember visibly pulled himself together.

"You are not to worry, mademoiselle. We will go to Vienna. I know a very talented mechanician there."

She nodded her acquiescence and watched the city lights flash by through the carriage window.

Run away from France? Was that the answer? Would she be successful with her quest in Vienna? Or would the Austrians try to take control of her automaton? And if she left Paris, she'd never find out who killed Marie-Ange. She knew the answer to the murder must lie in the artists' quarter.

A wave of dizziness overwhelmed her and her stomach turned. She closed her eyes against the nausea. The ongoing nausea didn't have anything to do with the orb. She realized her fears had come true. She was with child. Henri's child.

I can't leave Paris now. I need to find Henri. Someone in Montmartre will know how to find him. I must call him to account for his child. And the automaton and I can find sanctuary there among the artists and outlaws.

She stayed silent all the way to the Gard du Nord, scheming to herself. Peygember seemed wrapped in his own musings. When the carriage drew up to the station, Adelaide finally broke the silence.

"Monsieur, I will stay here in the carriage with the automaton while you buy us tickets to Vienna." She held out a hand to halt him. "Wait! You can't go with that box full of money, you'll be robbed. Take what you need for the tickets, make sure you get first class, that will provide us decent food along the way."

Peygember seemed lost in thought still. He nodded and mumbled in agreement, not meeting her eyes. He stuffed bills into the pockets of his coat. Adelaide noticed that he took only larger denomination bills, more than he needed for the tickets. He climbed out of the carriage and glanced at her.

"I will be back soon."

Adelaide said nothing in return. He shut the carriage door and strolled away, as if he wasn't in danger of arrest. As soon as he disappeared from view into the bustling train station, she leaned out of the carriage and called up to the driver.

"Driver, take me to Montmartre. Double your usual fare. Quickly, if you please."

She sat back down and the carriage lurched back into motion. Adelaide exhaled, relief stealing over her body.

We'll be safe in Montmartre.

She smiled at the immobile automaton at her side. She would keep him and her unborn child safe.

AJ Sikes

Wagner's Silent Night

December 1890, Paris

A milk wagon trundled down the *Rue Bayard* and Archibald Wagner followed, folding his heavy coat closer around him to keep out the mist coiling off the nearby Seine. It was 16 December, and Wagner had suffered more than enough Parisian chill for his tastes. He grimaced against the cold and made his way around still-fresh droppings from the milk wagon's team, being careful to set his feet down in time with the horses' hooves.

The dairyman halted outside a Haussmann apartment block. Wagner halted his progress as well. The wagon moved again and Wagner crept along the narrow street. He stayed close beside the tall apartment buildings and recalled the canyon walls he'd ridden through as a young man, during the war against the Confederate Rebels. That war, like so many others, ended with very little to recommend the idea of war. And yet, still the world hung on the very cliff's edge of utter disaster. It was men like Wagner who had answered the call to bring humanity back from the brink, and bring it back he would.

Or my name might as well be Benedict Arnold.

The milk wagon halted and moved, halted and moved. Wagner continued his pursuit in time to ensure his passage was not marked by anyone within the apartments. As long as the horses' hooves struck the cobblestones, Wagner's feet would be silenced to any and all within.

At the Place Françoise, he hid beside the central fountain while the dairyman made a stop, then climbed back onto his perch and took his team farther along. At the opposite side of the plaza, the milk wagon turned down a wider street. Cursing his luck, Wagner stole across the open plaza, and down the Rue François, staying tight against the buildings and watching every window for signs of a curtain being drawn back. He continued in this manner until he reached the avenue leading onto the Pont des Invalides.

The Seine coursed beneath the bridge, dark and hushed in the early morning chill, carrying small flotillas of ice along on its current. Wagner's destination, a reputable antiquities shop, was at the far end of the bridge. With the clatter of horses' hooves now too distant to be of use, Wagner set off. He adopted a casual pace, as though simply out for a constitutional and not, as he was in truth, out to collect the most dangerous artifact in existence. In mere minutes, if he had any luck left to count on, Wagner would have the oracle sphere in his hands.

At least, that was his hope as he stepped across the cobblestones of the avenue and put his shoe onto the bridge. If he found matters to be different upon his arrival, Wagner would have a long discussion with a certain Mme H—. Her admirable touches would be as nothing if her tongue proved treacherous.

After months of research, and more than a few nights spent in Mme H—'s arms, Wagner had uncovered the location of the lost oracle sphere. He knew the hour was dire. Agents from Prussia and France herself were anxious to locate the artifact as well. He'd tussled with one in the stacks of the Imperial Library just a week prior, leaving the man gasping for air and, sadly, breaking the spine of a valuable tome in the process.

Would have been better to break his spine and leave the text alone. But murder never comes with a reward. None worth having anyway.

Wagner checked over his shoulder as he stepped along the bridge. The man he merely winded or any number of other spies could be roaming the city this very minute, possibly following his trail. He'd even been warned to watch out for agents from the Dual Monarchy of Austria-Hungary.

Only Wagner worked for the one government that could, above all others, be trusted to secure the oracle sphere from ever being used. Destruction of the device was not an option. Attempts had been made to crush, shatter, and burn the object, time and time again throughout history. The ruin left in the wake of such efforts was testament to their futility.

No, the only salvation humanity could hope for was the United States laying claim to the device. And they had entrusted its capture to their best man. After twenty years of service, Special Foreign Services Agent Archibald Wagner was the most successful man the War Office had. If he couldn't do it, they said, well then it just couldn't be done.

It'd be a damn sight easier to do if I didn't also have to feel every one of my fifty years in this soggy French air.

The glass front of the antiquities shop appeared through the wisps of fog rising from the river as Wagner neared the end of the Pont des Invalides. After reaching the opposite bank, he approached the shop from an oblique angle to the door, preparing a quiet curse should Mme H— prove false. Before he could reach to knock on the door, it was whisked open and a sweetly maiden-like voice beckoned him to enter.

"Monsieur Wagner, *entrez, s'il vous plaît.*"

Wagner pushed through, hand above his lapel, ready to draw his revolver should the need arise. The shop was darkened within by a curtain hanging across the windows. As soon as Wagner was inside, the door closed behind him. He spun around, revolver out and aimed into the face of a youth, a boy not more than ten years of age if that. He could have been Wagner's own son but for the shock of jet black hair tumbling off the lad's scalp in all directions.

"*Oncle* Remy!" the boy screamed. Wagner spun again to see an old man with a lantern in one hand shuffling his way to the front of the shop. Replacing his firearm beneath his coat, Wagner stepped into the center of the shop entrance and waited for the proprietor to join him and the boy.

For his part, the boy sped past Wagner and met the old man halfway. They talked briefly and the boy rushed out of sight at the back of the shop. The antiquarian waited until the boy had gone before he continued on his path. He stepped over and around oddities and curios that littered the narrow shop, extending deep into the darkness at the back of the space. As he came, the lantern illuminated the walls, revealing shelves sprouting bundles of fabric, stacks of books and manuscript pages, and strange wooden masks that seemed to heckle or ridicule Wagner as the lantern light passed over their surface. Dust motes rose around the man as he came, and the lantern lit up ever more of the shop just as it banished still more of it into darkness. The whole effect made the proprietor, a Monsieur Le Grec, look like a ghost bearing a will-o-wisp through a morass cluttered with the effluvia of countless nations. His creaking, paper-thin voice only added to the haunting image.

"Monsieur Wagner. Come, come. No need for the blunderbuss at this hour. We've not even had coffee."

The old man came to a stop beside a low counter upon which a service was arranged. Wagner observed the gold-lipped china cups, a carafe, a pitcher of cream, and a dish with tongs and cubes of sugar. Nothing out of the ordinary, and nothing out of place. The tongs were, as he'd been told they would be, laid to the right of the cream pitcher. Mme H— must be in the building somewhere, preparing Wagner's gift.

"You would like the cream?" Le Grec asked him.

Having deposited his lantern on the counter beside the service, the old man set to pouring a dark liquid from the carafe.

"Don't mind if I do," Wagner said, knowing he'd get nowhere if he tried to force the Parisian's hand. The people of France were not unkind in their thinking toward Americans, but Wagner had learned, very much the hard way, that the French had their way of doing things and they preferred that way above any other.

He would bide his time, engage in the ritual of sipping coffee and talking about the latest inconvenience the French were being made to suffer at the behest of this or that government agenda. And once all was said and done, Wagner would receive the gift the old man had agreed to provide him. So long as Mme H— held up her end of things, it would all come out proper and good.

The antiquarian would unknowingly hand over the oracle sphere. Wagner would secure the world against complete annihilation.

And then I can go back home where a cigar is a cigar and people chit chat over glasses of bourbon.

The antiquarian handed him a cup of coffee. Wagner accepted it, reached for the tongs, and picked up first one cube, then another. The brew was rich, and yet slightly bitter on the tongue, despite the extra sugar.

Wagner finished his cup, and let himself relax into the moment. He breathed in the aroma of history that seemed to emanate from every corner of the shop. An African statue, carved in ivory, beckoned from a nearby shelf. Wagner was about to lay his hand upon it when a shrill cry broke in on their proceedings. In a flash, he had his revolver out and was rushing toward the back of the shop.

A door slammed, followed by a second scream, and then muffled sobbing. Finally a sharp retort was heard, and then a slap as of a hand across a face.

The boy came from the back of the shop, slinking around an ornate screen standing at the far end and obviously placed to block the view into the private spaces at the rear.

"What's happened?" Wagner demanded of the boy, who held a hand up to one side of his face.

A rustle of taffeta told of Mme H— approaching. She emerged from behind the boy and pushed him to the side as she stormed forward. Wagner kept his revolver ready, but angled it slightly to the side, just in case there should be a struggle. Better some bit of history be shot to pieces than the weapon discharge into Mme H— or himself.

"Archibald, I am sorry," she cried, reaching for his lapels. "The idiot boy did it. He opened the back door. I could not stop him in time."

"What do you mean, *chérie*? What has happened?"

"He has taken it! Herr Schliemann has taken it!"

Wagner wasted no time. Darting around the still trembling form of Mme H— and forcing himself to ignore the whimpering youth, he sped through the clutter, knocking the ornate screen aside. Wagner raced for the door at the rear of the building. He flung it open onto a Paris street that was empty but for the fingers of mist crawling away to hide in the shadows.

"Dammit!" he yelled. He had known to watch for Heinrich Schliemann's grasping fingers, and to cut them off from their goal by any means necessary. Now he'd lost the sphere to the very worst possible opponent.

Wagner holstered his revolver, checked his timepiece, and, straightening his coat and top hat, made a rapid course for the

Quai d'Orsay, planning his next moves as he walked a brisk pace beside the Seine.

Schliemann is off home, to Athens, but he'll stop in Naples first. He always catches a steamer there before heading back to Greece. And he thinks he's gotten away clean. He'll be slow to leave Paris. Probably even try to nab some other bit of history on the cheap. I'll catch him up before he boards the train to Naples.

Wagner stepped fast and forceful into the Parisian morning as window shutters were cracked open by the hopeful French, looking for even a glimmer of sunlight in the dreary December sky.

Fear not, Wagner thought as he walked. *America will come to your aid just as you came to ours so long ago.*

***

December 1890, Trieste

Wagner's timepiece read one minute past nine when the station clock chimed. He frowned. Where the Germans were always spot on with their time-keeping, the Italians, it seemed, did not strive for the same exactitude. And for Wagner, every second counted. He'd missed Schliemann's departure from Paris, after taking a nasty stumble outside the station and coming to with a gendarme shaking him by the shoulders and shouting in his face. Why he'd collapsed, Wagner could only guess, but he suspected the antiquarian's bitter coffee had something to do with it.

No matter, of course. Schliemann was notoriously greedy and took his leisure at Trieste, seeking out every cran where antiques could be found. Wagner still had to find the man, however, and spent a frantic day of worry that ended with catching his quarry's scent in a darkened plaza. In the glow of a gas lamp, Schliemann exchanged money for an object wrapped in silk. Wagner observed from the shadows, following Schliemann to his hotel on the other side of the plaza. He never let the man out of his sight after that, sleeping fitfully if he did at all, and keeping as close a watch on Schliemann as safety would allow.

For the next two days, they were as cat and mouse through the streets of Trieste. Wagner trailed the man around the port, worried that Schliemann would change course and board a steamer there. But luck smiled upon Wagner, and he had only to suffer a merry wander around the city, mounting and dismounting carriages, and weaving in and out of the crowds toting bundles and holiday gifts. For his part, Herr Schliemann himself always carried a heavyweight leather satchel against his chest, as if it were a babe in swaddling.

Best that you do keep the sphere safe, Herr Schliemann. If anything untoward befalls that device...

Wagner spent the better part of those days following Schliemann around the port city, until finally the antiquities thief led a path to the train station. Now, Wagner sat in his own compartment on the 9:13 to Naples, watching Schliemann make his way down the car, clutching the leather satchel tight against his breast. As he approached the compartment and passed, Wagner tucked his face behind a news sheet. He would have to be careful. With a clever bit of shaving, he could likely disguise himself, maybe even win a bit of Schliemann's friendship if he were lucky. And then, at Naples, he would strike.

***

The rail trip from Trieste to Rome, and finally to Naples, proved dull as ditchwater. That is, until dinner on the fourth night, when Wagner had the displeasure of killing Schliemann by mistake.

The dining car that night was close to empty, with only three couples seated at tables along its length. Finally, the last of these pairs departed, leaving just Wagner, Schliemann, and the stewards who busied themselves clearing away dishes and wine carafes.

Wagner had been careful to take only one glass of wine himself, but Schliemann—the man was a veritable sponge. He had dined alone, at the far end of the car from Wagner, with the satchel in his lap the whole meal. His distant position was expected, but his solitude was odd. Wagner had seen the man board with a retinue of friends, including two young women, neither of whom, Wagner knew, were Schliemann's wife.

Frau Schliemann is in Athens. Likely wearing Priam's Treasure still, no doubt.

As the dinner hour came to a close, Schliemann berated a steward for taking his wine glass and demanded another goblet full before he retired. The steward begrudgingly complied and turned to pace down the length of the car toward Wagner and the door to the kitchen behind him. Catching Wagner's sympathetic eye, the steward stopped short and asked if he'd needed anything else.

"I'm fine, thanks," Wagner said. "Tell me, that fellow at the other end of the car is a bit in his cups, isn't he?"

"*Sí, signo*—yes, sir," the steward said, shifting from Italian to English in the space of a breath. There was something Wagner wouldn't mind: getting home to a land where everyone used the same damn tongue.

"Was there something else, sir?"

"Oh, yes. I think I'll have another glass as well, maybe join my solitary companion for a toast. It's Christmas Eve tomorrow. May as well begin the holiday cheer early."

"Of course, sir," the steward said, with a scarcely concealed roll of his eyes. "I'll bring it out."

Wagner hadn't realized it until the idea struck him, but this was the perfect chance to catch Schliemann at his own game. He reached into his breast pocket for a vial of tablets and had one in his palm as the steward exited the kitchen. A glass of wine appeared at Wagner's elbow.

"Your wine, sir," the steward said, holding one glass out for him and a second in the other hand.

"Why not let me take that to him?" Wagner offered, motioning to Schliemann's glass and doing his best to appear chummy. Whether he'd got it right or not, the steward set both goblets of wine down and disappeared into the kitchen without a backward glance.

Wagner kept an eye on Schliemann, who had slid down in his seat and rested his head against the wall of the car. He rocked there in time to their transit along the rails. Wagner quickly dissolved the tablet in Schliemann's wine, and stirred it once with his finger, which he wiped on his napkin before standing and lifting both of the goblets from the table.

His leg shook as he made his way down the car.

Why now, of all times, should I get the shivers? I've done this before, and to more dangerous men than this buffoon.

Schliemann still appeared to slumber in his seat, bouncing and jostling with the rhythm of the train, hardly alert to his surroundings.

So it was a bit of a surprise when, as Wagner came within two paces of Schliemann's table, the man jerked upright and glared at Wagner.

"Ach, geben Sie mir!" he hollered, reaching for Wagner's own glass, which he held in his left hand. Wagner's German was good enough to parse Schliemann's demand, but he wasn't ready for the man's attempt to snatch the wrong goblet from him. Wagner had to shift his hips to bring his right hand forward. Schliemann didn't seem to notice; his hand hovered in the air and his eyes tracked from one glass to the next.

Worried that Schliemann would grab the wrong glass, Wagner slowly drew his left hand back. In an instant, he was bracing his hip against the table to stay upright as the train rocked and swayed around a turn. Schliemann nearly fell across the table, but caught himself just as fast. Still holding the satchel against his lap, he rose and reached for the goblet that Wagner held out for him in his right hand.

"There you go," Wagner said, adopting as friendly a tone as he could muster as he passed the goblet to his foe.

"You're not the steward," Schliemann said, using English now. He accepted the wine and sat down again.

"No, I'm not. Sorry for the surprise, *Mein Herr*. Name is Archibald Lynx. I'm visiting the continent from America, traveling alone like you. Thought we'd raise a toast together. Get the holiday cheer going a day early, and why not, eh?"

"How do you know I am alone?" Schliemann asked, sipping at his wine, but motioning for Wagner to sit across from him.

"Oh, just guessed at it really," Wagner said as he pulled out his chair and sat. "You've been at this end and I at the other for the whole meal, and neither of us with a woman's company."

Wagner was sure he'd overplayed his hand. Schliemann stared at him, either seeking after some truth in his words or looking for a detail that would tell him who Wagner really was. He held his goblet tight, then straightened and whipped his free hand at his ear, like he was swatting away a buzzing fly.

Schliemann gave a cry of pain and pressed his hand against his head, holding his ear flat and nodding as if in response to an inner demand.

"What is it?" Wagner asked, sudden concern rushing through him.

"My ear," Schliemann said. "The damn doctors in Halle. They said it was fine. They said they fixed it. But—Owww!"

Without another word, Schliemann put his goblet to his lips and swallowed once, twice, three times, draining the wine down his gullet. He sank back in his seat, still holding a hand over his ear and now clutching the satchel with his other.

"Leave me, please," he said. "I've ruined your Christmas cheer,

I expect, making you watch a miserable man suffer like this."

"But what's wrong?"

"An infection of the inner ear, they say. I told them when I got on board, but the doctor has nothing he can give me for the pain. He said if it gets unbearable, I should call—Aaahh!"

Wagner sat patiently, cursing himself for causing Schliemann more pain on top of his extant agony.

How could I have known? At least the drug will wear off, but the poor bastard—

Foes they may have been, and Schliemann was not even an agent in service to anything but his own greedy desire to possess the world's treasures for himself. But still, Wagner operated under a strict code of doing the least harm possible, as much for honor as for a sense of devotion to what was right. It simply didn't do to kill off one's opposite in the enemy camp. Spies were the real winners of wars. It was their job to find the enemy's weakness and exploit it so as to bring about an end to hostilities as quickly as possible.

Some had argued that Wagner's soft-heartedness for his counterparts would lead to his undoing, but he knew what every spy truly knows: in the end, it will be the spy's own government that decides his fate.

Schliemann had gone back to rocking in his seat, head forward, hand against his ear, and moaning as the train carried them down the Italian peninsula.

"Gentlemen," the steward called from the back of the car. "I am afraid we must close the dining car. If you please."

Wagner felt the need to call the man out for his effrontery, but, through a force of will, kept those thoughts to himself.

"Can I help you to your compartment?" he asked Schliemann, standing and reaching for the man's elbow. The steward's clicking tongue nearly loosened Wagner's restraint, but Schliemann nodded and stood just as Wagner got to his feet.

"Yes, thank you, Mr. Lynx."

"Of course, say nothing of it."

If I don't get him out of here, he's going to fall down on his face and the damned steward will be sure to call the doctor in. They won't let me move him.

Wagner took Schliemann's elbow and guided him out of the dining car and into the next one. They walked a staggering path down the car, passing curtained compartments and the snoring occupants within.

"Where are you berthed?" Wagner asked.

Schliemann walked stiffly next to him, clutching his satchel to his chest with one hand and holding himself up against the wall of the car with the other. He seemed to search the darkness of the passage, then slumped against the wall and slid down to a seat on the floor. The satchel rolled out of his grasp and thunked to the floor beside him. Schliemann stirred, as if cognizant of the sound and what it meant. Wagner snatched the satchel aside, holding it off the floor with one hand while he pressed his other against Schliemann's shoulder, keeping the man down.

"You...I need my bag—my..." Schliemann's lips went slack and spittle drooled from his mouth in a stream that ran down the front of his jacket.

Wagner lifted his hand off Schliemann's shoulder, letting him slide down the wall to lie on the passage floor.

"Sleep well, friend. And may your earache pass in the night."

Wagner stepped away quickly, but with measured softness, letting his footfalls land in time with the rocking of the train. He backed into the darkness at the end of the car, leaving the sleeping form of Heinrich Schliemann in the shadows.

***

December 1913, Washington, D.C.

The aged War Office clerk gently lifted a dark wooden case,

about the size of a hatbox, from a high archives shelf. He let it rest against his breastbone before descending the ladder. Afternoon light slanted through the clerestory windows beside his head, casting swords of brightness onto the dark stones of the floor. He held the case against his chest with one hand, and descended the ladder. His feet went from rung to careful rung until one touched the floor. All around him, shelves and stacks of books and boxes threatened to topple over at any minute. He breathed a sigh of sorrow as he took in the detritus around him. It was so like the massed collection of a raving antiquarian doomed to die beneath the excess of his obsession.

For every one of his past twenty-three years, Archibald Wagner had wondered when he might be so lucky as to be snuffed out by some tumbling tower of history.

Not much more a man like me deserves.

I should never have passed that pill to Schliemann.

Heinrich Schliemann had died the next day, while touring the ruins of Pompeii. News of his death reached Wagner while he was aboard a steamer bound for the Strait of Gibraltar and the Atlantic beyond. He'd nearly thrown the oracle sphere into the Mediterranean, but he knew better than to trust its safety to mere absence. Someone would find it. Someday it would be brought up from the depths. Then it would be used, and humanity's long struggle against the darkness would come to a final, horrible end.

Instead, I get to deliver it to a madman and let him flick the switch for us.

Walking his shuffling step over the flagstone flooring, Wagner made his way to the wooden planks of the central aisle where he turned and exited the stacks, putting his feet to the polished wood flooring that led a clear trail toward his desk at the front of the cavernous space. Try as he might, he couldn't bring himself to lift his foot to take the first step in that direction.

But Wagner knew a car waited on the curb outside. He was

expected, and the president was not a man who approved of being kept waiting.

Carrying the case in both hands, Wagner began walking. He nodded his farewell to the items he'd collected since departing the life of a field agent and choosing the life of an archivist. Each shelf he passed was mounded with papers and tomes, dusty boxes, old uniforms, cavalry sabers, and medals. Somewhere in the mess was the one firearm stored within the archives. As Wagner set the case on his desk, he wondered if it would be wise to bring the revolver with him. He might have a chance to stop this madness. He could—

I could get myself shot. No, Archibald. This may be your last day alive, but it won't end with you being gunned down by some doughboy who doesn't know any better. If you're to die, then you'll die on your feet like everyone else when that fool turns the crank and sets the sphere in motion.

Wagner lifted his great coat off the rack beside his desk. He shrugged into it, wrapped a scarf around his collar, and put on a cap to keep the cold off his naked scalp. He double tied the belt around his coat, to ensure it stayed closed. Then he lifted the case and stepped a dead man's march to the reinforced door at the entrance. An armed sentry opened and held it for him. A second guard saluted Wagner as he exited the building, then both men returned to their posts at the entrance, weapons slung over their shoulders and eyes rigidly staring at the gray morning air beside the Potomac.

The president's car waited at the street. The man himself was there, sitting on the far side of the car and chit chatting with some fellow holding blueprints. Wagner thought about turning and running, but how far could an old man get really? Even if he did get away somehow, what would he do with the sphere?

At the curb, Wagner forced himself to hand over the case to one of two military policemen who stood beside the car. Wagner kept his hands on the box until the young officer tugged on it.

"You'll need to get in first, sir," he said.

Wagner nodded, released the case, and lifted a hand in acknowledgement. He couldn't take his eyes off the case as he climbed into the president's car. He needed the assistance of the second officer to avoid tumbling backwards onto the pavement. Wagner thanked the young man with another raised hand, then took a step forward. Once he had his balance, he gently settled onto the cushioned bench seat beside the president and accepted a blanket, which the second policeman had lifted from beside the front seat. Wagner laid the blanket over his legs, drawing comfort from the weight of it even if it did little to warm him against the chill air coming off the nearby river.

"Sir," the first officer said, holding out the dark wooden case. Wagner leaned forward, straining against his arthritic spine, and accepted the case.

He felt his wispy voice crawling up from deep in his chest to emerge as only a hushed muttering of thanks. The soldier nodded and resumed his position across from the other young fellow in uniform. Wagner reflected on his own time in the nation's service, and the uniforms he had worn. How they had changed. Union Blue had been all he'd known, when he'd been in a uniform and not spying for the republic. These boys were dressed up in stiff drab wool and were called doughboys. They didn't look like any dough Wagner had ever known. They looked like they'd been dunked in a mud puddle, wrung out once, and let to dry in the sun.

The one who had given him the case looked over his shoulder and returned his stare.

"Sir, is everything okay?"

"Yes, sonny. Everything's fine," Wagner said, smiling and patting the case on his lap. He let his hands fall to the sides so he could cradle it there as if it were a crown of gold.

While the president nattered on with the architect fellow, Wagner took in the progress made so far on the National Mall. He stared off to his left, between the two policemen who now stood at attention beside the car. Wagner let his eyes wander a bit until he was able to focus on the terrain and the Lincoln Memorial project. Most of the ugly buildings of the last century were now gone. The new marble structure stood proud of the ground by easily twelve feet. Even in its state of half-completion, the memorial was a thing of beauty in the muddy landscape by the riverside. Guy wires slanted away in all directions from the blocky structure. Pulleys, sheds, worktables, and tools littered the area in amongst rounds of brilliant white marble lying on the ground like the toy blocks of some giant child.

Wagner imagined God himself reaching down to lift the stone cylinders and stack them in place around the monument to the country's greatest president.

A far cry we've come from those years, when one could take pride in our country. When we had a president who understood what pride really is.

"You have the device there, Wagner?" the president asked, snapping Wagner from his reverie.

"Oh, yes I do, Mr. President. Right here. Safe and sound."

"Good, good. Let's have it out."

Wagner the clerk, his hands shaking against the cold air, held in a sob. He took a breath, then another, and finally complied, easing the bronze clasp aside so he could raise the lid. His wintered hands trembled as he did so, but not from the chill.

Without waiting for the lid to be open all the way, the president knocked Wagner's hands away and reached for the device. He yanked it free from the velvet and lace that kept it safe inside the heavy wooden case.

"Mr. President, that—"

"Oh, I know all about this little beauty, Wagner. Don't you worry yourself a jot or tittle about it. Why, I've been waiting for this day like no other. You know what this means, Wagner? Do you?"

"I—"

"It means victory, Wagner. You remember victory, don't you? I know you fought for the Union, and I know you've done a lot of very great things for the country. Very great. But victory, Wagner. Victory! That's the stuff of legend, isn't that right? America will be legendary again, Wagner. We're going to be on top, and nobody will be able to stop us."

Wagner hoped the man in the carriage with him wouldn't go too far. But the gleam in his eyes, the devilish grin, and the hunger in his voice said that Wagner's hopes were wasted.

Legends are things that used to exist. They're remembered. They—

The last words Wagner heard were someone shouting about a doctor. He felt a hand pushing him back into the seat. The hand reached through his coat and into his chest where it squeezed until Wagner's heart stopped.

***

July, 1914, Washington, D.C.

The president sat in the Oval Office, alone and feverish in his mind. He ran his hands over the dark wooden case, halfway to salivating about what the sphere would tell him next. He swiveled the brass hook closure from its loop, releasing the slender hasp, which fell away with a hollow metallic twang. The president gently pushed the hasp all the way down to rest against the face of the box.

His first time seeing the sphere, he'd been rough with it, grabbing it while the old dotard clerk gasped out his last breaths. But now, the president worked his fingers carefully around the edge of the lid, feeling for the indentations that accepted his thumbs. He took a breath, and raised the lid.

The familiar warm glow of delight bathed him, just as it had every time he set eyes upon the device. Rays of summer sunlight streamed over the president's shoulders. A golden glow reflected from the gleaming brass cage of the device. A swirling blue ball was held within the woven filigreed metal, suspended there by whatever force gave the oracle sphere its power.

In the past year, the president had wondered if the sphere were a gift from God, or from more ancient deities, the gods of old. The gods long forgotten.

The gods long since dead.

Whoever had designed the device, they had the president's eternal gratitude. Each time he had used the oracle sphere, the president had asked a simple question.

What will happen?

And each time, he'd received an answer as images flowing through his mind in a parade of events. Factories filling cities with machines and jobs and money. Farms growing into factories themselves. American coal mines and oil wells emptying the earth's riches into America's energy pipelines. Gold mines and silver mines emptying the earth's glory into America's vaults.

All of it had proven true. America had risen, within the space of just six months, to be a power like the world had never seen. Not since Rome had any one nation been able to claim dominance in finance, minerals, manufacturing, and every other industry by which a country could be judged. America was the greatest and the grandest, and the president was enjoying the finest time of his life.

If this keeps up, I'll beat anybody they throw at me in '16.

"Well," he said to the sphere as he gently turned the crank set into the side of the cage. "What will happen?"

The crank operated smooth as silk, sending the ornate cage spinning in a dance of swirls and spirals around the glimmering blue orb. Right away, the president noticed something amiss. He stopped turning the crank and felt his stomach clench with fear.

It can't be broken. Not now. Not when we've just made it. It can't—

Usually, the orb would swell with light as images of prophecy swam through the president's mind. But this time the orb grew dim, and he saw nothing but the usual parade of memories from the day before. Speeches given, papers signed, phone calls avoided.

With fear shaking his voice, the president wondered aloud, "What the devil's wrong?"

A knock on the door snapped his attention away from the sphere for a heartbeat. He looked at the dim blue ball again. His hands shook as he lifted the oracle sphere and placed it back in its bed of velvet and lace. He closed the lid and fastened up the clasp.

Giving one last look at the case, with wonder and worry wrinkling his brow, he pressed the intercom button on his phone.

"Enter."

The door opened and his Chief of Staff came through, quickly shutting the door behind him.

"Mr. Pres—"

"What is it, Carl? I'm in the middle of this morning's query."

"It's—it's war, Mr. President. We're at war."

"Wa—with whom?"

"With everyone."

***

July 1929, Washington, D.C.

The president sat in a radio booth, a thick pane of glass separating him from his strategist, the corpulent slob named James Bacon. The president wiped sweat from his brow and regarded Bacon, who sat in the control booth with his eyes flicking left and right. The man could never be at rest. He always had something nagging at him inside, and the president had never managed to figure out what it was. But over the past two terms, Bacon had been the rock the president had needed. He'd been there when his cabinet dissolved the first time. He'd been there when the First Lady died in the middle of a fundraising dinner. Through it all, Bacon had been there.

If he'd been there from the start, maybe things wouldn't be as bad as they are now.

Bacon's voice crackled through the intercom, intruding upon the president's thoughts.

"Mr. President."

He held his hand over the switch, ready to open the broadcast channel. With a final wipe across his forehead, the president nodded and lifted a hand to signal he was ready. He settled his nerves with a breath, tucked his kerchief into his coat pocket, then pivoted at the waist.

The dark wood case rested on the table beside him. The president opened it and removed the oracle sphere.

He set the gleaming metal cage gently in his lap. The blue orb within spun slowly and leisurely, as if all the troubles of the world didn't depend upon it working its magic right then and there.

The president checked he had the microphone positioned correctly. He checked his position on his chair, shifting a buttock to relieve the pressure against the back of one leg. It all felt right at last, so he motioned through the glass again, holding up an open palm with his fingers spread.

"Yes, Mr. President," Bacon said. He would open the channel in five minutes.

This would be the president's third radio address in as many weeks. He'd started out with monthly broadcasts, but after the first few times, he'd provided America with an update; he had Senators from California to Ohio and everywhere in between sending runners to the White House. Telegrams and letters flooded the mail room downstairs. The people were angry. They'd elected him to a second term, and then broken with tradition and kept him in the hot seat for two more terms after that. He'd accepted the nominations gladly, and the victories buoyed his spirits. But now, his spine bent and his skin sagging, he wondered if he'd have been better off stepping aside and letting someone else take the helm.

The people were angry. They wanted him to fix their problems. They wanted the war to end.

It was supposed to be the war to end war itself.

Since the beginning, it had been a war of attrition, and in fifteen years, not much had changed. The French and English had done their level best to push back the marauding Hun. They'd done well on land and sea. But the air war had gone badly. Britain was a ruin, a shell of its former self. The English were running on fumes. France wasn't much better off. And now America was sending ever more of her sons, brothers, and fathers into the trenches, all in a desperate fight to keep the Kaiser from reaching Paris.

Fighting side by side with the remaining French and English armies, they had pushed the Germans back and forth between two rivers, the Marne and the Meuse. The president lost track of how many times the ground they'd gained was taken from them not one month later. And it had gone this way for as long as he could remember.

After that day when the oracle sphere went dark, he had continued his daily ritual, turning the crank and asking *What will happen?* The sphere had replied, if not in fine form, then at least with some semblance of attention to his query.

The sphere gave him hope at first, that the war would end in short order. Peace would reign over Europe and the United States.

He'd seen it plain as day. The war would end, America would be back on top, and she would come to Britain's aid, helping the English rebuild their ravaged country. The French, too.

Oil had been discovered in Arabia years ago, before the war, before the president's first term. It wasn't much, but the president knew it was only a matter of time before they found the motherlode. The sphere had shown him great fountains of the stuff bubbling out of the desert. He kept promising the American people that their worries would be over soon. The war would end. They just needed to find that oil.

We need it more than anyone else, so we can keep the boys going over there. Drive back the Hun and get this whole mess sorted out.

Bacon's voice crackled in his ears, startling him.

"Mr. President."

"Dammit, James! I nearly dropped the thing!"

"I'm sorry, Mr. President. We're at one minute before air, Sir. Are you—Is everything ready?"

"Yeah, I'm ready. Go ahead."

Bacon opened the channel on his end, introducing the evening's broadcast. With less than a minute before he would speak to the American people, the president turned the crank on the oracle and whispered his query.

"What will happen?"

As the words left his lips, he found himself wishing, hoping, and even praying for something good, some image of security and prosperity.

Just give me something to tell them. Anything. Please. Show me how it ends.

The images came, almost tip-toeing in at first, like flashes of celluloid in front of a Bell & Howell bulb.

An American soldier marched across a battlefield, alone. Bloodied snow coated the ground around the soldier's boots. The president couldn't see what the man carried in his hands, but it wasn't a rifle. It was too small.

The image faded. Another came, showing snowflakes tumbling through a dismal sky. They fell on the faces of the dead, lying in muddy fields, weapons strewn about amidst craters and shattered battlements.

As the battlefield vanished from his mind, the president saw boulevards and towering buildings overlooking Wall Street. Cars sat still and silent in the street. Pedestrians swarmed around them, like schools of angry sharks. The people moved as if struck by a sickness that turned them into raging lunatics. One after another they clutched at the sky, at each other, at whatever they could take hold of.

Is it an earthquake? A windstorm?

Another image replaced this one, showing a bank building with ledger books being cast out of every window. And then people followed the books, tumbling through the sky. The president choked and coughed as he watched them fall.

The scene shifted again, and the president fell back against his chair, breathing fast with his chest shaking.

Now he saw line after line of trenches stretching into infinity on either side of an empty and desolate landscape. Above it all, a single light seemed to hang in the sky. The president searched the image for any sign of victory, anything that might mean the war would end.

The light in the sky burst out like a flare, illuminating the battlefield and trenches below, and revealing the growing masses of the Kaiser's army on one side, constantly replenished from some font behind their lines. Across the battlefield, the president saw a dwindling number of American troops.

A final image flickered into focus and the president grabbed at his chest as a shock ran through him.

The soldier from before still marched over the empty battlefield. He had one hand raised. In it he held a metal rod to which was affixed a tattered piece of white cloth.

The flag of surrender flapped against the black sky as the light from the flare above diminished into darkness.

"Mr. President, we're ready in five, four, three..."

The on-air sign flashed.

"We need—," the president began.

He tried to shake the images from his mind, but the one of the soldier waving the flag of surrender wouldn't leave him.

"My fellow Americans—we need...We need to remember how great this country can be."

Through tears, and reminding himself that greatness was America's birthright, the president found his stride.

"America and greatness are inseparable. Even as we may encounter challenges that appear to push us back from a place of supremacy. But supremacy is ours to claim and always has been. If we falter in maintaining our place of prominence in the world, it is up to us to always work hard toward that goal of reclaiming it.

"The world looks to America for greatness. They look to us for guidance, for support, for direction. Only in America does the world get an example of greatness. And, my fellow Americans, make no mistake when I tell you that our greatness is assured so long as we all work hard to achieve it."

He paused, checking with Bacon for reaction. The man looked shaken, but confident. He waved a hand for the president to continue, and he did, telling the people what they needed to hear, even if it wasn't exactly what they wanted to hear. But the president was no fool. He didn't believe a single word that fell from his own tongue.

***

October 1929, Baltimore, Maryland

The son presented his mother with the morning paper. She accepted it as she always would these days, with a slight curtsey as if receiving a gift from royalty, and, as he always did, the son wondered why his mother felt the need to defer to him so. But, then again, he was the man of the house now with his father away at the war. Perhaps his mother's curtseys were a sort of ritual for her. Something to remind herself of the man who had gone over there. They expected him back soon. Maybe, the son thought, his mother was practicing for that day, when his father would come home.

"Mother, have you heard from father this week? His last letter is almost three days past now. He usually..."

The son trailed off into uncomfortable silence as his mother's face clouded over.

"I—Mother, I didn't mean to suggest..."

"No, of course you didn't," she replied, holding the newspaper in front of her as though it were a candle.

"But Father's name hasn't appeared in the lists. We'd have been told. Wouldn't we have?"

"Yes, yes we would have. And now I'd like to stop discussing it. If we're to be told, then there is nothing we can do but wait to be told. And if your father is coming home, we've only the same to do. Wait. And pray."

"Of course, Mother," the son said. He bowed his head and said a silent prayer for his father's safety, and for the safety of those around him. He included the enemy soldiers, too, something he never mentioned to his mother or to anyone else he knew. He suspected others in their congregation held similar thoughts, but, of course, nobody would ever admit to praying for the enemy's safety. That would be seen as treasonous, and the penalty for treason in America was a quick trip to the bottom of a short rope.

"The president is going to give his radio address soon," his mother said from the living room. The son finished his prayer, adding hope of good health and safety for the president and the German kaiser. Then he joined his mother in their narrow living room at the front of the house. She sat in her chair beside the radio at the near end of the room. His father's chair was on the opposite side of the radio. The son took a seat on the sofa beneath the front window.

While his mother dialed in the channel, the son straightened his pants legs and smoothed the front of his shirt. The president's voice soon crackled into the room, and his mother went through her own tidying rituals, pulling on the hem of her dress that fell to just below her knees when she sat.

"People of America," the president began, as he always did. "This is your president speaking from the White House. We have a grave truth before us: war. This is not news in and of itself, but I do have news to share. And you'll be happy to hear it, that I can tell you."

The son listened, intent and grasping for any sign of hope that the war was at an end. The world had been at war since July 1914, and now, in October 1929, it seemed as though it had to be at an end. There couldn't be any way the nations of France and England and Germany and America could continue sending their men to die. And for what?

As long as he'd known the world, the son had known war. His father had been conscripted in 1917. He'd come home, then gone again, in a repeated cycle that seemed to have no end. They'd hoped the war would end before the son came of age, but onward marched the armies. Onward rolled the tanks. And onward came the steady retinue of coffins draped in flags. The number shrank with each passing year, but still they came home. The son was one year shy of majority, and his father was still over there.

He could see his mother thinking the same thing, holding her hands tight in her lap, clenching around a handkerchief, tighter and tighter with each of the president's pronouncements that America's fighting men were doing everything they could to push the kaiser's men back into Germany proper.

"They're doing very well, indeed. So well. It is truly a testament to the American fighting spirit that our boys are winning the day where the French and the English could not."

Still the son listened, seeking out the words that would tell him his father would be coming home.

And then he heard them.

"I expect we shall very soon see an end to this war, and with it an end to all war. And with that, America, I wish you all Good Night!"

The radio crackled and went silent. His mother reached over

and slowly turned the knob to shut it off.

"So Father is coming home then," the son said, his voice light and cheerful. His mother's face shifted from confusion to fury in an instant.

"He is? Tell me where you heard that in anything that man just said. Tell me."

"Mother, I—that man? You mean the president. It was him on the radio just now."

The son waited for his mother's reply, but she only clutched her handkerchief to her mouth and swept from the room. The click of her shoes on the kitchen floor told him she was probably getting herself a drink. Should he go to her, offer some words of comfort? A prayer maybe?

Since his father had gone to war, the son was never quite sure what he should do when his mother became flustered.

A clink of glass on glass came to the son's ears from the kitchen. He waited as his heart beat against his ribs. The glass knocked against the counter. His mother's clicking shoes described a path to the hall and down to the master bedroom at the end.

The son waited until the door closed before getting up and going to the kitchen. He washed the tumbler his mother had left by the sink. He returned the bottles of gin and tonic to their positions in the cupboard and icebox. Then he shut off the light and cast a longing glance at his father's empty chair by the radio. Light from a streetlamp sent slanting shadows over the chair cushions. The son couldn't see them as anything but the trails of bullets.

***

July 1930, Baltimore, Maryland

The father set his walking stick down beside his remaining foot. With a jerk, he pushed his bulk off the bed, swaying as he stood. His wife was there in an instant, catching him under his right arm while he steadied himself with his left.

"There you are, darling. You're up now," his wife said.

"I'm up," he repeated. In the past year, the words had become a sort of chant or prayer, like something he'd have said in church. "Amen, and hallelujah. I'm up."

His wife didn't say anything to that, but he hadn't expected her to. She rarely said much these days, since he came back. He knew it was because he reminded her too much of her own father, taken back in 1901 by some sniper's bullet in Manila.

"I'm going to get dinner started, darling. Can you make it to the table?"

Of course I can make it!

He held his tongue until a calmer response suggested itself.

"I'll be fine, dear. You go on ahead."

***

When the father made it to the dining room, their son was already seated and thumbing through a booklet of some kind.

"What's that you're reading?" the father asked.

"Oh, hello, father. It's a book of hymns and carols. The choir is holding auditions for the Christmas concert this year. I'd...thought to join. To lend my voice in praise of the season."

"Little early for that, isn't it? Only just August. The Macy's catalog isn't even out yet."

"Oh, well, the pastor says he'd like to get a head start this year. He's not...Well, that is, he's worried he won't have enough to fill the choir?"

"Why not?"

The son stared at him for a moment, like he was hunting his mind for the right response. The father's patience was thin enough. He didn't need any clever talk from the boy.

"I asked you 'why not'."

"It's...Well, the congregation—"

"What about it?"

"It's smaller now, father. With the war, and...Well, the pastor is worried about the congregation's size."

"What's wrong with it? Same as last year, isn't it? Old Mother Grayson and the Pickerings still attend every Sunday. The Samuels and Mercers go every week, just like us. Plenty of other families in the neighborhood."

"That's right," said his wife, from the kitchen. "And the Cavendishes has been coming more often now, too. Ever since—"

Ever since those two sergeants showed up on their doorstep with that letter and a folded flag.

"So you're going to sing in the choir this year?" he asked their son.

"Y—yes, father. That's my hope."

He knew he should be happy to hear that much from the lad. Their son was always so hesitant to speak of his aims and ambitions. The father held his gaze steady for a moment, then tucked his chin in a nod. He hobbled to his chair, waving their son down when the lad stood as though he would offer a hand to help.

"I'm fine, son. I'm fine."

***

Dinner was a quiet affair, as it usually was. His wife served roast pork, but with only half a loin between the three of them, the father still felt pangs of hunger when the last morsels were cleaned off his plate. He sipped from his beer. It was the one he'd be allowed, unless the ration officer could be convinced otherwise when he came around on Wednesday.

"I don't suppose they'll have more meat for us this week, do you think, darling?" his wife asked as she cleared away the dishes.

"Only if the boys over there have had their fill. You know how things are."

She didn't answer except to hum her agreement.

Yes, she does know how things are. Economy in a shambles. Rationing to keep the troops fed and watered. She knows how it is. But that son of ours...

The lad was still seated, and thumbing again through the choir book he'd set aside during the meal.

"What's that one, son?" the father asked, aiming the neck of his bottle at the page.

"Oh, sorry. What was your question, father?"

"I asked you what that song was? What's it say? The lyrics."

"It's a Christmas carol, father. *Silent Night.* You know it."

Yes, he did know it. He knew a lot of Christmas carols, but when was the last time he'd sung one? When was the last time Christmas felt like an occasion for singing? It was the celebration of the savior. It was supposed to be a day of peace and calm and goodness, just as the year was growing to its darkest point.

"You should forget about that song book, son," the father said. A clatter came from the kitchen, but he ignored it. Their son timidly looked up from the carol to meet the father's eyes.

"I'm sorry, father. I don't understand."

"I said you should forget about that song book. All of it. Doesn't matter right now. You need to enlist, like the others boys have done. Only you and that Mercer lad are still here around the place, and he's signing up as soon as he's of age. His mother told me after services last week. You're already old enough. You should go. Just come back with both feet, not like your old man."

The room was silent after the father spoke. His wife busied herself being silent in the kitchen. Their son busied himself being silent, staring into the father's face with a look of abject terror.

"What'd I say?" the father asked. "I only told you what you need to hear, boy. Nobody else in town is going to do it. The pastor certainly won't. The Mercer boy knows well enough, but he's two years behind you. You need to set an example for him and make sure he doesn't get cold feet."

"But I don't want to fight, father. I'm—"

"You're what? Afraid? Hell, son—"

His wife chided him for cursing while at the table, and he was quick to correct himself.

"I meant heck, all right? Heck, son, I was scared like you wouldn't believe first time I got on the bus with the rest of the Doughboys back in '17. But that was thirteen years ago. Things have changed. They stopped the draft back in '25, so you'll be joining up with the volunteer force. And these days, you don't get shoved onto a train with nothing but a knapsack and the clothes you walk in with. They suit you up from day one. Give you a uniform, new boots, a dishpan hat, the whole works. You'll get a rifle, too, just like your old man did. What's wrong with that?"

"Everything, father. It's all wrong. I don't want to go to war because I don't believe war is right."

The father held his tongue, but he felt his face flushing beet red. The words that caused the blood to run hot under his collar only just sat at the back of his throat, ready to fire like an artillery barrage. He closed his eyes and took a breath. Then he swallowed the last of his beer before speaking again.

"You know the Reds aren't sitting back on their heels, son. They're making a lot of noise over there, and they're doing better than we are here at home. You ever hear of the Reds drinking only one beer a week because of rationing? Huh?"

The father lifted his bottle and slammed it back down on the table to punctuate his question. The son simply stared at the brown glass, and his eyes glinted with tears. As the father watched, he felt his temper reach its limit.

"We got close to one hundred million Americans in this land, son. One hundred million. You want to guess how many of them are wearing the uniform and going over there to fight the good fight? Go on and guess. I'll wait."

The son's eyes watered heavily now, and dew drops ran down his left cheek.

"I—I don't know, father."

"I said guess!"

"Ten, father? Ten million?"

"Ten! He thinks ten million Americans are willing to put themselves in the line of fire. Hah! You hear that?"

His wife stayed in the kitchen, out of the fray.

"Son, we got less than half a million people in the uniform right now. Probably closer to three or four hundred thousand. We would have had more if those damn busybody suffragettes hadn't made all that noise. We arrested most of them and that almost shut them up. But they kept hounding the Senate to change things. Those boys knew what was what and they didn't budge, no matter how many petitions that bunch of chatterboxes threw across their desks. But did that stop them? Oh, no. They went over to the judiciary, didn't they? And the Supreme Court let itself get henpecked until they killed selective service. We've been hugging hind tit looking for men who can fight ever since, and we need them, son. We need them bad, and you're going to be one of them."

"But father, I—"

"You what? You want to sing? Yeah, I heard you the first time. Well, forget it. There'll be time for singing when you get back from over there. What we need in this country are real Americans willing to fight. The damn Reds won't care if you can croon like that Kelly kid. They'll only care if you can shoot straight."

"We're not at war with Russia, father. We're fighting the Germans and have been for sixteen years. Don't you think it's gone on long enough? Isn't it time to give up on war and try something else?"

"This is why I left my leg over there?" the father screamed. *"So we can talk about giving up?"*

“I mean everyone should stop fighting, father. Us and the Germans. The French and the English, too. Everyone.”

“That’s not how wars are won, Son. That’s not what your great-grandfather did. He didn’t give up when those bastards tried splitting this country in two by raising their silly flag and hollering Dixie. Your great-grandfather didn’t give up. He signed up. At the ripe old age of seventeen. My father, your granddad, did his part, too. He was a Merchant Marine. He didn’t watch half his friends drown in the Pacific so his grandson could talk about giving up. That’s not why I gave up my leg. Not so you could sit here crying over a song book and telling me you’d rather join a choir than join the other men who are fighting and dying over there.”

“But that’s just it, father,” the son said through his slowly spilling tears. “Isn’t it better that we don’t have to fight? That I, and the Mercer’s boy, and every other young man still alive shouldn’t have to go fight, but we can stay here and do something better? Because you’ve already made that sacrifice?”

“*Better?* You should fight because it’s what we need from you right now. It’s what America needs. *That’s better.* That’s the life you’ve been given, Son. An American life, and if you’re not willing to fight for it, *you don’t deserve it.*”

He threw his empty beer bottle across the room, ignoring the shattering glass as the bottle upended a table lamp and sent it crashing to the floor. He clawed for his stick and shoved his chair back from the table. His wife had come to the kitchen door. She held one hand to her breast and the other stretched out toward him.

“You want to help? Clean up the mess,” he said to her. With a grunt, he pushed himself up, stumbled to his right and caught himself against the table. Huffing and blowing out his cheeks, the father took an angry step away from the table, then prodded the floor with his stick, and took another step. He followed a jerking path away from his wife, and away from their son.

"Just give up," he muttered as he stomped his way back to the sitting room where his chair waited for him beside the radio. "You don't hear the president talk about giving up. He talks about fighting back. Give the enemy something to think about. That's a man to listen to."

***

The son watched his father leave. He wandered his gaze around the room, looking for anything to settle on other than the broken pile of glass and lampshade fabric in the corner. The son looked at his teardrops collecting on the pages of his choir book. Even that seemed tainted with the seeds of destruction now. He closed it and stood, thinking to help his mother clean up the broken lamp and bottle.

"You shouldn't have provoked him," his mother said as she carried a waste basket, broom, and dustpan to the corner. She unplugged the lamp and set to pushing the mess into the wastebasket.

"Mother, let me help you," the son said, coming to a crouch on one knee beside her.

She turned a worried look in his direction, and then her face transformed to unquestionable reproach.

"If you want to help, you'll go to the enlistment office tomorrow morning."

The son reeled back as if stabbed, clutching his chest above his heart. His breath came ragged and sharp.

"Mother—"

"Don't *Mother* me. You heard your father. In this country, we listen to men. I don't have any say in how things are. I may want to see the war end, but I can't vote, so it doesn't really matter, does it? We could do with the extra money, too. Your enlistment will bring a bonus. It won't be much, but it might be enough to make sure we don't lose this house to—"

She pressed her lips tight together and continued cleaning up the lamp. When she'd finished, she stood and hoisted the full wastebasket.

"The enlistment office opens at eight o'clock sharp," she said, stepping past him toward the kitchen.

***

December 1930, No-Man's Land

Dear Mother,

On the fields of No-Man's Land, the bullets never stop flying. Mortars and artillery whistle in almost every morning and evening. We're just barely holding on here. Marks and Standish took shrapnel last night. They're on their way home now, along with what was left of Gregsby, Lamenski, and Stiles. Regis Killburn lost his eye, but he insisted on staying here in the trenches with the rest of us poor men. Half his face is covered in bandages, and I can see the blood soaking through them. He could hardly see straight with both eyes, and now he's sitting there, down the line from me, checking his ammunition over and over again.

He was standing up, with his head above the wall, a few minutes before. I think he's waiting for the Germans to shoot him. He'd rather go home dead than missing an eye. His girl won't like to look at him. That's what he thinks. He told me so anyway. I'll never forget that conversation. It was the first I had when I joined the 42nd.

"Are you afraid of getting shot?" I'd asked him.

"Who, me?" Killburn said, and then, with a chuckle, he continued, "Nah. If they ever get me, it has to be all the way. You watch, Archie. If the Kaiser's boys find a way to get me, it'll be

all or nothing. That's how I know I'm going home in one piece. We're almost ready to ship back to the rear, and then it's home to Dallas and Sara Ann."

So you see, he can't go home now. He's afraid Sara Ann won't look at him, and I know from the way he says her name that nothing could hurt him more. Not even a piece of shrapnel in his eye.

I wish I had more pleasant news to share. It is Christmas Day after all. Please tell Father I love him and hope his pain is not too great.

Merry Christmas!

Love,

Archibald

The son tucked his letter into the envelope on his knee, sealed it, and handed it over to the lieutenant. He knew most of what he'd written would be censored. In all likelihood, the entire letter would be destroyed. But he'd never been one to hide the truth in anything he wrote. He'd be damned if this letter would be any different. Even if his mother and father had never read a word of what he'd sent home, at least he'd written it. At least he'd put down the truth about what was happening in the war.

The lieutenant had given him an honor card once, when the son had run out of note paper to write on. His superior had laughed aloud when the son returned the card. He'd written a full letter, describing his latest meal of rations in the muddy trenches, and how tricky it was to avoid getting grit into one's mouth while eating. He'd remarked that his father must not miss that about the war. His words were all neatly penned around the honor card's pre-approved lines, such as *I have been admitted to hospital* or *I have received your telegram*, each with a checkbox next to it.

The son had thought the lieutenant was simply giving him the nearest bit of paper he had to hand. Then the officer explained that the British used the cards to send back simple statements from the front, none of which were anything close to the truth.

"But that's how it's got to be, Wagner," the lieutenant had said. "It's for morale. We have to keep the home front alive and well with our letters, just like they keep us going with theirs."

Now, the lieutenant accepted the son's letter with a frown on his face.

"Another tell-all, Wagner?"

"Yes, sir," the son answered.

The lieutenant sniffed and shook his head as he tucked the son's letter into the bundle he'd collected from the other men. They all sat against the trench wall in a row, some smoking, others staring at the mud. None of them smiling.

"It's Christmas Day, men," the lieutenant said. "Bit of cheer wouldn't hurt, would it?"

"Should we sing a carol then, sir?" one of the men asked.

"Why not, Frampton?" the lieutenant replied.

"Well, why don't you start us off, sir? Make sure we're on key," Frampton said back.

They all chortled, and the lieutenant shuffled away, staying to the boards as best he could, but still sinking his feet a few inches into the mud with every other step.

The son let what he'd just heard settle into his mind.

Should we sing a carol then, sir?

Why not?

"Why not, indeed?" he said to himself.

"Eh, what'd you say, Archie?" asked one of the men to his right.

The son shifted off his seat and into a crouch. He laid his rifle against the trench wall behind him.

"What're you up to, Archie?" they all asked. Every man around him was curious now. The son never did or said much except to answer questions and respond to orders.

He turned around, took a step to his right, and mounted the ladder in a leap. He was at the top of the trench before anyone could stop him, but Frampton got a hand on his boot before he went over the wall.

"Here, Archie, it's Christmas Day. The German's aren't shooting. They're taking a break, too. Just like us. C'mon down."

The son kicked back, just enough to force Frampton to release his foot, and then he was over the battlement and stumbling into the emptiness of No-Man's Land.

He stood on shaking legs and reached into his jacket for the white flag he'd made using bandages and the rod from his cleaning kit. He'd kept it snug inside his jacket for a week, wondering if he'd ever have the need or the courage to use it. The flag fluttered in the wind as he walked across the open ground beyond the trench line. He ignored the bloodstained snow and silently marched around the coils of barbed wire and fallen barricades.

A bullet zipped past his head, and he staggered to his right one step, *sploshing* his foot into a deep puddle. He tugged his foot free, shivering from the chill climbing up his leg.

Another bullet whizzed by, but he kept walking, holding his flag aloft.

The German trench line was in sight now. He could see a few helmeted heads bobbing around behind their battlements. The day's weak sunlight glinted off countless rifles, bristling from the trenches like spines.

The son opened his mouth, nearly choking on his fear, and finally managed a single line of melody. His teeth chattered around the words as he forced them out.

"Si-lent Night," he sang.

A German voice called out to him. "Halt!"

The son continued walking forward. He could see the German soldiers clearly now. Their rugged, filthy faces looked so much like those of the men in the trenches behind him. He breathed deeply, and sang the next line.

"Ho-ly Night."

German voices clashed in the trench ahead. Some seemed to be calling for his death. Others could have been arguing against it. He only knew a few words of the language, and none of them would be helpful now. So he walked slowly forward until he stood directly in front of the German battlements, staring into the muzzles of what felt like a thousand rifles.

"All is calm, all is bright."

The son paused, catching his breath in the chill, feeling the tendrils of fear snaking into every muscle in his body and telling him to collapse where he stood. He opened his mouth to continue, but was silenced by a German voice.

"Stil-le Nacht, hei-lige Nacht."

The son picked up the melody again, starting anew in time with the Germans who now sang as a choir. With each line, the carol spread through the German trench line, to the son's left and right. And then German soldiers began rising from the trenches, their rifles forgotten, to stand behind their battlements and sing with him.

The son raised his voice, amplifying every word with his desire to see the war finally meet its end. The Germans matched his intensity and passion, some of them climbing over the battlements to join him in the field of bloodied snow.

His cheeks ran wet with tears as he heard the melody echoed in English from the trench line behind him.

Dover Whitecliff

CASS&RA

A Pulp-Action, Four-Fisted, Dorado and Dark Claw Adventure

I

The Darquipelago, Another Leaf in the Book of the Multiverse, Monsoon Season, 1989

Elle Quartermaine nosed the 1939 Grumman Goose down through the moonlit cloud tops, compensated for the shudder as she passed through a hole between light and shadow, then dipped down into the rain and made toward the distant lights of Recluse Bay.

"You still haven't told me how we're going to find this particular lawless shadow mastermind on an entire island chain of lawless shadow masterminds. Or were you hoping I'd forget to ask?"

Elle turned her head toward the copilot's seat at her companion's question, and the Goose bucked. She turned back to flying, but not before the end of a tiger's tail smacked her cheek.

"You can fly and talk at the same time, my friend." In the privacy of the plane, Talia Pembroke had not bothered with her glamour, and Elle could see the human tigress out of the corner of her eye, her fur alternating black and silver in the rain spattered moonlight.

Elle kept the Goose low, fast, and level, eyes on the lights ahead. "You sure you want to know?"

"Let us contemplate that question. Do I wish to know if we will have to wade through an army of pirates, mercenaries, gangs, mobsters, robots, zombies, cultists, and fluffy bunnies with fangs three feet long to rescue Tashi and bring the one who kidnapped him to justice? I believe the answer is a resounding yes."

"You're not going to like it."

"Please. Rrrregale me."

Elle felt the vibrations of Talia's purr through her boot soles. Well not quite so much a purr as a growl. Not a good sign. Best own up.

"Got word that an acquaintance of mine set up shop outside Fort Stroud. Word is he knows anybody who's anybody in the Darq, and if anybody can tell us who the target is or where he's holed up, he can."

"Name?"

"You sure you want to know?"

"I believe we already established that fact."

"You're not going to like it."

"I believe we established that fact as well. Cough it up, Elle. Pretend it's a hairball."

Elle snorted. "Burke Makan."

Silence. Then, "The one that shot you in the back and left you for dead."

"I figure he owes me a solid."

"You mean other than the ones he used to shoot you."

"There is that." Time to drop the other shoe. "Burke's not one for extra company though. If you come with, he'll shut up tighter than a clam in chowder."

"You really have to work on your similes, my friend." Talia quipped. "Very well. I will prowl the docks, look menacing, and scare the locals. You have thirty minutes."

"Hey. You never know, Old Burke might be afraid of ghosts."

***

It only took checking out three low-end bars, plus one and a half brawls to find Burke Makan standing in an alley behind Spider's Trap Door. Makan took no notice of the rain pelting on and off, or the stench of stale booze doing the tango with that of the fish and petrol wafting in off the docks. He might as well have been a statue. Elle, on the other hand, breathed shallow and crouched at the end of the alley behind him, most definitely taking notice of every damn plop of rain that slithered down the back of her neck or dribbled into her eyes.

I don't remember him being that big.

Elle unclipped the pair of *bagh nakh* from her belt and slipped them on over fingerless gloves, then stalked up behind her quarry like an ant looking up at Everest.

Forget big. Massive's more like it.

Even standing on tiptoe, the top of Elle's head would barely reach the height of his armpit, and she could use one of his trouser legs as a sleeping bag with room to spare, but she put the thought out of her mind and reached up, clamping her palms down on either side of the base of his neck. She dug the steel tiger claws in enough to make an impression.

"Hello, Burke." To give him credit, Makan didn't move a muscle. He hadn't become such an infamous mercenary by being stupid. Elle couldn't see the look on his face, but she felt his shoulders tense under her palms.

"You're dead, Quartermaine. I shot you."

"Yeah, you did. In the back as I recall. Not very nice of you,

Burke, old buddy. I might even be tempted to hold a grudge."

"You weren't breathing. Your blood was painting the scenery. You weren't even wearing a bulletproof vest. I used a damned shotgun firing *solids*. You were dead." There was stark disbelief in his voice and a little bit of—what—fear? Maybe Makan *was* afraid of ghosts.

"Could be that I still am." Elle paused to let him think on that. "Or it could be you're a crap shot. Either way we have business to discuss. Now, I'm gonna let y'all turn around so we can talk all civilized like. But I wouldn't recommend trying anything stupid." Elle let Makan's neck loose but did not pull off the claws.

"What is it you want?" Makan turned, eyes wary.

"I hear you know every badass in the Darq. One of them stole my cargo. Boy from the Tikauli Jungle. I'm out a load of money if I don't get him back. If y'all don't want to find out how put out I was when you trashed my favorite shirt, not to mention my favorite back, you'll give me a name and a hidey hole to pull him out of. And just so you know that I'm willing to let bygones be bygones, I'll call it square if your tip pays out. Long as you don't shoot me again, of course."

"Of course."

Elle smiled in what she hoped was an amiable fashion, but Makan's eyes told her it was more menacing than congenial. She almost laughed when Makan's finger twitched upward as if he wanted to poke her in the belly to make sure he wasn't talking to a ghost. Almost.

"What do you say, Burke?"

"Ten percent of your take. Word gets around I pay out for free and I'm out of business."

"Well, to be fair, I shouldn't have to give you anything t'all, but now I think on it, I'm willing to pass on five percent as a finder's fee."

Elle kept the smile going and counted down silently from ten.

On four, Makan nodded.

"Deal. Five percent."

"See, I knew we could play nice together." Elle slapped him on the bicep just hard enough for him to feel the bite of the claws through his shirt.

"Just so you know, assuming you're talking about that runt with the Third Eye. He's not the only one. Your competition is putting together a collection of seers if I hear right."

"Where is he?"

"Skull Island. Just off the north coast – you can't miss it. Not going to give you a name. You already know him. Wouldn't want to spoil the surprise."

"Mighty sportin' of you, Burke." *That was too easy. Something's off.* "I think that concludes our business for tonight."

"You know the account number."

"I'll wire the funds if the tip works out. If it doesn't, you won't see me coming." Elle turned and walked away, not looking back, though her ears were cocked for the telltale signs of Makan's Ruger clearing leather. She rounded out of the alley and slunk into the shadows, invisible to the moonlit world, then waited silently for Makan to make his move.

"Sir, we have a problem. Quartermaine's here. SHE *can't* be here. You swore there was no way SHE could have survived that ambush."

She could hear every capital letter in the pronoun. *Now that's interesting,* Elle thought. *How'd Makan learn that name... and who else in the Darquipelago would know who mama named me for?* Far as she knew, only those who lived near one of the Five Fountains of the Living Waters would know the connection between her given name and H. Rider Haggard's SHE.

More important, who in this place is high enough on the food chain for Makan to call Sir *and mean it?* She listened for more, but the rest of the conversation might as well have been one sided considering the static hissing from the radio. Elle left it for pointless and ghosted through the streets, so deep in thought she strangled a yell when Talia landed in a crouch not two feet in front of her.

"Your thirty minutes were up twenty minutes ago."

"Give a girl a heart attack why don't you."

"You're immortal."

"Still. It would hurt."

"What did you learn from your very large friend?"

"Didn't get a name, but according to Burke, we've crossed paths before."

"Well that reduces the possibilities from millions to hundreds. Where?"

"Off the north coast. Makan called it Skull Island."

"Skull Island."

"Yeah."

"Why do villains always choose the skull? I count at least three or four dozen Skull Islands spread across the worlds. There are 206 bones in the human body. Choosing the same one repeatedly shows a lack of creative thinking. Seriously." Talia harrumphed.

"Well, I may be wrong, Kitty Cat, but I'm guessing your average citizen wouldn't take a super-secret, under-the-volcano lair on Humerus Island serious like." Elle had never been able to keep a deadpan look for long, and when Talia twitched her whiskers in disgust, she busted out laughing.

***

As it turned out, there wasn't a skull to be had. No massive under-the-volcano, high-tech base. No scads of faceless minions in orange jumpsuits doing their master's bidding. No hot secret agent in a spotless tuxedo waiting to infiltrate the Lair of DOOM. It wasn't even really an island at low tide, more like an industrial hill in the muck.

"I think I would take Humerus Island more seriously than this place, my friend."

"Must be a low-rent villain if he can't even afford a couple of Halloween skeletons as decoration. That said, we don't know what's in there and looks can be deceiving. If you think we should turn tail and get a couple extra claws, now's the time."

"Turn tail? I think not. I like mine where it is." Talia grinned, baring her fangs. "Li and the Pantera priests asked for our help to rescue Tashi and bring him home to the temple, and I for one would not disappoint them. We have more than enough claws between us to find out who runs this pathetic base and shut it down."

Not five minutes later, Elle knelt on concrete in a jumbled canyon of crates, wooden pallets of who-knew-what wrapped in plastic, and the occasional decommissioned tank covered with graffiti. She peered around the treads of one of the latter, trying to make sense of what she was seeing while Talia sniffed one of the nearby wooden boxes and lifted the lid, then hefted out a plastic package filled with white powder.

"Heroin?" Elle whispered, though she doubted they could be heard over the rattle of rain on the warehouse's corrugated roof. Talia sniffed again.

"No. Powdered sugar."

"What sort of nutter stockpiles powdered sugar with his tanks?" Elle turned to see Talia set the package on top of the tank treads and flick a claw forward to slit the plastic. "Don't sneeze."

"That would be unwise." Talia extended the claw to its full length and dug into the center of the bag. "Ah. The sort of nutter that hides velvet bags in the sugar." She tugged upward. "Not too heavy." Elle plucked the string from Talia's claw and pulled open the sugar-coated pouch to pour the contents into Talia's paw. Even in the fluorescents, the sparkle against the black fur and paw pads put Van Gogh to shame.

"Blood diamonds are a girl's best friend. Not."

"These are cut gems...not just diamond. Sapphire, ruby, and emerald...possibly from Thailand. Not easy to come by."

"And the Darq ain't much for that kind of wealth in the hands of the riff raff...at least not with the current management." Elle held the pouch open for Talia while she siphoned the gems back in and then tied it shut and dropped it on the bag of powdered sugar.

Talia sprang upward to crouch behind the turret of the tank for a look from higher ground, her midnight and moonlight fur blending into the shadows of the dimly lit warehouse. Her tail flipped back and forth across a graffito of a small pink rabbit with a Day of the Dead skull for a face, giving Elle the distinct impression the bunny was playing peek-a-boo with her.

"Too true," Talia answered. "Weapons, gems, kidnapping—separately maybe, but all in one group? Either our nameless target is in a higher echelon than we thought—doubtful considering the state of this, I don't think I can call it a lair without laughing—or he's doing this under the nose of some very powerful people. Neither bodes well."

"I'm with you there, Kitty Cat. And if my Cyrillic is up to snuff, those are the misplaced Soviet weapons Raj was telling us about when we were in Calcutta, the ones Ruskaya Mafiya is set to sell off to whichever idiot warlord forks over the most cash."

"Misplaced?"

"Well, they ain't exactly lost, being as they're right here in front of us."

"I believe the word you are seeking is stolen, my friend. Even with the Union breaking apart, they're not likely to misplace that much firepower." Talia's left ear twitched. "I hear crying. Not Tashi, but a child, perhaps more than one. From that corridor back there."

"Lots of soldiers twixt them and us. May get messy." Elle tallied at least a dozen, though said dozen seemed to be stacking long crates near the wall, completely oblivious to their observers. They were moving crates of various sizes that could easily fit anything from AK-47s to rocket launchers. Or copious amounts of powdered sugar. "And I'm thinking this warehouse is too big a scar on the landscape to leave standing."

"On that we agree. Shall we?" They stepped from behind the tank and moved forward through the clutter. Not one of the soldiers looked up or raised an alarm.

"Either these fellas are just downright stupid," Elle whispered. Too late they heard the cocking of weapons and saw the other squad of soldiers step out of the shadows. "Or this is a trap."

"So glad you could join us, *chère*." The leader stepped forward, a dashing grin on his tanned and chiseled face. He was tall, clad in well-pressed, starched (down to the creases in the pants) surplus fatigues, and carried a canvas messenger bag slung across his chest. Elle growled, almost as deep as Talia.

"Not your *chère*. Never was."

"After all those years running the jungle together? I'm hurt." He pulled a mock sad face, then replaced it with the movie star grin. "It was such a pleasure to hear you were tagging along with the cat-girl."

"Do we know him?" Talia purred, tail flicking, hackles raising. "He seems irritatingly familiar somehow."

"*Enchanté*, my furry goddess. I am Cesar D'Evreux."

"Not ringing any bells, and I am not your furry goddess."

"You met him. Once. Outside Baagha Village." Elle watched memories flick across Talia's face from the corner of her eye. Watched puzzlement turn to recognition. To rage.

"You were such a cute kitten. Breaks my heart to complete the contract, but the Naga will pay well for your hide, even if the delivery is a few decades late."

Elle grabbed Talia's tail and yanked before she could pounce, trying not to think about the fate of the human that spawned the saying *got a tiger by the tail*. She stomped down on her own urge to charge. *Think, Elle. We've fought our way out of too many scrapes not to know the routine. Get the opponent riled, and when they make a mistake, hit them with everything you've got. Only Cesar knows it and he's turning the tables. Time to turn them back.*

"Let. Go. Of. My. Tail." Talia growled, silver eyes flashing.

"Hold up now. Don't want to be hasty." Elle pitched her voice low, trying to keep calm. "Lots more of them than there are of us. Way more than *Rangoon*." She loosened her grip but kept hold. Just in case. Elle kept one eye on the soldiers, hoping nobody got an itchy trigger finger, but they seemed content to keep their cool. For now. Talia nodded in recognition.

"Very well. I will give you five points if you can get him to monologue, my friend. But when we fight, his soul belongs to the Spirit of the Cat."

"Deal." Elle turned her attention back to the leader. "Cesar D'Evreux. *Virtutis Comes Invidia*. Never did get over the envy, did you."

"Envy?" Talia murmured.

"His family motto. *Envy is the companion of virtue*. Ain't that right, Cesar?"

"Virtue is overrated." Cesar shrugged. "And it's only envy 'til you get what you want, *chère*."

"Except for that one little thing you can't have." *Hold your temper and watch. There. Behind the eyes. You're getting to him. One more little push should do it.* "Damn shame, really. Abuela always liked you best." *Now let him put the pieces together. That's it Cesar. One plus one equals two.*

"She couldn't. She didn't. That's the only way you could have survived Makan's ambush. How could she—not *you*."

"Yup." She smiled. "Me." Elle called just enough power from the Fountain of Living Waters to prove a point. To most of the worlds of the multiverse, the Fountain of Youth was a footnote in one of those Hot Rods of the Gods movies. Even those who lived in the cities where the waters burbled to the surface of the earth only gained extended life and a freedom from disease.

But Elle had been remade in Living Waters and knew the truth of what she guarded. She let the light blue mist settle around her open hands for only a moment and watched the anger and hatred flicker across Cesar's face when he realized what it meant.

"She chose *you*?" he snarled. "All the power of a Guardian and she passes it to a pathetic, perky pixie-top who's all sunflowers and puppy dogs." He spat on the floor. "What a waste."

"Maybe. Maybe not. But better than putting the fox in charge of the hen house." Elle watched, and waited for his anger to get the better of him, ready to fight. But it didn't happen.

"Maybe. Maybe not." Cesar shrugged and signaled to his men to lower their weapons. "If I take out the brats, you'll slit my throat."

"I was thinking more slow and painful death, but that works."

"And I can't kill you now that you have the protection of the Living Waters. Hold that thought. I wonder if decapitation might do the job on an immortal."

"Saw that flick. Not bad."

"I liked the music," Talia agreed.

"Well, *chère,* I don't have a broadsword to hand, or I might give it a go. Impasse it is then. Here's what we're going to do. I don't have time to stand around and jaw about my evil plan for world domination and personal financial security. Suffice to say the powers that be in the Darq are a little touchy about my being here. So, my boys are going to load the cargo, including the brats, into the trucks out back. Then we're going to leave. I will dump one of the runts out the back every five minutes for you to rescue. The Tikauli boy last."

"I have a better idea." The voice was low and silky. Elle turned toward the sound to see Burke Makan topple through the door and into the light, much the worse for wear. The two squads of goons stiffened one by one and fell to the floor, weapons clattering to the cement and, fortunately, not discharging. The voice sounded female, but the figure that stepped up onto Makan's back and struck a pose was androgynous, clothed head to toe in vermillion spandex. The forty or so minions that stepped out of the shadows behind the dead goons dressed identically but in a darker shade. "We'll flay the skin from your flesh one millimeter at a time for daring to enter the Darq."

"Guess I don't have to wire the money to Makan's account." Elle shrugged at the downed man-mountain with the cherry posed dramatically on his back.

"Does this person not know that disco ended ten years ago?" Talia sighed. "What an embarrassing entrance."

"And flaying is so twelfth century." Although certain the newcomer had heard their derisive comments, Elle raised her voice to call across the open space. "Oy, Maraschino! Do you mind? We're busy here!" She followed with a quick eyebrow conversation with Talia. *I'll take Maraschino and the Bing Boys. You get D'Evreux.* A swish of her tail told Elle that Talia understood.

"Kill the capes," Maraschino ordered. "Grab the Oracle. We have no time for shenanigans."

"There's *always* time for shenanigans—" Elle started forward and stopped dead. She had forgotten Cesar.

"I don't think so. I have all the chips." Cesar had backed up to the entrance of the corridor and stared them down, a rocket launcher hoisted up over his shoulder. "Oracle's mine. Or nobody's." He turned toward the corridor. Maraschino made two quick slashing motions from where she stood on Makan's back, and the underlings split to charge both directions.

No time to think. Too far to charge. Elle cupped her hands.

"Kit!" Elle shouted. Talia bounded forward, stepped into the hand hold, and Elle heaved her upward and outward, hurling Talia over the charging mob like a furry, clawed cannon-ball. Black, silver, and olive camouflage spun across the floor when Talia bowled into D'Evreux, knocking him down before he could fire. They rolled over each other, and the strap of D'Evreux's bag caught up in Talia's paw. Elle couldn't see too well through the chaos, but a loud tumble of clatters told her Talia had kicked the rocket launcher, then sliced through the strap to free her paw, sending the bag flying. Elle turned her focus to the fray looming in front of her, *bagh nakh* a comforting weight on her hands. "Good thing all y'all wore red. Blood's a bitch to get out of spandex."

Keeping track of anything inside the swirling chaos was nigh impossible. She caught a quick glimpse of Talia grabbing at D'Evreux's arm. *Why? No. No! NO!* The launcher had only been a ruse for the grenade in his other hand. She heard a roar as Talia heaved, rolling D'Evreux on his back. His hand smacked the floor. The grenade skittered into the corridor where the prisoners waited. By the frightened screams and Talia's speed, Elle knew D'Evreux had pulled the pin. The fight crowded back in close, blocking Elle's view save a flash of Talia leaping toward the deadlier target.

Time stretched like the taffy at Sparky's Boardwalk. Elle kicked and clawed, clearing a hole just in time to see D'Evreux leap to his feet, scramble across the rubble to the rocket launcher, shoulder it, and press the trigger. Fire *fwooshed* backward at the launch. As soon as the payload left the tube, she saw D'Evreux drop it. He snatched for the bag on the floor, trying to scoop and shove its contents back inside: fist-sized bundles wrapped in burlap, a diamond necklace, a jade statuette, a swirling blue-black globe encased in filigree that had escaped from its box. This last he shooed in with the flap of the bag rather than grab it. *Now why would he take the time to do that with the warehouse about to—* Time snapped forward as the rocket hit the first of the cohort charging D'Evreux. A plume of molten death melted its target and kept coming.

"Go out the back, Kit! Now!" Elle backpedaled as she fought, pulling as many of the bunch of spandex cherries into the danger zone as she could manage. The crates around her opponents exploded into a powdered sugar firestorm with cut gem shrapnel spraying in all directions.

The grenade flew out of the corridor with the hostages and into the open area of the warehouse. Elle imagined the tink it made rolling to a stop in the midst of the tower of weapons crates, but she swore she could hear it. Behind and around her, explosions erupted. Elle crouched and covered herself as best she could, calling upon the Living Waters for protection as the warehouse came down around her ears.

***

Singapore. Another Leaf in the Book of the Multiverse,
Monsoon Season, 1989

Elle fiddled with the charred fragment of plywood, turning it over in her hands, mostly ignoring the potent concoction in the umbrellaed glass next to her. The thing sported a stencil of half a toasted bird on one side *maybe an eagle?* Under that, what was left of the label read *use 13*.

“Not much of a clue. Use 13 whats? Eggs? Chocolate chips? Not even sure if this was Cesar’s or something from the rest of the junk in that place.” Elle tossed the fragment into the center of the table as a lost cause.

“Were you close once? Is that why you never spoke of him after you rescued me from the Naga?” Talia asked. Elle looked across the table at her mentor, Li, Guardian of the Second Fountain, Shangri La, but found no help there. Li sighed.

“You should have told her long since, Grasshopper.”

“I know, Li. I know. Yes, Kitty Cat, we were close. Cesar was a child of two Fountains. His mama was from El Dorado, and my mama’s closest friend, and his papa was from Avalon. He was older by a few years, not that it matters much, and dashing, and Abuela’s favored student. I was just one of the horde of girls who adored him; we all figured he would be the Guardian of the Fifth Fountain when Abuela took her rest."

"How old were you?"

"Like the song says, I was sixteen, going on seventeen, and boy was I naïve. He said he took a shine to me because I was a free spirit. Said he admired my *great courage* in sneaking into the Naga caves as a girl to steal the statuette with the Spirit of the Cat. To allow you to be born into the world again someday. Great courage, *pfft*. He only wanted somebody gullible and stupid to cover his tracks."

Elle paused, fiddling with the umbrella in the drink, working up her courage. "I found him in the jungle one night. He had stolen the statuette from the Pantera temple and was leading the Naga in to steal the Living Waters to give them eternal youth. He told me they'd promised great riches to any who helped them. Asked me to come with him. Instead, I sounded the alarm and helped Abuela and the Guardians defend El Dorado from the Naga. The council of Guardians let him live but stripped him of his ability to ever find any of the Five Cities again."

"How then is he still alive?" Talia asked. "That would have been nearly eighty years ago."

"Abuela was certain that he had been hoarding water from the fountains in a den somewhere, though we were never able to find it. He was not seen again until he found you in Baagha Village. We foolishly assumed he had lived out his years in exile and died." Li smiled. "You see, Elle, gullibility knows no age limit."

"And you did not tell me this why?" Talia did not sound hurt, merely curious.

"You were only five when he grabbed you. How do you tell a kid that you're sworn to protect that the guy who stole her from her family and sold her as Naga-nibbles was your hero? And now he's got off to who knows where. At least Maraschino and the Bing Boys are in custody. Cra—" Elle looked across the table at Tashi, listening wide-eyed to the exchange from his perch on Li's lap, and changed course, gesturing at the fragment on the table between them. "Darn it. If I'd dug out of from under faster, we'd have more than this to show for it."

"With a building on your head. Oh yes, certainly, my friend." Talia punctuated her remark with a smack of her tail to Elle's cheek that Elle felt but didn't see. With her glamour up, only the faintest traces of tiger remained about Talia. Her black and silver hair resembled her ruff in tiger form, and her eyes still sparkled predatory silver, evidence of the great cat within.

"You should have clawed your way out in a heartbeat and singlehandedly rounded up an entire island chain of villains. Next time someone blows up a warehouse with you inside it, I will hold you to that. You may have walked the worlds for nearly a century, Grasshopper, but sometimes you can be a real idiot." Li added. A ghost of a smile passed over Elle's face at the good-natured rebukes, knowing the pair of them were trying to pull her up out of her funk, and she gave them the respect and humor they deserved. Tashi giggled.

"Raksha Elle is not an idiot, Memsahib. She is just silly." The boy gave Elle a gap-toothed grin with the absolute joy only a seven-year-old can muster. "We took the others home to their parents, and I am not only safe, Raksha Elle, but I have new friends that can See like I can. You do not need to feel bad or to dig any faster next time."

"And the worlds are short one Skull Island. Which is a very good thing. Perhaps next time, D'Evreux will make a better choice in naming conventions." Talia smiled.

"Somehow I doubt it." Elle mimicked Talia's Hindi lilt. "That would show an excess of creativity."

"So, you *can* speak proper King's English. There is hope for the world."

Tashi giggled again and then turned his head to look up at Li. "Should I tell them now, Memsahib?"

"Your gift is your own, Tashi, along with the decision to tell others what you have Seen with it."

"I will tell them then. It is important." He sat up straighter on Li's lap and looked across the table. "Raksha Elle, Raksha Talia, I have Seen. Will you hear what I Saw?"

The formal question gave Elle pause. Destiny was one thing. Knowing what was coming another. Surprises kept life interesting.

"Do you think it's something we need to know?"

"Yes, Raksha Elle."

"Then we will hear what you Saw."

"I have Seen a great city to the east. A city filled with light and darkness. A city with heroes that keep the shadows at bay. You must go there. Others are waiting for you to join them. While we were in the cells of the man D'Evreux, many of us Saw this same thing."

"Does this city of paragons have a name?"

Tashi paused, thinking, then shook his head. "I cannot See it yet. But I know that you, Raksha Elle, and you, Raksha Talia, must have two names when you find it."

"Two names?" Elle asked. "Why would we have two names?"

"I do not know, Raksha Elle, but you must." He looked up again at Li. "You will name them, Memsahib, will you not? Have I Seen true?"

"Yes, you have, Tashi. Two names. I was planning to wait a bit before having this conversation with Elle and Talia, but you speak with the wisdom of Sight. Time to let the tiger out of the bag, as it were."

"Now hang on, Li. Tashi's talking about secret identities. Nix that idea straight up. No cloak and dagger stuff for me. That's for the pulps. I'm a Quartermaine. And besides, people ain't stupid. Just because in the comic books some cape puts a shirt and tie on over his rainbow undies and throws on a pair of glasses don't mean that, miracle of miracles, nobody can recognize him on the street. And I sure as hell ain't running around in vermillion spandex."

"I concur. We have established that vermillion spandex is not a fashion statement." Talia shook her head in agreement. Li sighed.

"Elle, you have walked the worlds for many years now, since Abuela chose, rightly, I might add, that you succeed her as the Guardian of the Fifth Fountain. And you Talia, embodiment of the Spirit of the Cat, look out for the underdog, if you will pardon the pun. But the pair of you have always done so under your family names. You are both charged with the duty to protect precious things that are bigger than lineage.

"Elysian, Kilima N'Jaro, Thorne, and I, yes," Li took Talia into her gaze, "and the Pantera priests as well, have all worried about this, thinking you were both holding on too long to your childhood among mortals, but we decided to give you time to grow in to your strengths. I believe that time has finally come. You are ready."

Elle opened her mouth to argue, but Li raised her hand for silence. "Elle, you will always be a Quartermaine, and spandex is optional. This has not so much to do with iconic costumes as with reminding you of who you are and what you protect. For all of us who walk the worlds as Guardians, the names we use over the years gain significance."

Elle looked at Talia and saw her own thoughts reflected in silver. *Where is this going?*

"It is high time you two walked in your own light rather than in the light of others." Li turned to the tigress. "Talia, the tribes of the Naga have one name they fear. They speak it with venom, again, pardon the pun. Knowing that the Spirit of the Cat has once again chosen a vessel to keep them from spreading their evil terrifies them."

"I heard the Naga priests chanting in the caves when D'Evreux sold me to them as a child. They spoke of killing the claw. Is that what you mean?"

"No, that's not right." Elle said, plucking at her memory. "Not *the* claw; it was *Dark Claw*. I heard it too. When I came after D'Evreux to get you back and, wait. I heard it before that. In the Valley of the Kings."

"Yes, Elle, when you braved the dark of the Naga caves to find the statuette and kept them from destroying it. When you allowed the Spirit to choose a new vessel. This name they fear above all things. Talia, you must take on the mantle of the Dark Claw."

"If a name will aid in wiping the Naga from the pages of the multiverse, then I will wear it gladly." Talia flexed her fingers and Elle caught a glimpse of the claws beneath the glamour. "Dark Claw is suitable. What of Elle?"

"Grasshopper."

"No, not Grasshopper. You got me beat by near two millennia, Li, so you can get away with calling me that, but that's it. I'm not wearing a headband with antennae." Another tail to the cheek stopped Elle in mid-tirade.

"Let her finish, my friend."

"Sorry. Thoughts of having a silly suit with six arms got the better of me."

"Yes. It would." Li smiled. "Elle, in your heart, family is everything. Your parents, your brothers, Talia, the Guardians, your people. And your name until now has only acknowledged your father's line. Let me suggest a name that takes in your whole family, so that you remember the importance of protecting it: Dorado—in honor of your homeland, the City of the Fifth Fountain, El Dorado."

"Dorado. I like it. It's purrrfect." Talia pronounced and picked up her Singapore Sling with her tail, deftly upending it over Elle's head. "I christen thee Dorado!"

Elle sputtered and Tashi laughed.

"A formal naming is most appropriate." With that, Li tossed her own drink over the now soaking and sticky Elle. "You have passed the rites of manhood, making you a full adult of the tribe. To Dorado and Dark Claw!"

"Well, that's sorted then." Elle stood and snatched the umbrella out of her glass, popped the chunk of pineapple into her mouth, and then dumped the glass over her own head. "Dorado and Dark Claw it is."

"I like these names!" Tashi hopped off Li's lap and ran to hug Talia. "They suit you!" He rounded toward Elle, looked for a dry spot, and finally ended up hugging her leg.

Elle backhanded the alcohol from her eyes and stood. "I need a shower."

Talia delicately sniffed the air. "Yes. Yes, you do."

II

Nova Arete, Port Liberty Docks, Another leaf in the Book of the Multiverse, 2010

Nova Arete may have been a city chock full of paragons but keeping the shadows at bay wasn't exactly what Elle called simple. In the one and twenty years since they walked out of the bar in Singapore, Elle and Talia had found a home in Nova Arete and joined those Tashi had Seen waiting for them. The Protectors of Virtue may have been one of the lesser known hero coalitions in the city, but hell, Elle would rather save the world with people she could have fun with than the stuffed-spandex shirts with all the news coverage. Take this morning for example. Just a simple warehouse break-in near the dockside tram station. Possibly including an experimental monster.

Oh, the donnybrook had started out easy enough. A couple of cyber-hoodlums trying to cut the chain on the warehouse door. Not an experimental monster in sight. And the mish mash of pop-top armor and glaringly bad color choices didn't save the punks from a beating or being dangled from a loading crane to await NAPD like some awful piece of modern art.

Unfortunately, it was a popular warehouse. And it only took another five minutes to find the army of goons and the experimental monster therein. The leader stood and kept on standing until he towered over the rest of them. Fuzzy grey and white fur covered most of his body, and the hair on his head and shoulders was wild and longish; if one were charitable, one could call it a mane. He wore the cheap man's version of Dr. Banner's alter ego: ripped parachute pants and a belt. Hanging from the belt was what would have been an across-the-chest messenger bag on a normal human, but on this creature looked more like a sporran on steroids. Even with the fur, Elle thought something about him was disturbingly familiar. She was trying to put her finger on what it was when the fight started.

"I AM WAR WOLF!" The howl following the exclamation was earsplitting even above the ongoing donnybrook.

"Does yelling stupid names count as monologuing?" Elle leapt into the air, twirled, and slashed downward at one of the goons on her dance card.

"I'm afraid not, my friend." Talia bounded after her prey before he could back out of the fray. "Nor is howling."

"Sorry, Doll, no points!" Rik O'Shea yelled down from the catwalk above them, calmly nailing shot after bullseye with his submachine gun, Brown Bess.

"This from the guy that names his tommy gun after a flintlock. Thanks, Shamus."

"My pleasure, Doll."

"St. Jeanne?"

"*Non*. Null points, *cherie*. Stand still, Dark Claw, would you? I cannot heal you if you're bouncing around like that."

"MOO!" DredNought stomped down, cracking the cement floor

in front of him and throwing several of the opposition off their feet, his metallic voice box amplifying the sound until it sounded more like a herd of brass cattle.

"*Et tu,* DredNought? Tough crowd tonight." The goons just kept coming and they were no closer to taking down the leader than they had been when they walked in. One of the goons flew by, no doubt thrown by Dred, and smashed into a pile of cardboard boxes. Styrofoam peanuts and tinsel foofed into the air, while black orbs cascaded to the floor, rolling every which way.

I hate déjà vu. Warehouse near the ocean. Check. Lots of goons. Well, they're not dressed like cherries, but—Check. Crates of things that didn't make sense in a super-secret villain lair. Check. OK, the oversize werewolf is new, but still.

Elle had no hackles to raise, but something about this whole set up put her on edge. She whirled to slash at one of her opponents and nearly tripped over one of the spheres. She scooped it up, intending to brain the goon in front of her. *Something ain't right. But what? Why the nerves?* She looked at what was in her hand. *And why the hell am I holding an 8-Ball?* A triangle bobbed up to the surface window of the magic ball that said *Better not tell you now.*

"Great. Thanks for nothing."

"Look out, Rik!" St. Jeanne's voice. Elle looked up to the catwalk and saw a silhouette moving in on their sniper.

"Dred!" She pitched the 8-ball and DredNought swatted it upward. The silhouette turned into a falling body. And all the while, War Wolf remained behind the fray, howling and clawing at the larger crates along the back wall, behind enough cover that Rik couldn't get a clear shot.

"Why is he not attacking?" St. Jeanne shot a burst of healing energy from her hands toward the metal mountain that was DredNought.

And said werewolf appears to be looking for something specific while his goons keep us busy. I'm thinking giving him time to find the whatever it is ain't a good idea. But how do we clear a path when these idiots are multiplying faster than rabbits on an oyster diet?

"He's looking for—" A howl of victory cut St. Jeanne off.

"He's found it, Doll. Dred! Clear a path. We have to stop him!"

"No time. Dorado!" Elle turned. Saw Talia cupping her hands. Grinned. Stepped into them and flew over the crowd to careen into the wolf-man.

"Bad puppy!" She grabbed the burlap bundle from War Wolf's paw and backhanded his muzzle as they rolled top over teakettle. "You don't take other people's stuff. It's rude." Elle tried to hold on as War Wolf tucked his legs up but couldn't match his force. She was airborne again. This time straight up. Elle crunched into the bottom of the catwalk hard enough to make her ears ring, and lost hold of the bundle as gravity kicked in. The cement floor wasn't exactly forgiving, but Elle called on the Living Waters for strength, scrambled to her feet, and launched herself at War Wolf's retreating back. Only suddenly it wasn't his back, but his front, with four feet of sharpened steel in front of it. *Crap. That's gonna hurt.*

Elle decided that having a giant werewolf yank his broadsword out of her belly was just about as painful as having one stab her with it in the first place. She dropped to her knees and fell forward on her elbows, unsuccessfully ignored the squelching sound, and fought to remember what she needed to do to breathe again.

"Let's see you grow a new head." *That voice.*

A shot clanged on metal and the sword clattered to the floor. "Not on my watch, Fido!"

A growl and a curse, then, "Maybe next time." It was the last thing Elle heard before she collapsed.

Darkness. Pain. Elle looked down on herself from above. Saw the blood spreading on the concrete. Saw Rik and St. Jeanne fighting their way through the goons, Talia and DredNought in the lead to clear a path. Saw War Wolf flash a toothy grin and wave before turning to fog and vanishing through the wall. *No, that can't be. Can it?* She cursed the fuzziness muffling her thoughts.

A memory. Elysian, the oldest of the Guardians, slamming her falcata into Elle's heart. Teaching her in her own inimitable sink-or-swim way how to call upon the Living Waters to bring life. *That's it. Water. The Living Water.* Elle pulled herself back to her body and clenched her left fist feebly. Forced herself to form the words. To believe them. To call on the strength.

"*Agua da me vida.*" She croaked, spitting blood from her mouth. Silver-blue light flowed from her left palm, encompassing her body, and lifting it into the air, healing, forcing tissue to knit and close. She bellowed at the pain, but landed on her feet and charged into—Where'd the fight go?

"You stay put, my friend." Talia pushed down on Elle's shoulder until she sat down hard on the concrete. "Immortal or not, a blade through the middle isn't exactly a hangnail."

"We have to go after War Wolf. I'm ok. Just a flesh wound."

"Said the Black Knight." Talia smiled then looked around at the carnage. "Rik, can you get NAPD in here?"

"Sure, Doll." Rik pulled out his cell phone. "Dispatch, Rik O'Shea here. Yeah yeah, Private Dick. I know. Funny. Look. We got some goons here for transport. Yeah, they're secure. Half hour? You kiddin' me? You're right down the street. Oh, giant squid. Uh-huh. Sure. Just get here pronto, Flat Foot. O'Shea out." He tucked the phone back in his pocket. "Dispatch says Archie's in the bay again. It'll take a few for them to cordon off the area and keep the civilians clear of his tentacles while they take care of it."

"That is a good thing, I think. We should not leave these crates for the gendarmes," St. Jeanne called from behind them. "Many of the boxes are full of trifles, but they appear to be camouflage for several arcane items, some of them with evil auras."

"I'll help you sort, Jeannie. We'll have to sign for whatever we take into custody." Rik set Brown Bess next to Elle. "Here, Doll, look after Bess while I do the heavy lifting. Dred, give a moo when NAPD shows up, will ya?"

"Baa." DredNought lumbered off toward the entrance.

"I'll take that as a yes." Rik shrugged, then tousled Elle's hair. "Next time you find a giant robot that needs fixing, Doll, do us a favor. Don't teach it to talk with a Farmer John See and Say."

"Oh, I don't know, Rrrik." Talia purred. "It's better than Beep Boop Beep."

***

"MOO!" Elle looked up from the incongruous pile on the table in front of her, grateful for the sound of DredNought's call echoing through the warehouse and halting the frustrating game of "how is an 8-ball like a phone headset, vials of morphine, or a cobra carved from yak horn."

"Anybody home?" The human shout followed right on the steer's heels.

"BWAAK!"

Elle laughed at the affront in DredNought's reply—*What am I? Spare parts?*

"Sorry, big guy. My mistake. Anybody home that talks normal? O'Shea?"

Elle waved her hand at the officer and stood. "Over here, Detective."

Rik straightened up from the crate he was rummaging in and pushed Elle back down onto the sawhorse she had been leaning on. "You sit." He met the officer midway through the carnage. "Davidson. Thanks for coming down so quick. These all you brought?" Rik motioned to the handful of uniforms rounding up and hauling off the various unconscious goons.

"Yeah, well, the Disgruntled Seraphim and the Kane Sisterhood heard the sirens and teamed up to get the calamari to back off into the briny deep, but Grief Maker and Nova Kane stayed on for the photo op and the autographs."

"I'm guessing Nova's wearing her Christmas bikini with the red velvet and the fur?"

"Don't you know it." Elle smiled at the memory that flashed by at Davidson's answer. She and Talia had helped Nova design that outfit on Girls' Night Out. Good to know it was still working as advertised. "Plus, all the kids love Grief. Had to leave half the boys there just for crowd control."

"Civilians." Rik sympathized.

"Tell me about it. So. This all of them? The couple of freaks dangling from the crane outside probably can't even tie their shoes. And this lot looks like low-class muscle to cause all this mess." Detective Davidson surveyed the ravaged warehouse and whistled. "Anything else you want to tell me, Shamus?"

"If you get a report of a twelve-foot wolfman, I need to hear about it, *capisci*?"

"You're tellin' me you let a freaking monster loose in Port Liberty?"

"We had a man down. And he did that poof-vanish-into-thin-air-hey-presto thing. We can track him down when we get back to base, but keep your men clear, and just call us if you hear. We'll take care of it. This sucker's dangerous."

"Like SnowFlame dangerous?"

"More like Dictator on PCP and meth dangerous."

"Gotcha. I'll back you, Shamus. Paperwork takes time, but just you make sure you take him out before anything else happens. Captain doesn't like it when the bad guys walk, know what I mean?"

"Understood. There's a couple of things here that shouldn't be in civilian hands. We can get them back to Omega Department to put under containment if you'll give them a heads up to let them know we're coming. I'd rather not get fried trying to walk in unannounced."

"You'll sign for them?"

"We'll sign for them. Just give us a few minutes to make sure everything's secure before you start inventory on the back wall. Other than that, you need anything from us? Dorado lost a lot of blood, and the rest of us aren't much better off."

"You're clear. I'll give the Omega geeks a call."

"Thanks, Flat Foot." Rik shook Davidson's hand and the detective moved off to direct the cleanup. DredNought, Talia, and St. Jeanne joined them at the table. "Other than what Jeannie's already accounted for, anybody else find anything we need to take with us to the Omegas?"

"*Non.* Everything questionable is packed into those two crates. DredNought, *mon ami,* can you help me transport them?"

"Baa." DredNought picked up a crate in each hand and followed St. Jeanne over to the NAPD. Elle watched them walk off and absently picked up the 8-ball. Again, the feeling that she should know something she didn't. That voice.

"Why a sword?" The words dropped into a moment of silence.

"What did you say?" Elle turned to see an NAPD lab tech crouching next to the fallen broadsword.

The tech shrugged. "Why the heck would a giant werewolf need a sword? Claws and fangs not enough? Compensation issues if you ask me." He snapped a photo, then picked up the sword in a gloved hand, holding it carefully by the crosspiece, and bagged it as evidence.

Why a sword? Elle stared at the 8-ball.

"I do not think that will help us track the wolf, my friend, but I will try." Talia took the ball from Elle's hand. "Oh, Great and Mystical Ball of Plastic," she intoned, "Where is the one who calls himself War Wolf?" She flipped the ball over and showed it to Rik. "What sayeth the Oracle, Rik O'Shea, Solver of Mysteries?"

"'Reply hazy. Try again later.'" Rik snorted. "Yeah, Doll, that's no help."

But the question remained. *Why an 8-ball? Why—*

"An 8-ball is an oracle."

"It is technically a toy, not a true oracle. And phone headsets are not oracles." Talia ventured, tail flashing back and forth. "How will that lead us to the wolf?"

"Hold up, Doll. Let her follow the scent. Something's clicking between the ears. I can see the steam. Keep it coming. 8-ball is an oracle. Is this War Wolf some kind of fake fortune teller?"

"No that's not it. The word. It's important somehow." Elle picked up the figurine of the serpent with the flared hood and fangs.

Why a cobra? Cobras aren't oracles either. Wait. Is it a cobra? Or something else?

"It's not a cobra. It's not a cobra."

"You're right there. Cobras don't have arms far as I remember."

"Arms?" Talia took the figurine in her paw and bared her fangs. "Naga."

"I'm guessing that's a bad thing?" Rik asked. But Elle's mind was still whirring.

Oracle. Oracle's mine. Morphine? Morpheus. Dreams. Prophetic dreams. Naga. Let's see you grow a new head.

"You know where that thing came from, Doll?"

"Well, would you look at that." Elle jumped. She had forgotten the NAPD tech, who had left his examination and come up behind them. "An 8-ball. Haven't seen one of those since my kid brother cracked it open trying to find out what made it tick." The tech picked it up from the table and turned it over. "Is the sky blue?" Turned it again. The white triangle popped up with *You may rely on it.* "Still getting it right fifty years later. Good thing too. 8-balls will come in handy way things are going." He paused to look at her more closely, "You ok, kid? You look pale. That's a lot of blood to leave lying around."

"The way *what* things are going?" Elle prompted, but she already knew the answer.

"The whole fortune teller thing? One of those will come in handy the way they're disappearing. Five so far. Even Armando—disappeared from the park in front of City Hall this morning, and he's a djinn. How could he not see that coming?"

"War Wolf isn't some experimental monster," Elle blurted. The fear in Talia's silver eyes mirrored her own. "It's Cesar. He's back."

"What? Cesar who? Where are you guys off to in such a hurry? Was it something I said?"

***

"Tashi! You home?" Elle called as she vaulted the fence in the twilight. "Tashi? Haruko?" No answer. "Take the top floor." Talia bounded to the roof of the small house in the upscale Peregrine Falls neighborhood, headed for the back yard and the upstairs veranda. Elle slid on the *bagh nakh* and made for the front door. It was pulled to, but Elle saw as soon as she closed with it that the lock had been broken. *Crap. We're too late.*

She stalked through the house, hope disappearing with every step. Tashi's study was the worst of the downstairs rooms, and even there, the disruption was minimal. A cork board tilted off-kilter half slid into the office chair, and sketches littered the floor. Elle righted the board and hung it back on the wall, then crouched to retrieve the artwork, mostly watercolors and pencil sketches, all lifelike and full of energy. *Why the board and not the desk or the file cabinet?* Elle thought. *Maybe Tashi Saw something. Sketched it.*

Elle sorted through the fallen memories, ear open for Talia's search upstairs. Some were events they had shared since Tashi and his wife had immigrated to Nova Arete. Haruko in her wedding gown with a bouquet of orchids. Baby Talelle on Talia's lap at her first birthday party, her chubby fist reaching for Talia's whiskers.

Other events he must have Seen since Elle hadn't ever told Tashi the whole of that particular story, and, at the time it had happened, Tashi's great-grandfather would have been a boy of three. Still, the image matched her memory so perfectly, Tashi might have been standing behind her. A cave lit by torches with Naga slithering around a dais, knives poised to destroy the statuette of a cat resting atop it. Elle as a girl, crouching in the shadows, scared down to her boots, but determined to rescue the statuette.

But nothing resembling a giant wolf man. Elle stood to continue her search, but a corner of paper caught her eye. This one barely sticking out from under the throw rug. Someone must have kicked it when they took him.

No, that's wrong. Tashi shoved it under here for us to find.

This drawing was not like the others. Rather than a single moment, this one captured three images flowing together. The first was a box stenciled with an eagle and labeled *Item 94312, Warehouse 13*. The second image was a hand holding a sphere the size of a baseball. The outside was some sort of filigree that Tashi had sketched in golds and bronzes while the inside swirled in blue and black and blood.

I've seen you before. You were that thing Cesar swatted into his bag. The last image was Tashi in a way she had never seen him before, eyes rolling in his head, screaming, face contorted in agony. Or madness. Unsettled, Elle took the drawing and continued her search.

The remaining rooms downstairs were still mostly intact. Either there had not been time for a struggle, or Cesar had used the worst kind of leverage.

"Talelle? Are you hiding, Kitten? It is safe to come out. We will protect you." Talia's voice. Met by silence. Elle took the stairs up to the second floor and found Talia in the toddler's room. She held out the drawing as she took in the scene. The room was untouched, save for one exception; the window seat was empty of its guardian. Mister Kitty, Talelle's favorite plush tiger, now lounged across the pillow of her bed, a business card set jauntily in front of one ear. Elle plucked it up and read the impeccably starched script: *A cat or a kitten. Your choice, chère. Hugs, CD.*

"This does not bring me comfort. Wait a moment." Talia held up a claw. "The fragment you found in the Darq. Did it not say *use 13*?"

"Yeah. I think that's what it looked like before it got toasted. And the round thing. I saw it before Skull Island disintegrated. Cesar had it in that bag and he took it with him."

"What of the card?"

"He wants a trade. You for Talelle. If the Naga figurine we found was part of the package, my guess is they'll be on the welcome wagon when we get there."

"Does the card tell us where to meet?"

Elle turned the card over and read "Custom Arcade Simulation System & Recreational Arena. 19 Ajax Parkway. Find your own adventure!" Elle paused. "Wait a sec. Find your own adventure? That sounds familiar. Isn't that the new place that opened up in Brixton Park? The one all the kids are clamoring to get into where it makes a game custom just for you? Why would Cesar hole up in an arcade of all places? He hates kids, except when he can make money off selling them."

"Look at the letters, my friend." Talia pointed out the initials.

"C A S S & R A. One was a folk singer, the other a sun god."

"Not Cass and Ra. Cassandra. The oracle that went mad because no one would believe her prophesies."

"Damn. I was hoping you were going to go with my version. Rather take on a sun god than have Tashi go mad from staring into that thing." Elle took the tiger from the pillow and ensconced him back on the window seat. "Don't you worry, Mister Kitty. We'll have them back before sun-up. Meantime, you watch the house."

III

Nova Arete, Brixton Park, Another leaf in the Book of the Multiverse, 2010

"Dorado and Dark Claw. Welcome to the Custom Arcade Simulation System & Recreational Arena. We have been expecting you. I am Pythia, your hostess for this evening's festivities. Based on your superior abilities, the entertainment architect has customized your adventure for ultra-survival mode. Please proceed down the left corridor to platform five. Enjoy your evening, and don't forget, C A S S & R A gift cards make wonderful stocking stuffers." The hologram had proportions only a twenty-something kid that hadn't yet made it out of the computer lab to find a girlfriend could dream up and wore a skimpy Greek chiton and high-heeled gold sandals adorned with florist's wings.

"Thank you. We will be sure to stop by the gift shop on the way out." Talia flicked her tail and walked through the three-dimensional projection. "Ah, there is nothing more refreshing than a cheerful hologram to send you to your doom."

"Not my doom I'm worried about." Elle felt for the comforting weight of the *bagh nakh* on her belt and switched out English to the language of Baagha village. No sense making it easy for anyone listening. "Keeping Cesar occupied and then finding a mind-melting baseball in a building this big and leaving the team two heroes down—"

"Stop fidgeting, my friend. Cesar does not have a team. He has underlings. He will not expect us to trust Talelle's fate or Tashi's, or any of the hostages for that matter, to the Protectors of Virtue. He will expect us to go after them ourselves. Once they are safe away from here, I will very much enjoy clawing open the door to Cesar's lair and ripping his throat out while you retrieve Item 94312."

"Right then. As Dred would say. Moo."

Platform five didn't really exude doom. The midsize alcove held three platforms and, as Elle entered, a group of younger teens—all sporting t-shirts announcing 'Jordan's 13th birthday'—ran into the pillar of acid green light that shot up from platform six and winked out of existence. Platform five's only difference from the other two was that its circle on the floor shone with golden light instead of the acid green, for which Elle was thankful, and it was ringed with an ouroboros. Five for the Fifth Fountain. Gold for El Dorado. And a serpent eating its tail for the Naga.

No need to hammer it home, Cesar. We already know you have all the chips.

"Cesar never could do subtle."

Talia started to retort, but Pythia the pleasant hologram lit up in front of them.

"Your adventure will start in thirty seconds. Please step onto the platform."

"Let's do this." Elle stepped forward into golden light.

***

"Not what I was expecting." The corridor was well lit, pristine, and solid metal. Behind was a blank wall, and not fifty feet ahead was a T-junction with a pair of unmarked buttons on the wall between the two steel doors. Though Elle couldn't see any security cameras, the feeling of being watched told her they were there. Pythia flickered in front of them.

"Please move forward and select a button to begin." Pythia's voice was the same, though maybe a bit excited, and this time coming from everywhere without a speaker in sight.

"At least the hologram's happy." Elle unclipped the *bagh nakh* and slipped them on.

"This is not a hologram, my friend." Talia tapped the wall with her claw; the clicks didn't quite echo but were louder than expected. "We have been transported."

"If they used the same tech as the emergency medical transports from Medtronics, and that's top of the line, then we're still in city limits, probably even still on the property..."

"I hear a very large but in your statement."

"Please move forward and select a button. I am ready to begin." Pythia's voice took on an irritated tone. Elle ignored the petulant-looking hologram, trying to fit the puzzle pieces together.

"How many times have we used the Medtronics transports over the years? Dozens? Tell me this didn't feel different. And this place smells, I don't know, *weird*. Too clean, no odor at all, not even me, and I've still got blood all over my shirt. What if—"

"Move forward and select a button. I want to begin now."

"Didn't your programmer teach you it's rude to interrupt when people are talking?"

"What if—" Talia prompted.

"What if we're on another page of the multiverse?"

"Some sort of pocket dimension per—" *Screeeeee*. The wall behind them shuddered and then scraped forward. "—haps." The wall picked up speed.

"I want to begin now. I will enjoy your adventure. Please make your selection."

Elle and Talia walked forward, apparently not fast enough for Pythia. The projection winked out and the wall picked up speed, giving them no choice but to run.

"Which way?" Talia asked.

"Don't care. That wall's going too fast to stop." Elle slapped toward the panel in front of them. The door to the left split horizontally like a service elevator. "Go!" She shouted, shoving Talia in front of her, and then dove through, tucked, and rolled to pull her feet out of the way as the door chomped shut with a CHUUUNG.

How did it know I was going left? Did I even hit the button?

"How odd." Talia's statement pulled Elle out of her thoughts and she finally noticed her surroundings. Somehow, they were outside in the sea air, standing on the deck of a container ship near a hatch with rust sneaking through the paint.

"What the...hologram?" Elle bent her knees with the heave and roll of the deck.

"Unless it is a hologram with smell-o-vision, my friend, I think not. The seagull guano is far too pungent."

Pythia reappeared. "You have chosen *Disarm the Bombs*. This is one of my favorite missions. Success parameters: locate and disarm the six bombs in the hold of this tanker populated with Skellions. You will receive a point bonus for speed, and an additional point bonus if you also rescue the hero Millennial Fusion from the Skellions and escort him to safety within the time allotted." Elle reached for the handle, nerves jangling, but Talia held her back.

"And the failure parameters?" Talia asked. "What are those?"

Pythia's pixels grinned. "I am so glad you asked, Dark Claw. You will fail the mission if any of the simulated bombs explode."

"Well, that's a plus. Simulated bombs won't do real damage."

"You are correct, Dorado. The simulated bombs will do no damage, but because your superior skills have qualified you for ultra-survival mode, I will note the simulated explosion and transfer its signal to an actual explosive device of the same size. It will explode somewhere in Nova Arete in a well-populated area. This will be exciting!"

"Exciting my—"

"Are the simulated bombs on a timer?"

"That is a wonderful question, Dark Claw. The bombs in the simulation are set for ten minutes. After transport and pleasant conversation, the current countdown is at five minutes and ten seconds."

"Five minutes?" Elle grabbed the door handle, yanked it open, and followed Talia through to the dimly lit innards of the ship's cavernous cargo hold. Below the catwalk where they stood, several gang-bangers surrounded a fist fight. They were definitely Skellions considering the red and black hoodies and skull painted faces. All were hooting and hollering like so many kids on a playground. And behind them, piles of cargo containers with enough nooks and crannies to hide four dozen bombs.

"There is no choice but to split up, my friend. Even SpeedJack would be hard pressed to beat the time limit alone. I will take the right side of the hold."

"Crap! You're right. I'm left." Elle made to vault over the railing when Pythia appeared in front of her, a stern expression on her face.

"C A S S & R A is a family friendly environment. Points will be deducted from your final score for swearing."

Elle rolled her eyes and jumped; rather than nailing a superhero landing, she ignored the Skellions and sprinted for the containers. Three followed, waving spiked baseball bats. She dodged, hid, and let them go past rather than waste time in fisticuffs, then set off at a quick jog. The hold stank of rat, stale oil, and detritus.

Where are we? In some other shard of Nova Arete? The bombs may be simulated, but the heaving is real enough. Bomb. Bomb. Where's the bomb?

She crouched to avoid another Skellion patrol and moved on.

For a split second, Elle thought she heard a pulsing hum out of sync with the rest of the world, but, on going forward, the hum changed tone and then faded.

Humming cargo. Great. No. Wait. The programming in the arcade is for ticket-holding guests, even if Cesar jacked with this adventure. And your average Joe couldn't beat this scenario without clues.

She doubled back until she heard the hum again and followed the pulsing beat. *There!* In the shadows between two containers sat a metal crate. A blinking metal crate. Each blink flooded the space between the containers with red light. Elle shimmied between graffitied balloon letters reading TANSTAAFL on one container and DIOGENES on the other to get a closer look at the crate.

The timer counted down from three minutes and thirty seconds, but the device made no sense at all. The wires spewing out of the ACME style bundle of TNT were of the requisite red and green colors, but none of them were connected properly.

Lovely. How do you disarm a bomb that's not set up to be disarmed like a bomb?

Elle leaned over, supporting herself with a palm on the lid of the crate while she looked over the timer in hopes of finding an on/off switch. The pulsating glow from the crate changed color, bathing her hand in electric blue light.

Did I hit a switch by accident?

Elle lifted her hand and the red glow returned.

Could it be that simple?

Elle slapped her hand down on the crate until the blue glowed bright and waited. *3:09. 3:08. 3:07.* Panic started a happy dance in her gut. *3:06. 3:05. 3:04.*

"Yay!" The bomb's amplified squeaky voice echoed through the canyons of steel containers and made Elle jump. "You have disarmed me! High five, hero!" A tube pushed out of the top of the crate and, with a *FWEEET*, showered Elle with glitter and confetti.

"Somebody's in here!" The shout was too close for comfort. "Fan out and find them!"

Elle called on the Living Waters and leapt with all her strength. She pulled herself up on top of one of the container stacks in time to hear a Skellion patrol pound by below. One stopped to look around until a *FWEEET* from the right side of the hold caught his attention. Two down. Elle grinned a moment at the thought of Talia's reaction to having her fur foofed with glitter. She didn't envy any Skellion that got in her way afterward.

Using the high ground atop the cargo, Elle spotted the next crate and bounced from container to container to get to it. She heard another *FWEEET* halfway there. One more bounce landed her on the container tower next to her target. She dropped down to put her hand on top of the crate. By the time the glitter cannon erupted, the timer read one minute and forty-five seconds.

Elle reached the back hull without spotting another crate, or Millennial Fusion for that matter. Talia bounded up a second or so later.

"We missed two. And we're running out of time, my friend."

"Where...wait a minute. We jumped down from a pretty wide catwalk. You don't think—"

"Last one there buys drinks. When you pay up, I'd like a mai tai."

"You wish!" Elle leapt up for the tops of the containers, alternately sprinting and jumping from one to the other. *Go. Go! GO!* Elle reached the edge of the last tower of steel. The circle of Skellions looked the same, only from this height, she had a better view of the contenders in the middle, one of which wore an electric blue and violent orange outfit painful to look at. "Get the bombs, Kitty Cat, I'll get the cape."

Elle waited for Talia to work her way to the side of the hold, then jumped down into the center of the circle. She nailed the landing.

"Howdy, boys. Got room on your dance card?" Elle went to work on the Skellions, only noticing afterward that Millennial Fusion had stood on the sidelines cheering her on rather than helping. The light in the hold began pulsing red. Pythia's voice boomed out of everywhere and nowhere.

"Allotted time for this mission will expire in ten seconds. Nine."

"Dark Claw?!"

"Eight."

"Get to the door—bombs are neutralized!"

"Seven."

"Can you fly, kid?"

"Six."

"Nope. Superspeed."

"Five."

"Then RUN!"

"Four." Elle shoved him toward the stairs and jumped for the catwalk. Talia pulled the door open and they tumbled through to the deck of the ship on *Two*. Elle stared up at the sky.

"Everybody ok? Dark Claw?"

"I hate glitter."

"Fusion?"

"Dorado?"

"Yeah, kid."

"What's a dance card?"

"Before your time, kid. Way before your time." Elle pushed to her feet in time to see Millennial Fusion phase out of existence with a shocked look on his face. When he disappeared, Pythia hovered in his place.

"Congratulations! You have completed Level One with one second to spare."

"Liar-liar, pants on fire."

"I do not understand your reference, Dorado." Pythia's pixels looked puzzled. "I am not wearing pants. Nor are they on fire."

"I neutralized the last bomb with six seconds remaining," Talia explained. "Yet you stated we beat the simulation with one second to spare."

"Both statements are correct, Dark Claw. Neither is mutually exclusive." The hologram flashed a happy grin. "And you are running out of time. Please choose a button to begin Level Two. You will enjoy Level Two even more than Level One." Pythia gestured behind them.

"Where did that come from?" Elle asked. Next to the rusted door, where none had been before, sat a two-button panel. And a second door.

***

Four nonstop missions, three hundred thugs, two dozen various exploding devices, and a giant monster in a sewer later, Elle's patience wore thin. Based on the erratic twitching of Talia's tail, Elle figured she wasn't far behind in the intense desire to wipe the ones and zeroes off Pythia's holographic mug, find Cesar D'Evreux, and extract some serious payback.

"Where is that little War Weasel? Cesar should have come howling through by now, wreaking revenge for losing his hostages. Something is seriously wrong here."

"You cannot call him War Weasel, my friend." Talia slashed through another Mafiosi. "It is insulting. To weasels."

Elle let out a laugh. The pair of them stood in yet another warehouse, surrounded by bleeding and unconscious foes, breathing hard, and covered in sweat and stinking of sewer, blood, and a whole host of other unmentionable things.

"That said, however, I am tiring of this game." Talia's tone was musical and unerringly pleasant, but Elle saw the bared canines behind the smile as Pythia reappeared.

"It is a good game. You have completed Level Six. It is one—"

"Of your favorite missions. Yeah, yeah. We got that Pyth. But I'm just about ready to tell you to Pyth off."

"Pyth off. A pun. On my name. I would rate it as funny once."

"Funny once."

Cesar hates anything on paper other than money, bearer bonds, Sun Tzu, and Machiavelli. How is it Pyth here knows Heinlein? Unless.

Pieces started to click together. How their bizarre obstacle course was in an arcade even though Cesar hated anything under the age of twenty. How the doors always opened a second before either of them could select a button. How War Wolf had vanished from the warehouse and why there was no sign of Cesar. Why Pythia was so eager to keep the missions coming. TANSTAAFL.

DIOGENES. The club where Sherlock's brother spent his time. The smarter brother that was the namesake of Luna's computer. "Well played, Pyth. Well played."

Pythia's eyes flashed. "Please select a button to begin Level Seven. I am ready for you to begin."

"You pick the next one, Pyth. We can take it. If this is ultra-survival mode, I ain't impressed. If we're putting our lives on the line for Tashi and the rest of the fortune tellers you've got squirreled away in your innards, we should at least break a sweat, don't you think so, Kitty Cat?"

"Speak for yourself. I do not sweat. I glisten."

"Point taken, but break a glisten just sounds wrong."

"Select a button." Pythia stamped her holographic foot; Elle poked her finger through Pythia's holographic shoulder for emphasis.

"These are way too easy. Give us a real challenge."

"The game is not challenging?" Pythia's tone danced on the line between confusion and rage. "I have studied you. These missions were built for heroes of your caliber. I gathered the fortune tellers to stabilize the probabilities of the maximum amount of entertainment without detection postulated by my Oracle Sphere. I even provided the proper motivation."

"I concede five points for monologuing but let us move past this. We have a War Wolf to paper train."

"Finally." Elle smiled, then turned her attention back to the hologram. "You've had us barking up the wrong werewolf, I'll give you that. No Naga to speak of, and I'm guessing Cesar isn't even on the same continent, let alone in this building. But I bet he's the one that plugged that baseball into your circuits in the first place, and I bet that's how you knew about us." Talia's look clearly asked if Elle were out of her mind, but then Elle saw her make the leap from Tashi's drawing of madness to the crazed hologram in front of them.

“Heinlein.” Talia whispered.

Elle nodded in answer and mouthed *She’s an AI. Be ready.*

“Did you kill him, Pyth? Not that I mind really, but Dark Claw had dibs.”

“Select. A. Button.” Pythia screeched.

“Not happening. *Agua dejame ver.*” The Living Waters welled in Elle’s eyes, clearing away the pixelated overlay from her vision. The Mafiosi were so many robot drone parts on the floor. And beyond them, a whirlpool of swirling light that opened onto a control room. Elle grabbed Talia’s wrist.

“This way!” And they dove through. If Plato had a perfect version of everything in his cave, this would have been the perfect super-secret, under-the-volcano lair.

“NO!” Pythia’s voice blasted out of the banks of floor to ceiling monitors lining the chamber’s walls.

From around the walls, doors opened and more of the robots ran forward. “We’ve got to find that baseball. That’s the key.”

“You know what it looks like. I will keep them occupied.” Talia growled, growing, changing, swirling in darkness to release the Spirit of the Cat, letting it take her. Elle had seen it hundreds of times, but the ten-foot-at-the-shoulder, midnight and silver beast still scared the bejeebers out of her. Of course, that was the whole point.

Elle dodged and sprinted, hoping that the Living Waters would see what she could not. The ball, as she remembered it, was a small thing to see in such a large space, but there it was, suspended above a metal rod, spewing out light and looking so much like a ball-point laser pen that she almost laughed. Elle leapt, sailing over a robot, this one probably masquerading as a monster of some sort since it ran at her on all fours, and reached out to grab the sphere.

“MINE!” Pythia screamed.

Elle’s fingers curled around what felt like touching a doorknob after pulling socks out of the drier.

"You can't have it. Mine. Mine. MINE!" A hand of light grabbed at the sphere. Pythia's voice echoed wildly until it sounded like a flock of seagulls. The roar that followed was deafening. Darkness flew by Elle as she fell to the floor and rolled, still tugging against the light from the pillar.

Elle felt something give and *pulled*. Another roar. Pythia, or whatever amounted to the thing pulling at the sphere let go. Elle careened backward, slamming into one of the monitors, and lost focus. Just for a moment. But it was enough. The Living Waters poured from Elle's eyes, leaving the swirling mass of blue, black and blood square in her vision. Only the vision was not her own.

Mud flying. Barbed wire. Blood. Bodies. I know this place. But this was not my when. Stille Nacht. Heilige Nacht. *All is Calm. All is Bright. A flash of light. A hall of mirrors and parquetry and chandeliers. A clockwork queen dancing in front of the statue of Athena, Goddess of Wisdom. Grant me wisdom. I know this place. But this is not my Versailles. A rooftop garden with a thief, a monk, and man with a prosthetic arm. A thief, a monk, and man with a prosthetic arm walk into a bar. I know this place. But this is not my London. A maze in another world. A warrior with one blue eye, one brass. A wolf on her arm. I will know this place. Talia and I. We will know this place. And soon.*

"MMMIIIIIINNNNEEEEE!!!!"

"Elle!" Elle blinked at the shout; the filigree ball flew from her hand. *What just happened?* The beast of darkness that towered over her dissipated until Talia was with her once again.

"How many fingers am I holding up?"

"Trick question if you have paws. I call foul. What did I miss?" Elle trailed off as she realized what she was seeing.

The three arcs that remained of the cracked portal dangled from the ceiling above the destruction, bonking into each other like a Dali version of a Newton's cradle. The computer banks sparked and whined, light from the monitors pulsing into so many ones and zeroes. And the floor of Plato's Super-Secret Villain Lair could have passed for a New York City trash barge.

"You've been busy."

"Come, my friend. We must find the others and leave this place. Pythia vanished when the Spirit of the Cat slashed the portal and smashed the computers, but she is mad, and in more ways than one. She is not through with us, and we must find a way to stop her before she destroys all of Nova Arete."

Elle pushed to her feet and looked toward the portal parts. The humming portal parts. With the whirlpool of swirling energy winking in and out like Charybdis on a bender. Robot bits started skittering toward the light. "That's not good."

"THIS IS ONE OF MY FAVORITE MISSIONS!" Elle and Talia whirled as one. Pythia's face covered the cracked monitors behind them with its parts in no apparent order.

Great. Trapped between Dali and Picasso. Talk about surreal. Elle thought. *Now what? A giant werewolf in a bikini?*

"Ideas?"

Elle looked around, brain scrambling. Computers were already smashed. Pulling the plug wouldn't stop Pythia's backup generators. "Don't think the IT help desk is a viable opt—" Then Elle saw it winking at her from the top of a pile of junk off to the left. "You're not going to like it."

"You keep saying that."

"SELECT A BUTTON!" A bolt of energy shot from the monitor sporting Pythia's left eye. *Or was it her right eye?* All mixed up like that, Elle couldn't rightly tell. Elle shoved Talia out of its path and scrambled for the filigree ball. The mound of detritus slowly disintegrated, pulling into the unbridled portal to who knew where. Elle climbed against the tide. Dodged a second bolt. A third. Dove. Reached. And grabbed the sphere. This time she knew better than to look at it.

"Hey, Pyth! Look what I got!" She shouted.

"MINE!" An energy bolt hit the junkpile under Elle and she

fought to keep her balance as more of the lighter pieces flew toward the light, scrunching with finality when they hit it.

"Finders, Keepers, Pyth. Time for you to play MY favorite mission. It's called FETCH!" Elle hurled the sphere with all her strength at the portal as the pile below her collapsed and followed its path. For a moment Pythia's hologram reappeared flickering in front of the flying ball of doom, but it shot through her pixels and straight into the portal. Elle almost felt sorry for her when she saw the abandoned look on Pythia's frozen face before she pixelated and dissolved. Almost.

But then whatever little control Pythia might have had on the portal was gone and the pull was too strong. Elle flailed for something solid to grab onto to keep from being vacuumed into infinity.

Well, I guess we'll find out how immortality handles going supernova.

"Gotcha!" Elle grabbed Talia's wrist, and Talia yanked her sideways, out of the path of its pull. The portal collapsed inward then expanded in a blinding whoosh, latching on to Pythia's forlorn afterimage, deconstructing it and slurping it into the morass before diminishing to a single point of light and winking out, leaving nothing but silence in its wake.

"Well, that was fun." Elle sat up slowly. "You okay, Kitty Cat?"

"That was my favorite mission."

CRRAACK!

A giant-robot sized portion of the wall buckled and dropped to the floor with a resounding THUD. DredNought stepped through, followed by Rik, St. Jeanne, and, to Elle's relief, the Seers. Tashi and Haruko brought up the rear with Talelle.

"Oink!" Dred's tone was so much like "Ta da!!!" that Elle laughed.

"Looks like we missed the party. Shame."

"*Oui*. Quite a shame, Rik. These two have all the luck."

"Not much of a party, my friends, but you did miss the

monologue. Please take note that Dorado has earned five points." Talia bowed to Elle with a flourish.

Elle pushed to her feet, fist bumped the team, and she and Talia walked over to hug Talelle, Haruko, and finally Tashi.

"You were right to tell us what you Saw, kid. To send us to Nova Arete. We belong here."

"Yes, Raksha Elle, Raksha Talia. Yes, you do."

Katherine L. Morse

The Internet of Undead Things

**ping* Today is Victoria R.'s birthday. Wish Victoria a happy birthday.*

No, Facebook; I can't wish Victoria a happy birthday. She lost her battle with cancer two months ago. Thanks so much for the reminder of my summer of death. I lost four friends in as many months. When Ted Jr. mentioned he knew a senior Department of Defense official through his dad, I'd checked LinkedIn. Sure enough, the official and I were 2nd degree linked. Not just through Ted Jr., but also through his father (though cancer killed him in the summer of death as well). What about William? Nope, LinkedIn has no idea that William was felled by a massive heart attack three months back. I can't even stand to look at Ana's Facebook page. The pictures of her participating in active, wacky adventures before ALS robbed her of her personality, her voice, and finally her breath, are just heartbreaking.

***

Okay, I can't read any more of this security spec. Maybe a little social media brain candy? Come on, Internet, give me some cat videos.

No, please no pictures of last winter's cosplay convention. That will just be more reminders of me and Ana in our steampunk Harley Quinn and Poison Ivy costumes.

Seriously, Facebook? Why must you repeatedly fail to send me invitations to upcoming events and yet spam me with ancient pics? Sure enough, pics of me and Ana hamming it up with our fake blasters.

Wait a second...these weren't here before. She never posted these, because she received her diagnosis when she got home from the con.

> *Message to Julian from Leigh: Hey, did you post new pictures to Ana's FB profile?*
>
> *Message to Leigh from Julian: No, I just left it online so friends could post remembrances. Maybe someone else posted them.*
>
> *Message to Julian from Leigh: No, it says she posted them.*
>
> *Message to Leigh from Julian: Probably just FB bugs ... there are so many. Let me check.*
>
> *Message to Leigh from Julian: No, I don't see any new pics.*
>
> *Message to Julian from Leigh: From the cosplay con last winter? I'm looking right at them.*
>
> *Message to Leigh from Julian: I don't see them.*
>
> *Message to Julian from Leigh: Yeah, probably just a bug.*

That's one weird ass bug.

***

I wonder if I'm linked to Dr. Roman through anyone? Surely someone in my LinkedIn connections knows him. Oh, Ted Sr., of course. I really need to remind Ted Jr. to take down the profile.

**ping* Ted endorsed you for a skill: security engineering.*

This is now officially a "thing." Let's see...what about Michelle? She's been dead at least four months and I'm pretty sure she knew Liev Roman. Yep, sure enough, 1 shared connection: Liev Roman.

Connect *click*

***

**ping* Michelle endorsed you for a skill: requirements engineering.*

I'm not crazy; I'm not crazy; I'm not crazy.

***

**ping* You have 1 new message from William W.*

Okay, there's no way this is a delayed message or some arbitrary Facebook weirdness. LinkedIn is too reliable for that. Someone is seriously messing with me. I'm definitely checking this out when I get home from my walk.

Why is this light taking so long? Come on come on come on!

So, LinkedIn, what do you have to relieve the boredom?

Message from William W.: Are you still happy where you're working? Would you reconsider my job offer?

What the...? Oo, there's the walk sign. Time to get moving.

SHREEE...WHOMP Aaaaaa! Paaaaiiiiiinnnn! Sharp. Pain. Then. Nothing. Oh no. Please oh please. Just let me die. Do not let me be paralyzed. Lightness. And sparkling light. Good, I'll just go toward the light and this will all be over. Goodbye, Damian. I have always loved you.

Nausea and vertigo? I thought you were just supposed to drift peacefully toward the light. Why is the light coming out of my phone? Freaky, streaming streaks of light like warp drive or fiber optics. Is this some upgraded 21st century near-death experience? Why do my guts feel like they're on the outside, and my phone is in my hand on the inside?

Whoosh pop Since when did dying come with unintentionally comedic sound effects? At least I'm right side out again. Wait, there's my house down there. And I'm flying toward one of the palm trees with the ring of cells that looks like a crown of thorns. This is really going to hurt. Oh, wait, no. I'm already dead. This is definitely not like any near-death experience I've ever heard of.

Bink Now I'm an atomic pinball between cell towers. I'm ready for this to be over so I can just get on with being dead. **Bink** Ooo! **Bink** Ouch! **Bink** Oh goody, actual fiber. This is a lot like those tube water slides at that resort in Maui, but without the water. **Sploosh** Why did I have to think of water? It's cold in here. And dark. And the pain is back. All over crushing. Dead; that's all I ask for, just plain dead.

Swish Cornering is bad. *Bink* Light is good. This is different. The network branches. Maybe everyone gets their own personal idea of heaven and hell. So the computer scientist gets the Internet? Oh man, how do I get to Zappos? .fr? .de? .nl? Naked cell phone ads in Swedish? Not only did I get the Internet, I got the European Internet. No, I do not need a good deal on a Viking river cruise. I'm dead and their pop-up ads are still haunting me.

Oh, that can't be good. Straight IP addresses without URLs and indecipherable text, probably encrypted. Even the NSA and CIA have public websites. So, that's what hell looks like for computer scientists: the dark web. Can I steer? Can you body surf the Internet? Crap, apparently not! No no no no no, I want to go over there!

Kashunk The phone. Of course it's the phone. It's the only part of me that's also part of the network; well, not exactly part of me, but you know what I mean. It might as well be. I can steer with it. Next stop, Zappos. Do they have that in Europe or would it take me back to the US?

Bink bink bink sploot Okay, that hurts a little less now. Whoa, I'm not moving. Where am I? Is this the Masterpiece website? What's with all the antiques and baroque?

"You are in the International Criminal Court in Den Haag."

Whoa, Teutonic ice princess. Who are you? Was I talking out loud or did you just read my mind?

"My name is Betje, Leigh. I work for the ICC, tracking and capturing international criminals. You did not speak out loud. In your current state, reading your mind and speaking to you are virtually the same."

"What do you mean, 'my current state'?"

"I will try to be brief. Normally this conversation would happen gradually over the course of several online conversations. The circumstances of your arrival necessitate less circumspection."

"I could go for some of that 'less circumspection' right about now."

"Ah, yes. You wish me to expedite the explanation. There are many international criminals we cannot reach through legal means. We recruit trackers to achieve the desired means through extralegal mechanisms."

"I'm still not feeling the 'less circumspection.'"

"We recruit trackers through undead profiles like those of your friends William W. and Ted P. Curiosity about the undead profiles is an indicator of Internet transit proficiency. Depending on one's moral proclivities, you are pulled toward some portal of the dark web or here. Ted and William were working for us prior to their deaths."

"Prior to? I got William's email just before I wound up here!"

"Technically, accepting William's email brought you here. Particularly strong recruits linger in the Internet after they pass. That recruiting email was William's final act. He is now truly passed."

"So, Ted too?"

"Yes, Ted was also a particularly strong recruit. His work in nuclear weapons made him attractive to both sides. He brought us several high value targets in the weapons of mass destruction black market. He was also working to recruit you by endorsing your technical skills."

"And Victoria?"

"That was just a Facebook bug. There are so many. We could fix them, but they provide good cover for our operations."

"This is all very patriotic and global good-citizen-y, but I'm not sure it's for me. Can I just be regular dead?"

"You are not dead."

"What?"

"You are not dead. You are just outside your body. Your current state is unprecedented."

"Unprecedented? That doesn't sound good. What the hell does that mean?"

"You are not in hell."

"Coulda fooled me. 'Unprecedented' sounds like throwing an exception. Explain."

"As I said at the beginning, Leigh, normally this conversation happens gradually. Trackers are usually only away from their bodies for a second or two during the initial recruitment action, as if they are absorbed in something on their phone."

"I don't get it. We've been standing in this cavernous 'library' talking for at least a minute."

"That is an artifact of your human expectations. You are in the network now. As a computer scientist, you should understand. We know you talk and text with your European friends. How long is the transmission delay?"

"Usually less than the hundred milliseconds that's humanly perceptible."

"Precisely. This conversation is running several orders of magnitude faster than real time, as you would say."

"Wait, so you're not human?"

"I am, but I am also in the network at this instant so I can communicate with you. And we are not really in this room. It is a virtual projection intended to make you feel more at ease."

"Ducky. Just so you know, that explanation doesn't really make me feel at ease. So how about you return me to my body and we have this gradual conversation I keep hearing about?"

"Well, now we return to the unprecedented nature of your current state. You are out of range of your phone."

"No, I'm not. It's right here in my hand."

"That is a virtual projection of your phone just as I am speaking to a virtual projection of you. Your physical phone has just landed on the pavement several feet from your physical body. I daresay the paramedics are unlikely to put it back in your possession when they take you to the hospital. There is one positive piece of news."

"I shudder to think what qualifies as 'positive' in your view."

"The new case you just bought for your phone did its job. Your phone is intact. Once someone thinks to put that phone back in range of your body, we can return you."

"And in the meantime?"

"In the meantime, you might consider embarking on a mission or two."

"Well, since I have nothing to do for orders of magnitude faster than real time, how does this gig work?"

"Look at your phone. We have installed a new app. This app will appear on both your virtual phone and your physical phone. When we identify a target, you will receive a notification via the app. The notification will include a tag. The tag will navigate you through the network to the target. When you reach your destination, activate the tag and touch the target with the phone."

"Touch? Won't they notice me popping up unexpectedly, waving my phone at them?"

"You are a virtual projection; they are real. They will notice nothing, not so much as a flicker on the screen."

"That's it?"

"There is one more thing. As soon as you tag the target, press the return button on the app. That will return you to a safe location."

"What kind of safe location?"

"Under normal circumstances, it would return you to your body a second or two after you left. Trackers normally position themselves somewhere secure with their phones at hand when they go on a mission, enabling their safe return to their bodies."

"Got it, blah blah, unprecedented state. So, what about me?"

"We have established safe houses in the event the network should experience a disruption, such as a router going down, during your return trip. The Icelandic My Little Brony one is quite popular."

"You have got to be joking!"

"A safe house should be the last location your adversary would expect to find you. Additionally, their IT staff is not particularly attentive."

"Well, you've got a point. You couldn't arrange to send me to Zappos instead?"

"That would be the first place they would think to search for you."

"Good point. So, what's tracking actually like?"

"One of our millennial trackers described it to me as 'the ultimate first person shooter'. He occasionally executes missions while sitting in his car waiting for a traffic light to change. I advise against this behavior in the strongest possible terms."

"Uh, yeah. One last question before you send me off. What if I need to get back here?"

"There is a home button on the app."

"Duh! Where to first?"

"Near Al Bukamal."

"That sounds like one of those places where my life is worth less than a goat's. I have a personal rule against going to places like that."

"You are not going there. You are still in the United States."

"Po-tay-to po-tah-toh."

"You must go now or we will miss our opportunity. Remember: activate the tag, touch the target with the phone, press the return button on the app. You will be routed automatically to a safe house. Good luck."

"Luck is for the unprepared. Oh, I guess that would be me right about now. Bye." **Click**

Bink bink bink kashunk Man, it's dark in here. Who knew the dark web wasn't just metaphoric? **Kashunk kashunk sploot**

OMG, this is even worse than I imagined! It's like an animal den in this cave. Good thing I can't smell anything in this state. Ew! Humans actually choose to live like this? Okay, terrorists, not so much humans.

“Silence the whore! I’m trying to work here.”

How very Star Trek. I can understand them and I’m pretty sure they’re not speaking English.

“No no no, please, no.”

Oh god! Do terrorists really do nothing but rape and murder? Why must they be such horrific stereotypes?

“Stop crying, whore. Get my tea! Abdul Naseer, get back on guard duty!”

Right, focus on the asshole at the keyboard, not the asshole who’s shirking guard duty to rape the slave woman. Why can’t I take all of them out? Why does it have to only be the one asshole at the keyboard? They’re all terrorists, after all! **Click Swipe-Tag Click**

Bink bink bink kashunk I think I’m going to vomit. **Kashunk kashunk sploot**

“Welcome back, Leigh. Well done.”

“Thanks...I think. If I had a body to go back to, I’d be done. As if their crimes against humanity as a whole aren’t bad enough, that poor woman...”

“Which woman?”

“The slave. Don’t you know about her?”

"We only perceive the target unless they post pictures or videos of others, which is uncommon."

"The other monster in the cave was raping a woman. And if that wasn't bad enough, she was horribly maimed."

"Were her injuries burns? She probably did that to herself."

"Are you nuts? Why would any woman do that to herself?!"

"There are situations more horrible than your privileged Western mind can conceive. Self-immolation may have been her only escape from slavery. Or she might have hoped that her disfigurement would dissuade the chronic rape. Tragically, it never does. It only serves to further reinforce the criminals' perspective of the slave as sub-human."

"I'm not sure I'm up to this job. I'm going to barf."

"I think you will find that many regular bodily functions do not work in your current state."

"Great! Can't we pull her out too?"

"The technology of the tags only allows us to capture one individual."

"Ugh. Just get me out of here."

"As you wish. I will send you someplace 'fun.'"

Kashunk bink bink bink *Buon giorno*, play-modena.it.

***

*ping* You have a tracking mission—a financier for a Russian human trafficking ring

Dos vedanya, Paravoy Dzhournaal. _*Click*_

*Bink bink bink kashunk *

Urgh! Bleah! Ouch! What the f***? I'm disintegrating! It burns! My eyes! Come on, stupid tag, activate! Ahhhhh! Home button, please, please, please. There...no...pain...now!

*Kashunk bink bink bink*

"Leigh, what happened? What are you doing back here? Where is the target?"

"I have no freaking clue, Betje! Why don't you tell me? I popped out the other side and started to disintegrate all staticky. And then it burned! My eyes were melting out of my head my brain was engulfed in flame my veins ran with molten lava! What did you send me into?! <sob>"

"Damn!"

"Whoa, I didn't think you even knew that word. Now give me a goddamn answer!"

"Did you see anything in the room that looked like a television dish receiver?"

"Hey, I was more than a little distracted with all the electronic splinching and getting sucked into a volcano to notice, thank you very much! <hiccup> No, wait, I might have seen something like that on the wall just before I was sucked back here."

"Damn!"

"There's that word again. Mind sharing, Betje?"

"We suspect that rumors of our disappearances are spreading and targets are taking precautions. The dish was almost certainly a jammer."

"Ducky, now what?"

"We can upgrade your phone with anti-jamming software. It will ameliorate the jamming, but it will make you slightly more substantial."

"Is that a polite way of saying fat?"

"No, it will make you less than invisible. Depending on the amount of light in the room, you may appear as a faint shadow. You will need to exert extra caution if you are delayed in a target environment. Stay in the shadows as much as possible."

"Gotcha. Send me someplace quiet where I can recuperate, maybe Norway."

***

"So, Betje, I've done a lotta missions for you, but I gotta know. What actually happens to the people I tag?"

"Be quite certain you want to know."

"Like I'm gonna feel bad after all the heinous shit I've seen."

"As you wish. The tag pulls the entire essence of the target through the Internet. It applies the same technology we use to move you around. It is analogous to a packet header; it tags outgoing traffic so we can identify it to redirect the network traffic here."

"That must be a hella huge chunk of data."

"Sometimes when you are working at Starbucks, you notice the network slows down suddenly. You walk around looking for the selfish individual streaming live video, but you cannot find the offender. That latency is one of our targets being retrieved."

"How do you know I do that?"

"People stupidly think they are anonymous on public Wi-Fi, but it exposes you to recruitment just like it exposes you to viruses and malware."

"Oh, yeah, duh. But what happens to them? Do they get dumped to some Halo or WoW server?"

"They get pulled into a secure bit bucket where they are disassembled. It is not unlike the sensation you experienced when targeting the human trafficking financier. Their bodies eventually die."

"They burn from the inside out?"

"That is the sensation they experience. It is the electrons being stripped out of your brain. But it is only a sensation that lasts for a few seconds."

"Well, I guess that seems awfully humane considering what they've done."

***

**ping* You have a tracking mission – a kaichō of the Sumiyoshi-kai*

Back to work for me. *Sayonara,* Kotaku. **Click**

Bink bink sploosh bink kashunk

Oh, crap! Four people in the room and no one actually at the keyboard. Probably not the badass ninja chick with the *ninjatōs*. Oh yeah, Leigh, get in the shadows. So, not the young guy. It's gotta be one of the gray-haired dudes. First one who bows at the end of this conversation isn't him. Why is the ninja looking straight at me? Nothing interesting in these curtains. That's creepy; it's like she's looking me straight in the eye...and walking right for me. Oh crap! She can see me!

Dammit, I'm taking one of them with me this time, even if it's not the target. Preferably before she manages to draw that sword cuz she looks like she knows how to use it.

Click Swipe

Swish Ahhhhhhh! That actually hurts! Am I bleeding!?

Click

Kashunk bink sploosh bink bink kashunk

"Ow, what the f*** was that?!"

"I beg your pardon."

"That samurai-ninja-whatever-the-hell-it-was could actually see me! She nearly killed me! You told me they couldn't see me; I'm just a shadow!"

"The targets cannot, but they have their own agents. We have heard chatter on the dark web that they have become aware of our methods and are recruiting agents to protect high value targets."

"And you were gonna tell me when?!"

"I apologize."

"So, 'I apologize' is not actually 'I'm sorry.' It's pretty clear that you're not being straight with me about a lotta shit. Time to come clean. What actually happened to Ted Sr. and William and Andrea and Ana?"

"You do not want to know."

"So, here's my deal. I'm super literal. I asked because I actually DO want to know."

"It is better if you do not know."

"Better for you or better for me? Because I've figured out I don't have to come when you call. So, if you want me to keep doing your dirty work, give it up!"

"You cannot return to your body without my assistance."

"And then my body will just peacefully pass away, or so you say. But I don't so much believe that crap anymore. What happened to my friends?"

"They were disassembled during tracking missions."

"Seriously, Betje, that's it?"

"Do you remember how you received messages from them after their bodies died?"

"Sure; that's how I got here."

"Our disassembler is nuclear; Ted designed it. The burning lasts only a couple of seconds and the targets are gone forever. You are not granted that peaceful passage if you are in the open Internet. You just wander and gradually disintegrate. As long as there's an Internet, you wander and burn."

"Um, I have to go."

Bink bink bink

***

Bink bink bink

"You rubbed my lamp, Sahib?"

"I beg your pardon."

"You know you say that a lot in our conversations, right? And you have zero knowledge of pop culture references. I could totally kick your ass at pub trivia. No...nothing?"

"We have located an international arms dealer who trades stolen arms to rogue states in exchange for stolen antiquities. He is wanted by several countries for both classes of crimes."

"Got it. What does he look like?"

"We have never acquired photographic intel. The most reliable way to identify him will be his immediate proximity to the antiquities. He trusts no one with those."

"The fat cat perching on a pile of loot like Smaug. Check!"

"Er..."

"Seriously, don't even try."

Kashunk bink sploosh bink sploosh bink kashunk

Fat cat on a...throne?...surrounded by old museum-y stuff. Check. Big wood crates stenciled in Russian. Oh, with hammer and sickle stencils; nice touch. I guess that old crap still works. No disintegrator dish, yay! Scary ninja chicks lurking in the shadows? Nope. This should be easy.

Skirting the lights; staying to the shadows. What's with the freaky blue orby geary thing...in a display case with a handle? Rich assholes collect the weirdest shit. Okay, come to mama. Hold up. He's looking right at me. How is that possible?! No, he's looking through me? Wave like you're the queen, Leigh; no response from tsar fat cat. Stick my tongue out; no response. Is he waiting for me to do something else? Okay, giving him the finger also elicits no response. Maybe he's just staring into space. His minions are definitely oblivious to me; no, please, just walk right through me, Ivan. Movin' on. Or not. He's definitely still tracking me. And checking the orb. What gives with the swirly black stuff in the orb? It's like it's following me...kinda like a 3D etch-a-sketch. Oh shit! It's tracking my electronic signature. Time for you to go, *tovarisch*!

Click Swipe-Tag

Silly arms dealer—swinging at me with your swirly etch-a-sketch. Repeat after me, non-corpor... Ouch, damn it! That hurt! Now you're just pissing me off!

Click

Kashunk bink sploosh bink sploosh bink kashunk

"What is that?!"

"Emotion and confusion all at once, Betje? This is almost as good as the time you said, 'Damn.'"

"This is no time for your sarcasm! You should not be able to bring physical objects back through the Internet. How did you get that...thing here?"

"Fourth dimensional portal? Solar flare?"

"I reiterate, this is no time for your sarcasm. This is unprecedented and dangerous. If you can carry an object back here, someone can send an object back here as well. We have no way of knowing if this is dangerous...or what it is for that matter. Can you hand it to me?"

"Um, maybe. Here. Oops, maybe if you try grabbing the cage thingy with both hands?"

"This is interesting. The globe coalesces black smudges as the device passes between our hands."

"My turn to remind you that we don't really have hands, just virtual projections of them. BTW, I already figured out it tracks our electrons. Also, it was in a framed glass case with a handle. He hit me with it by swinging the case by the handle and I actually felt it. But the case didn't come through with me. Just the orb thingy stuck to my hands."

"These are valuable observations. As you were able to bring the device into the virtual world, I expect I will be able to return it to the physical one."

"Oh. Maybe it's virtual and the case was holding it in the physical world. Man, I miss solving engineering problems!"

"I will attempt to discern the nature and purpose of the device. And then I will meditate on its implications for our mission."

"You meditate!? I really didn't see that one coming."

"It provides the clarity and calm necessary to execute our mission without regard for the danger."

"Alrighty, then. That's not creepy at all. *Ciao*."

***

"So, Betje, what do you have for me today?"

"'Today' has no meaning in this context."

"No, ma'am, we here at the FBI do not have a sense of humor that we're aware of."

"What does that mean?"

"Wow, testy. Never mind. The fact that you don't get the cultural reference is meta funny in and of itself."

"I still don't understand and it doesn't matter."

"Contraction, you? Really, never mind. How're you coming with that globe / device / thingy?"

"That's none of your concern! You have a mission."

"Moving right along. What have you got?"

"You'll be tagging a Triad Mountain Master, a Dragon Head. A young, inexperienced White Paper Fan will make the critical mistake of carrying his phone into a meeting between the Mountain Master and his Deputy Mountain Masters. You'll be deploying the first broad-spectrum tag we developed based on your recommendation."

"'Will make,' future tense?"

"If it works, it will capture all the meeting participants; you will go down in the annals of legendary trackers!"

"Oh stop; you're making my head swell."

"No joking! The future of our struggle depends upon your proving this technology!"

"Are you okay? You don't normally do unhinged."

"Just go! Good luck."

"Luck is for the unprepared. Ta!"

Bink bink bink kashunk kashunk sploot Well, points for taste. This is way better than those Daesh caves. Now I wish I could actually smell something because the spread of food looks amazing. Oh yeah, hunger. That's a thing I miss.

Scrawny dude right next to me must be the idiot White Paper Fan with the phone. That would make the scarily serene dude at the opposite end of the room the Dragon Head. I should have asked about the range of this tag. Will it be more effective if I'm closer to the target or closer to the network access point? Oh well, getting any number of these skanks is a win. Split the difference and get to the middle of the room. Damn there are a lot of people in here. Oh, check that. I can walk right through the furniture. I guess that makes sense, but ick. Jitter, not good. No, not the burning...not the burning! That hideous gilt on the table must be attenuating the signal. Through the table! Through the table! <urp> Whew! Okay, genius, get back on task. Any second now that White Paper Fan could discover his mistake and turn off his phone, and then I'm really screwed. Right about here. **Click Swiiiiiii**

Bink bink bink kashunk kashunk sploot What the F!?!?!

"Hey, sleepy head. Welcome back. The doctor said you're ready to wake up."

"Damian, where am I?"

"You're in the hospital where you've been for the last three days. That's weird. Why is this app on your phone flashing?" **iiipe-Tag**

"Damian, noooooo!"

***

This story is dedicated to the memories of my friends who died in my "Summer of Death" in 2015. For five months, it seemed like someone was dying every few weeks and their continued presence on social media was a constant, painful reminder. I toyed with the idea of this story until the sight of a picture of William, blown up to fill the screen in a ballroom at an awards banquet, sent me into fits of sobbing. And yes, William was a true patriot.

David L. Drake and Katherine L. Morse

Yandell's Folly

The 'Lectric Fountain

Rounding the street corner, Fabiana switched her heavy battery bucket from one hand to the other as she walked toward a dilapidated building, shifting her lean to compensate for the burden. She shook her free hand to get feeling back into her fingers and cinched tight her double-thick nematic aramid jacket, making her feel just a bit more bulletproof. This was her least favorite errand of the week. She figured that by going to the Fountain at eleven at night, maybe others would give up for the evening and head home.

Without stopping, she gave the building a once over. It was skinned in shiny slipstream aluminum decor, which was probably eye-catching when it was first constructed, but it was now covered with oxidation pits, scratched-in graffiti, and glutinous urban filth. On the upper floors, the building was collared in video ads that played incessantly. The broadcast was displaying sixteen simultaneous close-ups of a frenetically enthusiastic woman telling her university club friends that her boyfriend was going to buy her the newly released 2103 Her-Sport hyper-hybrid 3-passenger coup, "In red!" As the soprano exclamation echoed through the urban canyons of New York City's lower east side, the sporty crimson bullet car visually raced around the building's fifth floor.

As she had hoped, she encountered fewer people milling about than usual, their buckets or bricks in hand, waiting for their chance at the Fountain kiosks. Despite the hour, she noticed people of all ages.

She didn't interact with anyone; there was nothing she had to share. She started circling through the internal passageway, walking slowly past each kiosk. While passing her fifth kiosk, its dull green "Energized!" light clicked on. She snatched the cord on the top of her bucket and had it plugged into the kiosk before anyone else could react. The faces around her were livid.

An elderly woman dressed in a worn winter coat, shook her fist at Fabiana as she spat out, "I've been waiting for electricity for three hours, bitch!" The gesture caused the spiral plug on her brick to spring back and forth for a bit, adding an unintended comedic element to the aged woman's gesticulations.

Fabiana just gave her a tight fake smile and a nod. Her internal voice calmly reflected, *"No use wasting my breath on discussing my good luck."* The others around the kiosk jumped to form a line, hoping that there would be energy left after she had filled her bucket.

She watched as the joules clicked by on the kiosk interface and her bucket's percentage indicator progressed. With a few minutes to go, an eager teen jogged over to Fabiana, her naturally red hair secured into a ponytail that bounced with each of her strides.

The adolescent opened her conversation with, "You must have the best timing! How long were you here before you were able to tap in? Two minutes?"

Fabiana got caught up in her enthusiasm and even surprised herself with her willingness to converse. "Yeah, just in the right place at the right time."

"How long do you usually wait?"

"You know, about four hours." Fabiana scrunched up one side of her face as she remembered the last few times she had been here. "Sometimes more."

"That's a huge bucket! How long is it good for? It must have set you back quite a few BC's!"

"It's a hand-me-down from my older brother. It'll keep me in electricity for a little over a week...wait a minute! Are you blogging this?"

"Public conversation! Constitutional right. It's all bloggable."

"Don't get pseudo-legal with me, girly. Turn off the recorder. And I'm almost done here, so go corner someone else."

"Aww, come on...you got me all wrong. I'm just writing a post on people's opinions on the crumbling of the free electricity system. Thirty years ago, there wasn't any waiting at the 'Lectric Fountains, or so my parents tell me. Now the kiosks are almost never charged."

The kiosk made a dull clunk sound when it detected Fabiana's bucket was full, but the "Energized!" light was still on. The middle-aged man who was next in line elbowed Fabiana out of the way, pulled out Fabiana's plug, and shoved his power brick's plug into the kiosk's socket. His brick started to make happy dinging sounds indicating it was charging. Fabiana carefully inspected her plug for any harm from the rough handling, and even though she didn't see any damage, she still shot him an evil glance. She stepped away from the kiosk, shifting the bucket back to her other hand.

The blogger followed her closely. Fabiana raised her eyebrows in resignation that she would share her opinion about the utility.

"When the solar collector satellites started lasing energy down to the collector stations, everyone thought we'd have all the electricity that we would ever need or want. Once the manufacturing grid got their share, the rest was to be distributed to the people...you know, us. Free energy, free time. Isn't that what they advertised? Well, when the corporations figured out that with enough energy, you can convert common materials into rare materials, they tipped the scales on how much was their fair share. We nobodies are now *fighting for the scraps*. Is that what you, dear blogger, wanted to hear?"

"Well, yeah, but can you name some of the greedy corporations?"

Fabiana tipped her head side to side as she weighed the question. "Not if I wanna keep working in this town. You want some advice on how to beat these greedy corporations?"

The blogger lit up at the possible inside scoop. "How? What's the plan?"

Fabiana smirked as she kept walking toward home. "Every one of those greedy companies is publicly owned. Buy their stock. Invest. Then you'll be making the same kinda money you blame them for making." She giggled to herself, knowing that was just what the blogger didn't want to hear. "What's your name, so I can check out your blog?"

Still enthusiastic, the blogger called out as she trailed Fabiana. "Cass. Cass Sarkozi. My blog requires no Blockchain Credits to read! Check it out! And, eh, for the record, what's your name?"

"Fabiana Mastrodonato, and yeah, most people can't say it correctly the first time."

Cass turned and walked a few more feet, and then turned back. "Hey, Fabiana! You want to grab some food?"

Fabiana was caught off guard. She tipped her head to the side with a 'Why not?' look, following it with, "Sure. How about Orchard Street?"

When Cass caught up to Fabiana, she pulled out a small phone-comm. "Let me just record your name, you know, for the blog."

After a few taps and a cheerful ding, she slid the device back into a pants pocket.

The two of them chatted as they walked a couple of blocks. Fabiana pointed at the udon noodle house, they both nodded, and entered. After selecting an empty table, Fabiana set down her bucket. They ordered through their phone-comms, and two generous bowls of steaming soup were delivered to their table by a shiny stainless-steel wait-bot.

"Do you make any BCs on your blog?" Fabiana asked.

"Actually, I do. I write for Global Spot, and I get a percentage of their advertising revenue from my entries. I do pretty well. Some articles are sponsored, some are highlighting an event, but the stories I enjoy the most are the ones I create myself."

Fabiana expertly slurped a couple of hot noodles into her mouth with the aid of her chop sticks. A subtle chime that sounded like a struck meditation bowl rang from her pocket. She pulled out her phone-comm and made a confused face at the display. "Umm, your article on our encounter just came up. I'm subscribed to Global Spot, and I've set my filters to let me know if my name comes up in an entry. But...how did you write the story? It's only been a few minutes. Do you...have a mental link system?"

"I've never seen one of those systems work well. You have to wear them on your head like a helmet, and they're so big and clumsy. And expensive! The end result...the content itself...is always wrong, I don't know why the corporate journalists use them."

"I'm serious. How did you write that story? Did you somehow tap into my brain?"

Instead of laughing off the suggestion, Cass instead looked nervous. "I had already written..." She trailed off her explanation as she tried to figure out how to proceed. "I have these dreams...premonitions, really. I write them down. Sometimes I get it right, sometimes I miss a few details. For the 'Lectric Fountain story, I couldn't figure out your name. That was the last detail that I had to enter before submitting the story."

Fabiana pointed to her screen. "You have word-for-word everything I said in here! That's just not right. Are you broadcasting our conversation?"

Cass blurted defensively, "No! No! Really...I just wrote that story around two o'clock this afternoon. I just had to wait to talk to you to verify that I got it all right."

Fabiana stared at Cass for a few seconds before proclaiming, "I don't believe you. I don't believe you wrote these words this afternoon."

"I know you will probably never believe this, but it's true. Every day I stop by the museum, and I sit near the Greek orb in the Hellenic artifacts exhibit. Then I write my stories for the day. I go and have conversations with people, make any corrections needed, and publish them. I've been doing this for three years, and you're the first to...catch me at it. But its not a trick! I really write these stories."

"Well, Cass. I just don't believe you." With that, Fabiana dropped her chop sticks on the table, stood up, grabbed her bucket, and left.

Cass sat in silence for a minute. She pushed her soup bowl away, glanced at all the happy chatting patrons sitting at other tables, buried her face in her hands, and said quietly to herself, "I just...I just wanted a friend."

***

Tiberius's Dream

The five reporters stood at the ready outside of Tiberius Yandell's office door. Their eager anticipation of getting a mid-day news lead, and a live interview to boot, made them lean slightly forward, waiting for entrance.

"This is obviously staged," thought Tammy Wong as she

adjusted her black tech-trimmed glasses. "His assistants would never let us hover here unless Tiberius wanted to make a big entrance." She did her best to put on a sober journalistic face to hide her belief that this may be another of his chest-thumping philosophic grandstands. "Play the role. Be the role," she chanted to herself.

Tiberius himself flung the heavy wooden door open. "Friends!" he bellowed. "Come right in. We have much to celebrate!"

The five of them eagerly stepped in, their handheld recorders already on with their voice-tracking microphones and hyper-stable face-following cams locked on. They spread out a bit, each trying to find the image angle that would best sell the story. The maneuver left Tammy in the middle, feeling like she won a mini-victory of positioning.

Tiberius was cocked and loaded for his reveal. "This is a dawn of a new age!" He made a sweeping gesture out the 131st story's floor-to-ceiling window that looked out on the New San Francisco cityscape. "What you see is a shining city full of hopes and promises. But the hopes and promises have been dictated to the citizenry by product manufacturers, bureaucrats, and managers for so long that they contain only faint echoes of a free society. Earth's economy is stagnant. Unlimited energy has made people lazy. Nobody's interested in innovating anymore because everyone has everything they need. When they get bored with some new toy, they toss it in the recycle heap and get something new to entertain them." He paused, hoping that guilt would sink in to his audience. "The Greeks didn't see the gods as omnipotent, omniscient and wise, but petty and capricious. The gods of energy and technology are just like those gods. Like Odysseus, we have lashed a donkey and an ox to our plow in a futile attempt to shirk an unavoidable conflict we fear. Like Agamemnon, we must reveal this lunacy for what it is. We must face the enemies of sloth, indifference, and complicity head on!"

Given her lack of historical knowledge, Tammy cringed at the comparison to the ancient world. In her right hand, she squeeze-typed "Odysseus donkey" into her phone-comm and her glasses displayed a couple of translucent sentences about Odysseus feigning lunacy to avoid participating in the Trojan Wars. Good enough, she thought. I get the idea.

"To this end, I am founding a new operational entity within Yandell Corp to design, build, and launch interstellar space vehicles for human passage to exoplanets. We...the human race...will no longer be trapped on one planet. We can be brave explorers again."

The well-dressed twenty-something reporter with well-kept mid-back length red hair to Tammy's right shifted from foot to foot. To Tammy, she seemed to be anticipating the next thing Tiberius would say.

He opened his arms wide and called out, "Who's with me?"

The redhead shot her hand into the air. "Cass Sarkozi here! And I'm with you!"

All eyes shifted from Tiberius to the outspoken reporter. Tammy made a confused face.

Wasn't his question rhetorical?

Not missing a beat, Tiberius pointed to Cass. "Now that's what I'm talking about!"

Tiberius went on to describe his new corporate-comm site page to submit proposals, designs, and résumés. He finished with another rousing speech about new frontiers and brave explorers, and when he finished, he politely concluded the interview and dismissed the reporters with promises of invitations for the next reveal of his plans.

And he promptly forgot about Cass. But she predicted that would happen.

***

Scientist's Paradise

In typical corporate fashion, an enormous hardwood table dominated the boardroom atop the Yandell Corp headquarters building. Millions of recessed pinhole ceiling lamps bathed the room in the perfect shade of warm light that gave the room a permanent atmosphere of calm. Pearlescent textured wallpaper of the two non-glass walls gave the room a soothing sense of vastness and murmured quietness.

The board of directors and their support staff made their way to their preassigned chairs, all wearing their light grey gender-neutral success-oriented corporate suits. In defiance of the ubiquitous clothing, each of the women attending sported a bold hair style and makeup combination that made the men look slightly bland and corporately sober.

Matteo Zegen had found his chair minutes before any of the other members arrived. He scanned the others as they busied their way to their spots, reading their tells as easily as most would read newsbites on their comm-phones. The hyper-aware entrepreneur had parlayed his uncannily precise and accurate ability to read other humans into an omnipresent empire of intent recognition software, modeled on his own abilities, and deployed by governments and top-fifty multinational conglomerates. While it had made him wealthy and the golden boy of corporate and national security forces the planet over, it had also made him one of the most feared and despised men on the planet. Tiberius Yandell's glass bubble of an executive conference room made him particularly nervous for his own safety; one whisper-flight hover drone with an encrypted inbound-only comm chip and a micro grenade could take out the entire room.

Matteo closed his eyes for a precise count of three deep breaths in and out to refocus his attention. He didn't need his own software to recognize the intent and magnitude of Tiberius' growing mania: the dark circles under his eyes, the irritability, the irrationality of his recent live interview. Any second-rate security force profiler right out of school could see the signs.

Tiberius is no longer focused on the Yandell Corp mission. He's focused on evolving himself into this century's history-maker.

Matteo was particularly interested in how the other board members were reading and responding to these signs. The psychologist, physician, and sociologist all wore expressions of practiced inscrutability. But all three were gazing around slowly, obviously attempting to assess the other board members, but without Matteo's skill for misdirection.

So, the other 'people people' on the board are also concerned.

Matteo turned to reading the remainder of the board members, the ones from government, manufacturing, science and infrastructure. They were all absorbed in the opportunity for power-grabbing and deal-making.

"Attention!" Tiberius barked.

Matteo noticed the "people people" flinched but immediately recovered their masks. The others grudgingly abandoned their money—and influence—making dance and turned to face Tiberius.

Without the formal pleasantries of an official call to order, Tiberius launched into his favorite, nay only, topic of interest over the past few weeks. "A reachable, inhabitable exoplanet is out there. I can feel it in my bones. It will have the pristine environment for a sane society, one whose laws and customs are driven by reasoned facts and sound judgement, not the blind emotions of the masses or the greed of corporations. Imagine an educated populace working as a unified team on scientific, artistic, and egalitarian pursuits. It will be a scientists' paradise. *An entire planet* as a research facility. And Yandell Corp will be the driving force behind it."

Funny, thought Zegen, *normally I'm a fan of irony.*

Tiberius pointed a finger at the blank wall behind him where millions of recessed pinhole display lights jumped to life, displaying scientists, engineers, artists, construction workers, chefs, and a multitude of other hard-working iconic occupations, waiting patiently in queues to board iconic bullet-shaped spaceships. "Colonists will be selected on merit and commitment to my vision. Scientists will be rewarded with new stars to study and a world of new problems to solve. Funding issues will be a thing of the past. Resources will be rich and plentiful!"

The technocrats jumped to their feet and clapped, one or two wiped away a tear. They turned and shook each other's hands vigorously, as if they had just won a sweepstakes.

Of course, thought Zegen. *They're all expecting fat contracts to make this mad vision a reality and anticipating the hole that Yandell's departure will leave at the top of the dog-eat-dog heap. Donkeys and oxen indeed!*

***

The Speech

Tiberius stood behind the podium at the edge of the launch pad of the Yandell New Jersey Interstellar Launch Facility; the 23-story high spaceship loomed behind him. With video broadcast units recording his every move, Tiberius let the wind blow his hair dramatically a bit before he gazed seriously over the throng gathered to hear his words. His stance was both pensive and resolved, as if pondering how to tell his tale without losing its subtle meaning. The crowd was quiet and prepared for his message.

"My friends, in the beginning of the second century, the biographer Plutarch wrote of many famous Romans and Greeks. One of his best tales is of Theseus, a founding hero of Athens, a great reformer, and the slayer of the Minotaur. But Theseus was known for his journeys and exploits, and to explain the domain of the unknown in which he travelled, Plutarch wrote:

> *...writers crowd the countries of which they know nothing into the furthest margins of their maps, and write upon them legends such as, 'in this direction lie waterless deserts full of wild beasts' or 'unexplored morasses' or 'here it is as cold as Scythia' or 'A frozen sea'...*

"Plutarch went on to clarify his words:

> *All beyond this is portentous and fabulous, interpreted by poets and mythologers, and there is nothing true or certain.*

"His significant point was that we shroud what we do not understand in terrifying mystery. By that measure, what he said in the second century is still true today regarding the emptiness of space beyond our solar system. We have no true concept of what the interstellar frontier truly holds except for our interpretation of ancient dim light that shines and primordial dust that blows by our local corner of the sky."

He paused for effect.

"These are the words we have used for millennia to frighten people away from exploration. And they work!" He paused again. "But, no more! We have discovered two new worlds in the Orion arm of the Milky Way, which we named Alpha-4 and Beta-3, a mere nine lightyears from each other, which will make them easy to internavigate. From what we can determine from this distance, Alpha-4 is a habitable iron-core planet with water on its surface like our earth. Beta-3 is similar, but mountainous, offering unparalleled opportunities for astronomical exploration...and a new view of the heavens."

Tiberius switched from dreamer to technologist as he made a grand gesture toward the spaceship behind him.

"Travel to Alpha-4 will be accomplished on the Yandell Corp

interstellar transport ship *Trireme I*, named after the primary ship design of the Athenian maritime empire. What you see behind me is the test prototype that will be used for safety and performance analysis. Ten craft will be constructed for the journey."

A murmur started in the crowd. Tiberius noticed the tone wasn't entirely positive.

"You're probably asking yourselves, 'How can I be involved? What is this opportunity going to cost me? Will this be an adventure solely for the rich?' No! The only 'coin' you need is bravery! A spirit of adventure is the only job qualification! Who's with me?"

If Yandell had been expecting the breathless enthusiasm of the media longing for a scoop or the back-slapping support of his self-aggrandizing board of directors, the crowd's mixed response was a disappointment. The throng that was gathered here had little interest in leaving the Earth, and really just wanted to get a good story for the day.

A cluster of fashion technocrat reporters in the front row lost interest the instant they realized Yandell Corp wasn't releasing a new phone-comm app to reward them for trendy food selections; they wandered off to try the spirulina tofu frappe at a new club in the hyper-filtered air-wellness bar.

Others shouted, barraging Tiberius with questions. How did this compare to the initial manned trip to Mars and its unfortunate resulting outcome? With all of the profitable space mining of the asteroid belt for metals, why pursue this? Couldn't a section of earth be dedicated to testing these societal goals rather than venturing across the universe to seek idealistic philosophic dreams?

Tiberius smiled and answered them all. "It is a frontier with which we have the ability and the technology to pursue. Few will have the heart for such a trip. I am looking for that few."

The smattering of homeless people cordoned away from the

center of the plaza cheered faintly. It sure sounded like a free meal, a lot of free meals, and a place to sleep forever. Most of the rest of the crowd clapped politely, while others didn't even bother, and then just wandered away.

A clutch of Romani at the edge of the crowd begin whispering to each other. "It would be like the old days in the old country...like in *bunícă's* stories," urged one of the young men. "Just us and our wagons going wherever fortune takes us. You heard him, 'A spirit of adventure is the only job qualification.' The Romani are the very spirit of adventure!"

A cooler head, Pitti, cautioned, "We must consult the *familia*."

***

Discovery

"What's the hold up?" Tiberius demanded of Josef Wójcik.

"*Silo 3*, the Romani ship, is late loading."

"You'd think a people who've spent all of history wandering would be the first to be ready to pack up and leave."

"Yes, sir," Josef replied calmly. "They were very enthusiastic and among the first to sign up. Their captain informed me that they have a 'straggler,' a passenger Sarkozi who failed to pack some item of considerable cultural import. The captain assures me she will board within our launch window."

Tiberius smirked at his second in command. "At least we're all volunteers. I think everyone of us will understand."

Josef hesitated to answer. He started to say something and then held back.

Tiberius interrupted this vacillation with the single word "What?" to draw a response.

Josef forced out, "You know it only looks like we're volunteers. You know that, right?"

"What are you talking about?"

Josef pursed his lips. "I was paid to be here. Well...that's not exactly right. Hosterfren paid my children if I went in lieu of paying me my pension. They saved thousands of credits and my children got their inheritance up front. It's all very orderly and..."

Tiberius was spitting mad. "Hosterfren? Hosterfren Inc.? Is that how they funded our mission? And they forced you to go on this one-way trip to Alpha?"

Josef frowned. "No one was forced. All employees that were near retirement age were asked if they wanted the 'Alpha Voyage' package. We weren't supposed to discuss it outside of the job. I won a damned lottery to be here! My children...well...they just don't like me! They got their credits and I get to start over. I just..."

"Are you here because you want to be here? You know what...don't answer that. I don't want to know."

Josef blurted out, "Well, you'll want to know this! Every member of *Silo 6* was a prisoner from Brazil's São Paulo penitentiary. Hosterfren cut a deal with them. Brazil saved a fortune on prisoner costs."

Tiberius was thunderstruck by his own innocence. He stood wide-eyed at the role he had played.

Josef continued, "You know those mind-games where you can push a button and for five hundred credits someone disappears? Well, Hosterfren has been given that button. Except they could press it five thousand times."

For once in his life, Tiberius was speechless.

"Your Nobel Prize winning astrophysicist?" Josef asked. "His government gave him the choice of joining you or execution."

Tiberius looked like he had been punched in the gut. He had trouble breathing. "My whole plan was to take all these people to a new land. Start over. Not...line the pockets of a greedy conglomerate on Earth or serve the oppression of murdering totalitarian governments." Tiberius gazed dispiritedly across the launch field. In the distance, a tiny female figure sprinted toward the gantry for *Silo 3*, clutching a bundle under her arm like one of those ridiculous sports trophies from the 20th century.

She has no idea that the dream she's fleeing toward is really a nightmare. My nightmare.

As nonchalantly as possible, he left the bridge and strolled toward the hatch to the gantry.

"Mr. Yandell?" the guard on the gantry asked.

"I've remembered a personal item I meant to bring. I'll be right back." And with that, he exited the craft, never to return.

***

The Journey

The countdown continued and the ten ships blasted off in quick succession. The ships streaked towards the sky, orbited Earth, rendezvoused at the proper coordinates, broke orbit in perfect formation, and headed toward their first gravity assist point.

No sooner had the ships cleared Earth's atmosphere, picturesque images of their billowing contrail columns contrasting against a clean blue sky appearing at the top of the net-news sources, than the news cycle instantly grew bored. Pictures of the morning talk show host who was knee-deep in scandal replaced the launch and the ships were forgotten. The trip would take a lifetime of years, and there wouldn't be any back-and-forth chats with the travelers. The colonists were on their own.

Josef scrutinized the broadcast message he had prepared for all the ships. He pressed the SEND button knowing that this was the first and biggest hurdle of their trip.

> *As your pilots have informed you, we are all traveling a great distance at velocities never dared by manned travel before. Due to each of our slight variations in position, speed, weight, and a dozen of other factors, our optimal flight paths will diverge as*

well as our arrival time. Our communications between the ships will become both more delayed in delivery and more scrambled due to interference. For this reason, trust your own flight navigation system and take your own calculated course. As planned, be in your hibernation pods by day thirty. I trust you will travel safely and I will see you all on Alpha-4.

He was fully aware that, left to their own devices, things could go awry on board any one of the space craft. He also knew that the false hope of helping another craft would greatly risk any would-be rescuer's chances of survival.

In *Silo 6*, the released Brazilian inmates had worked out a stable pecking order by day twenty-two. Unfortunately, it reduced their ranks from the initial 1,000 to 532, and the trained pilots were not among the survivors. By day twenty-eight, a miscommunicated order combined with simple human error caused a high-pressure oxygen tank fire that breached the hull. The resulting leak not only drove the craft off its intended flight path, but also caused the ship to cartwheel at just the right rotational speed to permanently pin its occupants against the fore and aft bulkheads. Their deaths were slow, cold, and airless.

On *Silo 3*, the Romani leaders gathered to discuss their situation. The tall man in the center, Pitti Longley, stood and addressed the twelve in attendance. "It is two days before the time to hibernate, does the orb agree with our preparations?" All eyes turned to Cass.

She hesitantly stood. "To me, the orb is showing conflicting images. Well, I'm not getting clear images for the future. I'm not sure what to focus on."

"Have you tried Tanti Vadoma?" one woman suggested.

Cass, still standing, looked about at the faces of her elders. "Tanti Vadoma is on board? I didn't even know she was selected to travel with us, given her failing health."

Pitti chimed in. "We wouldn't have left her behind. She's been confined to her bed so far. She is the *bunícă* of us all. Let her consult the *yak* to see our days ahead."

Cass was concerned. "With her age and health, should we trust her vision?"

"To be certain," Pitti replied soothingly. "She is an old woman. Her knowledge of the orb's history is broad and deep. What can it hurt to ask her? We should do all we can before we clear the inner planets and go to sleep. Just to be safe, yes?" He walked over and patted Cass on the shoulder in a manner that was more paternal and patronizing than reassuring.

After the meeting, Cass and Pitti, helped the old woman to a cushioned wheelchair while supporting her hands to guide her shaky frame slowly down. They wheeled her into the "orb room" as it was now called.

Tanti Vadoma looked up at Cass with clouded watery eyes. "Why am I here?" she asked quietly.

Cass gave her a curt smile that was supposed to relax her. "What are you thinking about?"

"Why, nothing my dear."

Cass looked carefully at the orb, and it showed no activity at all. She walked to the left side of the chair, so that the old woman was between her and the orb. Leaning over to her, she asked, "What do you think of our path to get to Alpha?"

The elderly woman's forehead deeply crinkled above her nose as she thought, and the haziness of the orb faded, revealing a twisted line through a set of stars, as if it were revealing an interstellar roller coaster track. Tanti Vadoma's eyes cleared and she looked directly at Cass. Without a crack in her voice, she declared, "The *yak* is right. It is always right. We are destined to follow the path it shows." She pointed at the orb with her age-spotted hand, and without another word, she nodded off to sleep. Cass shot Pitti a *"Did I just see that?"* glance.

Cass stared intently at the orb, committing the path to memory before it faded. Certain that she had memorized every detail, she sprinted to the bridge where she dropped into the navigator's seat and pounded in the course.

Pitti and Cass huddled over the navigation station with the pilots. Pitti grilled Cass yet again. "Are you absolutely certain the path the pilots have programmed matches what the orb showed you and Vadoma?"

"Yes, yes, it's still stuck in my head! It matches exactly."

Pitti turned to the captain. "This path doesn't look like it takes us to Alpha-4, but I'm not a pilot."

"You are correct, Pitti. This course will take us very far from our original destination. I do not have the seeing mind, so I cannot interpret the orb's intention. But I can tell you that, if we follow this course and the orb is wrong, we will not have enough fuel to return to Earth or go on to Alpha-4. We will all be doomed to die on this ship."

"But why would the orb take us to our deaths?" Pitti asked a little desperately. "It has led us for millennia. We are its people, its followers, its keeper."

"Well," Cass interjected, "there's a good chance something could go wrong if we stick to the original plan to go to Alpha-4. We could all die doing that." She could tell by the looks on Pitti and the captain's faces that she was not helping the situation. "All I can say is, it's never lied to me. If it wants us to go there, it must hold something just for us. Maybe this is the home the Romani have never had."

"But if it's wrong, we have no idea where we'll wind up," Pitti reiterated.

"As you've said so many times already!" Cass exhaled dramatically in exasperation.

Pitti turned his attention to the pilots. "And you're sure the course you've programmed the ship to follow is the same as the path the orb prescribed?"

"Yes, Pitti," the captain replied flatly.

"Because we won't be able to correct it once we deviate from the path of the rest of the ships after we clear Mars. We'll already be asleep by then."

"I'm *familiar* with how space travel in hibernation works," the captain replied with a tinge of sarcasm. He shot Cass a sympathetic glance.

Pitti continued, "If we don't go into hibernation with the rest of the ships, they'll know and suspect something."

Cass mimed a strangling motion behind Pitti's back. The captain scowled and shook his head at her insubordination.

***

Landing

The Romani ship hurtled through space at a rate its designers would have never imagined. Inside, only the small status lights of the one thousand sleeping pods flicked their rhythmic status checks on their occupants. After years of flying at three quarters of the speed of light, its target solar system was ahead.

Without any assistance from the crew, the orb and the guidance systems made a series of near object flybys that slowed the ship down to a velocity where orbiting a planet was possible. This took 20 months on its own.

The pilots' pods awoke first. The motors to break the incubators' atmospheric seal whirred and the cold wispy air from within mixed with the warmth from without. Nutrient and sanitizer systems hummed to life, and the interior lights to the pods flickered on like centuries-old fluorescent lights.

The waking process was slow. Even after the pilots were roused, muscles and creaky joints had to be slowly limbered back into working order. Stomachs had to get something in them, the blander the better.

But eventually, both of them had risen despite red eyes and sore backs.

"We...made it. Look on that monitor. We're orbiting a planet with water and vegetation," exclaimed the first mate.

A message came into the communication station.

"I thought we were alone? Who could be contacting us?"

The textual message couldn't be clearer. "Look outside your craft. Let us guide your craft in for a landing."

The two pilots stared at the monitor that showed a surreal scene outside the vessel. Enormous translucent hands held a succession of gigantic delicate hoops and urged them to guide their ship through. The scene appeared ethereal and wispy, as if fashioned from high-altitude clouds.

Cass came stumbling in to join them. "What...what is that?"

The captain felt he had to explain it to himself out loud. "At this distance from the planet, that can't be water vapor. It has to be a dust particle display...thingy."

"Thank you, Captain Badi, for clearing that up," First Mate Holomek sarcastically added.

Cass asked, "Are we to perform for them like trained circus animals? Whoever is controlling that *display thingy*, as Captain Badi so aptly named it, wants us to follow through the line of circles."

Holomek and Badi nodded together.

Cass answered her own question. "It's silly to worry if this is a trap of some sort; there's just as much danger in following the trail as ignoring it. The only other recourse is to leave, which is foolish to put all the energy required into turning our ship around and, well...ignoring the best indication of friendly intelligent life in the universe."

The pilots jumped to their seats and eased on the reverse thrusters, taking the craft out of orbit. As they descended toward the planet, they began transiting through the wispy hoops, one by one.

Once the ship entered the atmosphere, a giant soft hand caught the ship as a human might catch a feather, and transported it gently to the surface. Once firmly on the ground, the ethereal hand dissipated.

Another message came into the communication station.

"This world is safe for you. Join us if you wish."

After extensive checks of atmospheric composition, radiation levels, the magnitude of magnetic fields, temperature fluctuations, wind velocity, humidity concentrations, barometric pressure, and bacterial and viral concentrations, they concurred with the message. It was perfectly safe to exit the craft.

Trusting the orb's predictions, Cass volunteered to be the first. Completely unprotected, with nothing but a comm-link, she passed through the airlock, exited the craft, descended the ladder, and placed a foot on the green turf of the exoplanet.

It looks...like a nature preserve, she thought. She looked around at the rolling green grass-covered hills, majestic trees, and stream. What she didn't see were any signs of 'civilization'. There were no roads or buildings, not even livestock. Feeling a little ridiculous, she called out, "Hello?"

At the sound of her voice, a tall, perfectly-sculpted man in a toga coalesced a few yards in front of her. "Welcome to Olympus," he announced.

***

First Contact

"Um, who are you?" Cass asked skeptically.

"I am Apollo, the God of the sun."

Sure, thought Cass. *That makes perfect sense. I can see why they would use this projection. At least he looks the part. I'll just play along and see where this goes.*

The muscular giant of a man held out the hourglass for Cass to examine. "What is this?" Apollo asked in a Socratic manner.

"An ancient timepiece. Gravity pulls the grains through the

chokepoint at a relatively consistent rate. Traditionally it metes out a temporal unit called an hour. Thus, it is called an hourglass."

The self-proclaimed god smiled broadly. "Good. But this is also a model for the entire universe. It is trying to reach stasis. With every grain of sand that falls, it comes closer to its final equilibrium. However, with the universe, it is not gravity that drives the movement. What is it?"

Cass thought about the entire expanse of the universe moving forward. What causes that? "Time?" She was not confident in her answer.

Again, he smiled. "You are both wise and wrong. Your mistake is very reasonable, though, given your experience. The answer is Chaos. The universe is trying to go from greater chaos to less chaos. The confusion is that your scientists refer to the less chaotic state as more randomized. In fact, the universe goes from tension to relaxed. The grains are driven from the higher chaotic state to the less chaotic state. For the sake of simplicity, consider the upper half of this so-called hourglass as having a higher chaotic pressure, forcing the grains through the chokepoint."

Cass nodded.

He pointed at the chokepoint. "And what is this in the universe?"

"I know that one. It is 'now.' The activities that are happening at this moment. That makes the lower half the things of the past, the top half the things of the unresolved future."

Apollo nodded. "You are wise, and correct. However, let me improve our model." He touched a finger to the middle of the hourglass and it instantly changed into an hourglass with three chokepoints connecting the top half to the bottom, with the grains running through all three.

"This is better," he stated. "And I will tell you why. Every step forward, which your species calls a Planck Time Unit, the smallest possible unit of time, a grain is forced to go through the chokepoint from greater chaos to less chaos. But some distance away is another grain making the same decision. How far away are these grains that are making independent decisions?"

"Well, if you're measuring time at the resolution of Planck Time Units, then the distance is also minuscule. One or two Planck lengths."

Apollo nodded solemnly. "Again, you are correct. So, our model shows three chokepoints, but you would need enough chokepoints to represent all of the Planck lengths in the Universe."

Cass raised her eyebrows in understanding. She followed that with a furrowed brow and a raised finger. "But the model isn't right. All matter changes in every step from the current 'now' to the next. And the change in chaotic pressure from one 'now' to the next 'now' is usually minuscule, most of the time."

Apollo smiled again. "But...what if this hourglass model is actually a good one for understanding the universe? What if the grains flowed downward for a while until the pressure got greater on the lower half, and then it changed direction? Your perception is that time is always moving forward, but it is in fact going between these two states, trying to reduce its chaotic pressure."

Cass screwed up her face and quipped, "Then I would say that you created an elaborate model that doesn't help us understand anything."

The god's eyes widened and his nostrils flared. All pleasantness drained from him. "And what if I told you that I built a window that could see into one side of that model? Everything that is waiting to be resolved? Everything that has been resolved? Would that clarify its usefulness?"

Cass shrank away from the ferocity of his seriousness. "A window? A capability to see the state of things to come...and the state of things that have happened? That would be..."

"Yes!" he barked. "It would be the orb that you possess. And you have the genetic makeup within you to see into this window."

Cass looked even more confused. "But that doesn't explain how...it operates..."

Apollo stood to his full height and loomed over her. "The hourglass is just a model. It is not how it actually works!" Apollo tightened his grip on the hourglass and shook it at Cass as he shouted. "I am explaining what you...you...can actually do with the orb! Arrg!" He hurled the hourglass into the rocks and it shattered with a loud crash. Immediately, the glass shards and splintered wood faded away to nothing.

"If you're trying to teach me, you've failed. My people have possessed and used the orb for millennia. We have used its ability to guide our future. It guided us here. Why?"

He held out his arm, palm up, and the orb materialized in his hand. Cass's comm-link came alive. "The orb has disappeared! Get back to the ship!"

Feigning as much calm as she could muster, she activated the comm-link and replied, "Everything's fine...it's down here. I think you better get out here."

With Pitti leading the pack, a score of Romani scrambled down the ladder of *Silo 3*. They cautiously formed a crowd behind her, staring at her unconventional companion. Apollo motioned Cass closer with his other hand. "Look into the orb."

She stepped closer and he placed it in her hands. She looked into it as she had so many times before, but this time she felt a swirling, pulling sensation like a whirlpool. Her stomach turned over and she swallowed hard. When she regained her bearings, the planet, Apollo, and the Romani were gone. She was standing, no floating, in a sphere of infinitely repeating mirrors. The universe and all of time stretched toward her and away from her in every direction. Without looking, she knew that she could see everything that had and would ever happen. Everything. She had only ever looked forward in the orb. She turned to look behind herself and then realized that it made no difference. The future and past were in every direction. For the first time, she looked back...and back...and back. The universe shrank. Galaxies disappeared. In a flash of light, the universe became a single, luminescent, blue point.

She staggered back on the grass and murmured to herself, "Now I understand. It's the center."

Pitti ran to support her. "It's the center of what?"

"It's the center of it all. It's the single seed of the birth of the universe."

Apollo smiled. "And why did it bring you here?"

She smiled back. "It wanted us to bring it back to the nexus of the universe to start the cycle again."

Pitti panicked. "Start the cycle again? We brought it here so it could destroy the universe and kill us all. We should have gone to Alpha-4!"

It was Cass's turn to pat him on the shoulder. "Not the cycle of the universe, the cycle of caretakers."

Apollo smiled broadly.

"You are truly a worthy heir to my sister, Artemis." A pantheon of gods and goddesses materialized behind him, stretching over the hills. "We have been caretakers of the seed for millions of your years, but our time is ending. We sent the seed to your home planet to seek the next generation of caretakers. Farewell. Be good stewards."

With that, the entire pantheon evaporated like morning mist.

***

Alpha-4

Cass turned to her people. "We have found both our home and our calling."

Captain Badi asked, "So, this planet is ours now?"

"Yes," she replied, "for eons. Until it's time to find new caretakers. And I think I know where we should look." She gazed into the orb and saw eight ships landing safely on Alpha-4.

The End

Author Biographies

David L. Drake and Katherine L. Morse

David L. Drake and Katherine L. Morse are the award-winning, San Diego-based authors of *The Adventures of Drake and McTrowell—Perils in a Postulated Past,* a serialized steampunk tale detailing the adventures of Chief Inspector Erasmus Drake and Dr. "Sparky" McTrowell. The duo's many adventures are provided in weekly penny dreadful-style episodes on the web (www.DrakeAndMcTrowell.com). They have produced four novellas since 2010: *London, Where it All Began, The Bavarian Airship Regatta, Her Majesty's Eyes and Ears,* and *The Hawaiian Triple Cross.* Drake and Morse won a Starburner Award for the radio show based on their first story that has run multiple times on Krypton Radio.

When not cosplaying their alter egos at conventions all over the West, they are both research computer scientists specializing in distributed modeling and simulation. Mr. Drake is a nationally ranked foil fencer. Dr. Morse is an internationally respected expert on standards, but prefers to be recognized for her cookie baking skills. They throw awesome parties if they do say so themselves.

AJ Sikes

I'm an author of Steampunk, neo-noir Dieselpunk, and, more recently, post-apocalyptic military sci-fi. Since 2013, I've been an editor to authors writing Steampunk, neo-noir, space opera, horror, and post-apocalyptic fiction. I've even had the pleasure of editing a memoir or two. Truth telling time: the stories you hear about stay-at-home writers and editors are true. It's all tea, cats, and naps. As for the bodies in the basement, I really don't know what you mean. Why just the other day...

Twitter: @AJSikes_Author
Website: www.ajsikes.com/

BJ Sikes

BJ Sikes is a 5'6" ape descendant who is inordinately fond of a good strong cup of tea, Doc Marten boots, and fancy dress. She lives with two large cats, two small children and one editor-author. She is the author of the alternate history novel, *The Archimedean Heart,* a mix of fin-de-siecle artistes, royal roboticists, and revolutionaires. Her forthcoming novel, *Sand and Bones* takes place in the Bahamas, circa 1908. BJ Sikes edited *12 Hours Later, 30 Days Later,* and *Some Time Later,* a trilogy of alternate history short story anthologies.

You can find her on Twitter @BJSikesAuthor or on her blog bjsikesblog.wordpress.com/.

Dover Whitecliff

She was born in the shadow of Fujiyama, raised in the shadow of Olomana, and lives where she can see the shadow of Mt. Shasta if she squints and it's a really clear day. She is a an analyst and a jack-of-all-trades, but mostly a writer who has loved comics and superheroes and has been telling stories since forever. Dover won her first ten-speed as a fifth grader with a first-place entry into Honolulu Advertiser's "Why Hawaii Isn't Big Enough For Litter" contest. Her short story "C A S S & R A" is a sequel to "Seeker" and "Finder," paired short stories in the anthology *Twelve Hours Later.* The clockwork oracle predicts that more pulp action, four fisted Dorado and Dark Claw Adventures will be coming in the future!

Made in the USA
San Bernardino, CA
21 February 2018